Rheingold

Born Fatima

A Rheingold Novel

By Kelly Lewis

Hardcover ISBN: 978-1-7378758-3-3

Library of Congress Control Number: 2021922022

First Edition

For information about special discounts available for bulk purchases, or educational purposes contact Lewis Strategic, LLC., Kelly@LewisStrategic.com

Printed in the United States of America

Author's Note

A special thank you to friends and family that took the time to read this book and offer comments, suggestions, questions, and ideas to make the book more impactful. For protection of privacy and relationships, no names of living people are mentioned herein.

JR shared valuable ideas, clarification questions, and edits. Relatives in NC shared their kind enthusiasm and thoughts. NJL and his friend CMM shared opinions on several sections.

The woman who inspired Sydney provided much needed written comments, objections, admonishments, opinions, and most especially encouragement. Sydney also provided her special inspiration to complete the work and see it through the portal. In person, we enjoyed our reconnaissance for Joan Shepp and Sophie Curson. No matter the age, women look spectacular in clothing and accessories from both places. Equally cool, the reconnaissance led to visiting Holt's Ashton Bar with friends. It's easy to say, every time I walk and drive in Philadelphia, I'm reminded it's a special place.

A special thank you to several teachers, Gilbert Dunning who once told me, "Don't you ever stop." He was an inspiration and friend to many students. Dr. Bernard C. Dill for being tough on me in school, and a friend and mentor in life. Mrs. Barbara Tucker, my kindergarten teacher, who wrote me the only thank you note I received after I left eight years in public service. Her note was easily the kindest, sweetest letter I've ever received.

For most of us, there are no short cuts in life. My sports coaches, teammates, and fraternity brothers were/are major influences. You still inspire me to get motivated and get psyched. Yes, damn straight there was hazing, yelling, and screaming. But all of it, was the greatest preparations for my biggest challenges and victories in life.

Thank you to my twin, my siblings, their spouses, and children, for your inspirations, unending competitions, great laughs, stories, and love. Thank you to my parents, and grandparents for your determination, love of diversity, kindness to others, long talks, support, and love.

Thank you to my two children, my inspiration and love since the moment you were conceived.

I've been fortunate in my life to have the support of thousands of supporters and hundreds of campaign volunteers that gave me wings to help others. For this, I've felt honored and blessed.

There's been special people on my life journey, they know who they are, and this book is dedicated to them.

Finally, this book is dedicated to the proposition that our brutally savage civilization will work together to end this curse in our lifetimes.

"Silence in the face of evil is itself evil: God will not hold us guiltless. Not to speak is to speak. Not to act is to act."

"We are not to simply bandage the wounds of victims beneath the wheels of injustice, we are to drive a spoke into the wheel itself."

Dietrich Bonhoeffer

4:35 pm, Thursday, Corporate Boardroom, 50th Floor, 1735 Market Street, Philadelphia, Pennsylvania.

1735 Market Street is the crown jewel of Philadelphia's business district with powerful views in four directions of Philadelphia. The 54-story, 1,286,936 square foot, trophy building is widely recognized for its trademark pyramid crowned top that stands far above City Hall's once building-height limitation statute of William Penn.

The ultra-secure 50th floor has its own high-speed elevator from its own private car garage accessible only from JFK Boulevard. Guests were scarce, by invitation-only. Those privileged to work there or visit the 50th floor, were immediately struck by the sheer audacity of its ultra-pure white walls, furnishings, and furniture. On sunny days through architectural brilliance, sunrises and sunsets illuminated the 50th floor unlike anything on earth.

Most people didn't know, but outside of the White House and Pentagon, this was one of the most powerful offices in the world.

Wearing a black Philadelphia power suit, designed by her designated student team at the Philadelphia Fashion Incubator, The Heiress stood in front of a team of equally attired men and women. The men in dark bespoke suits, ties, and polished shoes. The women in black or dark navy suits, shoes, and jewelry, also designed by their designated teams at the Philadelphia Fashion Incubator. There wasn't a better dressed board room in America.

Most of the team were former special forces. The women were some of the first women in the world to be special forces in their respective nations.

Standing next to The Heiress, Kimberly was unofficially the first female Navy Seal and first female to complete Marine Special Operations training. Unofficially, because she completed the programs before females were officially permitted to apply. Kimberly was the test-case to prove females could complete the grueling U.S. Navy Seal officer training course and Navy SWCC (Special Warfare Combatant-Craft Crewmen). For the past seven years she has been bodyguard, administrative assistant, and senior vice president of The Heiress enterprise. Everything and everyone seen by The Heiress, goes through Kimberly, no exceptions.

Roz was the second woman to unofficially complete the Navy Seal program. Roz also completed the Navy Seal program before women were officially permitted to apply. Five months after Roz completed Navy Seals, she gave birth to her first child. Her husband Dance was one of the instructors. They were well-known as the most athletic couple in the Navy. In one of those marital "bliss" moments, Roz bet her husband she could complete Navy Seals after she unofficially learned Kimberly had unofficially started the Seal program. Of course, Dance wasn't permitted to be a part of any of her training. Yes, he was razed by the guys. But no one was more of proud of her, when the Team-6 commander told Roz, "I saw what you can do. No matter what is official or unofficial, in my book, you are a Navy Seal." In any conversation about tough pregnancies, Roz could always modestly proclaim, "my first two months of pregnancy, were the last two months of my Navy Seal training. I didn't know I was pregnant, but I gave new meaning to morning sickness for Navy Seals."

Roz and Kimberly had a special bond. They were the pioneers. They were the first two. They were the leaders The Heiress recruited into her inner circle.

The aura of The Heiress radiated in the room. Instead of volunteering for military special forces like everyone else in the room, The Heiress paid handsomely to design and build a Special Force training center. Then she completed the equivalent training programs for Navy Seals, Delta Force, Marine Special Operations, Air Force Special Warfare training, Britain's special boat service, and Israel's Sayeret Matkal. Now, she, Kimberly, Roz, and the others train daily at the center with her growing team of special forces retirees.

In the boardroom The Heiress spoke, "Roz, thank you. Your report on Project Poppy is exactly where we need it to be. We're roughly six weeks from deployment. Have your team stay the course."

"Last order of business, are there any questions on tomorrow's game plan to Harrisburg and back?"

"For the flight team to Harrisburg. Team of 12, are we set?"

The room nodded affirmatively. "Remember, before, during and after the flight, no eye contact with Rheingold."

"The Rheingold bio is attached to your read-through. Big sky version. Rheingold Craven is a former state legislator, turned lobbyist. He's unorthodox, unpredictable, with a strong track record, usually against formidable odds and disadvantages. Along with Shannon, he's our top VIP this weekend, with many activities designed to get him on our team."

Turning to the secure conference call phone, "Reed, have the tickets been delivered to Rheingold?"

"Yes, everything is set. He's rarely on-time, but he'll be on that flight. Kelby sends her love to all of you. Reminder, Kelby won't arrive until midnight. Confirming, Jack will pick-up The Heiress at the airport hangar."

The Heiress continued with a succinct business cadence. "Great. The only thing left is for Rheingold to get on the plane. In Philadelphia, if Rheingold recognizes Jack, we'll go with plan A to convince Rheingold to meet Reed at the party. If he doesn't recognize Jack, we'll go with Plan B, and I'll figure out a way to convince Rheingold to trust me and come to our party.

Addressing the conference room, "Team, our training and life experiences have prepared us for this weekend. With more than 700,000 expected guests on Sunday, we can't guess every contingency, but let's stay focused on our mission and assignments. Working together with city police, FBI, and the secret service, plus our team of 250, I'm confident we can stop almost anything they throw at us."

"I've briefed Shannon. She's definitely scared about Saturday and Sunday, but she is definitely excited to meet Rheingold on Friday. She asked me to personally thank all of you. She knows the personal risks all of you are undertaking."

"I echo the same sentiments. From the bottom of my heart, bless you all."

Scanning the room, "Seeing no questions, we are adjourned."

0630, Friday, Heiress Special Forces Training Center, undisclosed location, Philadelphia suburbs

That morning, Roz, Kimberly, and The Heiress did their weekly 3-hour burn workout. Each week, the 3-hour burn workout was crafted to combine some of the most challenging physical aspects of the world's special forces training, that didn't involve ocean water. By tradition, the three women would undertake it first, then the rest of the week, everyone else would gruel it out. The guys were smiling when the center's spectacular sound system blared out, *Angel in the Morning*, by Juice Newtown, as the team's started their 3-hour joy ride. 3-hours later, mud-covered, in combat gear, they finished with tired, exhausted smiles.

3:55 PM, Friday, Harrisburg International Airport

Harrisburg International Airport maintained a few flights to Canada to maintain its cache as an "international" airport. To a few Harrisburg people, being an international airport was a big deal. But most people in central Pennsylvania loved this airport because they could park under a roofed parking deck only 30 yards from the airport walkway, making it super-easy to get in and out.

The problem with an airport that's easy to manage, is it tempts you to test the boundaries of getting there on-time. So, as Rheingold was running through the airport, he was laughing at his ridiculous situation called "life." Once again, it was a Friday afternoon, and he was hustling his ass-off to board a puddle-jumper to Philly for another promising weekend with a half-filled itinerary.

As Rheingold was racing across the terminal walkway, he reached into his suit coat pocket, relieved that he remembered to bring both his flight ticket, and the gold ticket to Saturday's black-tie event at the National Constitution Center. *Fuck it,* he thought, *any weekend planned by Mr. Reed Caputo, Esquire was going to be legendary.*

As usual, Reed had given Rheingold the briefest of instructions, but it seemed straight-forward enough. "Dude, your flight ticket will get you past security, and they'll direct you to Gate C. At Gate C, get your sweet-ass on the private plane with about 12 other people." Rheingold smiled; his shiny flight ticket simply read: Gate C – Private – Seat 2.

As he rushed up the steps to the jet plane, he was still catching his breath, oblivious to everything around him. His brain quickly acknowledged he wasn't stepping onto an ordinary jet. He thought to himself, *damn, this plane is posh.*

Just as he was noticed there were no seat numbers, an attractive flight attendant was pointing him to seat number two, "Sir, your seat is right here." He was instantly psyched to be sitting next to a stunningly beautiful woman. As he was excusing himself to step to his window seat, he sucked in his gut to try and look 15 years younger. He noticed everyone else on the plane was well-dressed, in great shape, and buried in their laptops. As he was twisting into his seat, he realized the woman sitting next to him was staring at him. She was stunning with captivating and dreamy eyes.

Under his breath, he whispered, *thank you brother Reed Caputo. Very well done!*

Without making a fuss, Rheingold sat down, and leaned closer to her to pull out his seat belt. Instantly his nostrils were sending earthquakes to his aching brain. *Code red, code red, this woman smells exquisitely amazing.*

"Excuse me love, but would you mind having a glass of Champagne with me on this dreadful flight? You know it's Friday and I hate drinking alone," she coyly suggested from the seat next to him. Already mesmerized, Rheingold was unconsciously nodding his head up and down. She added in a purr, "Frankly, it's good to see a man dressed in a bespoke suit. The world is dreadfully casual these days."

As if on cue, the stewardess was already pouring two glasses of Champagne. Thinking back, he remembered everything started to percolate at a faster cadence, the moment he sat down next to this woman. The existential shift she brought was significant enough of a demarcation that he had notched it in his brain, forever.

Some moments you never forget.

What's in a Name?

After some small talk, Rheingold quipped, "Forgive my rudeness I never asked you your name?"

She smiled. "Yes, I suppose I have a name, but all my friends call me The Heiress, and you are now my friend." Her surprisingly strong hand and fingers grasped his muscled thigh for added emphasis.

They talked like long-lost friends. Right then, he could have told his friends he fell in love with her.

Simply put, The Heiress had a glow about her. One moment she looked radiantly Italian, then another moment changing to Scottish or Irish, then African, Asian, or Indian. Her beauty evolved in front of you. She was a beautiful blend of Audrey Hepburn, Diana Ross, Ali McGraw, Carly Simon, Rachel McAdams, Iman, and Michelle Yeoh; articulate, cute, adorable, stylish, abundantly sexy, and absolutely alluring. But immediately in her presence you knew she was different than anyone you ever met. She exuded an expression of power and confidence that was rare, captivating and intimidating. Simply put, she had a powerful presence!

Powerful: a word you might use to describe a mob boss, union leader, or dictator, but powerful is paralyzing when it's packaged in style, grace, and stunning beauty. And yet, as she spoke, he saw someone so wholesome, honest, and disarming. Someone strong and brave but also kind and gentle enough to bring home to meet your mother.

A Black Tie Event

"Rheingold my new friend, what are you doing this evening?" she tenderly asked, as she playfully skipped to Plan B.

"No plans tonight," he responded. "However, on Saturday night, I'm going to a black-tie event in Philly at the National Constitution Center. Tonight, I'm just headed to the Rittenhouse."

"Look darling, this evening I'm having a small gathering at my house, and I insist that you come!" As she again touched his strong thigh.

"Well, I…" he stammered.

"No, it's going to be great fun, and I won't take no for an answer," as she snuggled even closer to him. "I insist you come."

She shifted her leg against his leg, "Now tell me all about this black-tie event?"

Rheingold shifted forward and got into his famous story-telling mode. His friends and detractors would later relate that Rheingold could retell a story twenty times, and every-single-time he'd still pull you in, hold you in a joyful suspense, until everyone burst into laughter. Other times Rheingold would tell a new story, and everyone would lean-in to learn his latest escapades.

"So, I know this guy, another lawyer, Reed Caputo. Reed's the one that gave me this plane ticket and the ticket for the Saturday night gala. Reed and his beautiful wife Kelby are great fun! You'd love them. Everything about this man and woman define the word, fun; and everything they do is always carefully planned and executed.

They plan the greatest parties, they are gatherings, really. But unlike most gatherings, Reed and Kelby envision the dynamics, cadence, flow, guest list, food, wine, even the dessert orchestration. Years ago, they redid an old farmhouse with a bank-barn. For their gatherings, they pull together a fabulously fun mix of people, with once-famous bands from rock n roll to Motown. Every gathering delivers fun and an abundance of great wine."

The Heiress listened intently. She reveled in his dancing eyes, enjoyed his pronounced gestures, and fond recollections. What Rheingold didn't know was The Heiress already knew every detail he was revealing. More than Rheingold could ever imagine, The Heiress had thought through and planned the most incredible details he was about to experience first-hand. Now in motion, she loved it when her plans started coming together.

In-person, sitting next to him, The Heiress unexpectedly began to experience the allure, adventure, and essence of Ryan Gold Craven. And, even more than she imagined, after falling in love with him months ago, she *really* liked him.

"Oh, good, we're here," The Heiress gently interrupted, as the pilot asked everyone to buckle up for the landing.

Philadelphia

Philadelphia Airport is notoriously the worst in the nation. Even if it's not, it wouldn't matter because Philadelphians are notorious for demanding perfection and expressing their unfiltered opinions! They are famous for loving victory and despising the mediocre. Their football fans are fully capable of booing Santa with snowballs. In Philadelphia, grown men argue over the best cheesesteaks, restaurants, wine, and of course, sports! Life-long friends continuously banter between themselves. Outside of Philadelphia they'd call it hazing, and whine, but in Philly anyone bold enough to join in the banter, becomes family. You just better have thick skin!

In Philly, money talks and bullshit walks.

Entrepreneurs, athletes, and politicians understand one thing about Philadelphians: even if you achieve success, greatness, or championships, you still have to earn the greatness moniker, every single day!

Unlike the rest of the world, Philadelphians openly express great love for the things they love, and in return, they have never-ending expectations!

Since 1930, when Pat's created the cheesesteak and became the King of Steaks, Philadelphia's internal competition for the best cheesesteak has reached larger-than-life proportions. On Facebook, 61,000 cheesesteak gurus engage in brutal debates over the best cheesesteak in Philadelphia. Through conversations, Rheingold and The Heiress would later learn they both loved hot beef sandwiches from the Cherry Street Tavern.

Here, after the Magna Carta, Philadelphia was the birthplace of the Declaration of Independence, the continuance of the enlightenment, the start of the civil rights movement against hereditary rule with the Revolution, to its continuation that established the abolition movement to defeat slavery.

Rheingold lived in Philadelphia during his law school summers. He used to walk the city, proud of his family roots here, and Philadelphia's history for freedom and freedom fighters. In law school he wrote a paper about the burning of Pennsylvania Hall on May 17, 1838. He was in the crowd in 1992 when the Pennsylvania Historical and Museum Commission erected a marker at the Hall's original location at 109 North Sixth Street. The marker reads: "Built on this site in 1838 by the Pennsylvania Anti-Slavery Society as a meeting place for abolitionists, this hall was burned to the ground by anti-Black rioters three days after it was first opened."

Later, he won some of his biggest victories in the city. Here, The Heiress knew every player, with research files inches thick. If she permitted it, she let a few rarified people meet her. In widely disparate ways, they thought they knew Philadelphia.

Little did they know their families had 300-years of intertwined histories and deep roots in the City of Brotherly Love.

Tonight, however, this flight wasn't connected to the always-clogged Philadelphia airport terminals. Instead, their jet sped to a private hangar away from the main concourses. Quickly, the crew and passengers were unbuckling. Standing up, everyone on the plane was acting like this was business as usual. While he was in mild admiration, he easily recognized the passengers knew the drill. He also noted that no one was paying attention to him, except The Heiress. Everyone was polite and happy, and this was Philly. *What gives?*

He thought, *who are these people, why are they happy, and why the hell were they in Harrisburg?*

He stood and followed The Heiress. Elegantly, she reached back for his hand as they left the plane to walk down the stairs. Her hand was soft and strong at the same time. After they reached the ground, she continued to hold his hand, where she guided him to a waiting black Lincoln limo.

As he slid into the back seat, he thought he recognized the driver, but couldn't place it.

Let's Crash that Black-Tie Gala Together

During the flight from Harrisburg, The Heiress had provocatively declared she'd love to go as Rheingold's date to the black-tie evening. At first, he hesitated, since he knew he was a guest of a guest and only had one ticket. Her eyes gleamed as she recognized his reactions to his lack of two tickets. "You know most of the people going to this event have two tickets. Because it's such a big event, they rarely ask for tickets at the door!" She mentioned four or five famous couples she knew would be there.

"Let me crash it with you!"

As he paused and pondered, *I just met this woman, she's dazzling and beautiful, and already she's asking me if she can crash the biggest premier fundraising event of the year with me.*

Then Rheingold abruptly stopped thinking and barked, "Yes. Yes. Why not?"

Her smile grew as she revealed a few more details about the small, little gathering she was hosting at her house outside of Philly. His eyes were drawn into hers like melting chocolate.

Hold On. Wait Just a Minute. That's Jack!

Despite the two glasses of fabulous Champagne on the jet plane, his brain was starting to reconnect some of the dots.

Holy shit, that driver definitely looks like Jack. His mind was starting to think clearer...or was it fuzzier? Jack was Reed Caputo's driver, and Rheingold was with Reed and Jack on Tuesday night. *Oh dang.* Rheingold remembered Tuesday was one heck of a school night.

Tuesday Night at the Harrisburg Country Club

Yes, yes. Tuesday night, a couple of friends had invited Rheingold to attend a banking function at the Harrisburg Country Club. As he walked into the country club, Rheingold was pleased to see they had done a good job fixing up the historic country club compared to most renovation projects. He mused, *nicely done*. The evening turned into a reunion with dozens of former work and fun friends, and even a few blushing smiles from several past loves.

As he was leaving and saying his goodbyes, Rheingold saw Reed out of the corner of his eye and immediately knew the evening was going to rapidly change. Reed Caputo, Esquire saw Rheingold and bellowed to the waiter, "Hey brother, better make it two more bottles of my red wine." With Reed, there was always a magnetic effect with his hellos and high fives. For close friends, after he hugs you, he does that Italian thing of kissing each cheek. Straight away the whole party knows Reed holds you in importance.

Reed barked, "Dude, what the hell are you doing here?" as he grabbed Rheingold's arm for shaking hand purposes, "This is George, the leader of the credit union, and Michael the Chief Experience Officer." They shook hands.

With knowing smiles, Rheingold and Michael did high fives, laughing about the last night they partied together. Dang, Harrisburg produced a lot of fun nights. It was no surprise to see Reed holding court, entertaining the players within a ring of smiling, happy people, and great wine.

Reed and Rheingold held court for another hour trading legendary stories and laughs. After everyone left, Reed, Michael, and Rheingold started walking to Reed's luxury van in the country club's parking lot. As soon as they got behind the van, Reed bellowed to the moon, "What a fucking glorious night when the fucking stars light up the midnight sky!"

As they climbed inside the van, Reed asked Rheingold to open up two bottles of a luxurious Italian red wine he described as, "sublime, unworldly, basically, you're going to fall in love with it." Rheingold carefully opened the two bottles. Over the years, Reed had taught Rheingold about the Denominazione di Origine Controllata e Garantita (DOCG) classification. Of the 74 DOCG wines, somehow Reed was able to get the very best and rarest vintages. As the bottle's fragrance filled the air, Rheingold thought, *damn, Reed always serves the best wine, all night long.*

Refocusing Rheingold and His 1,000 Mph Mind!

Intuitively, from the airport Rheingold felt the black Lincoln Navigator Limo heading south on I-95. The Heiress knew Rheingold's mind drifting. To reconnect, she slid her luscious body against his. They didn't break eye contact as she seductively opened a bottle of red wine. Her smile, her lips, and her eyes became more intoxicating by the minute.

But Rheingold's mind couldn't stop trying to understand what was happening. For a split second, his brain flashed back to something

Reed had said about the pending weekend in Philadelphia, "Look you gotta come on Friday. You need a Friday night in Philly, I got you a room in the best hotel. You gotta come on Friday..."

His mind drifted, *Fucking Reed.*

When your mind is questioning things, it's one fucking syllable Reed. But at any gathering, you could tell how well someone knew Reed, by how long they pronounced his name, "Reeeeeeeed."

Rheingold laughed to himself, *well to me, he's fucking dude.*

Prove it All Night!

Rheingold's little déjà vu moment was interrupted when The Heiress said, "Siri, play my music!" Instantly, the first chords of "Prove It All Night" by Bruce Springsteen blared on the limo speakers. Rheingold almost shit his pants with musical elation and joy. *Damn, this woman is smart, hot, and likes Springsteen. How cool is that?*

The wine plume filled the limo with a deep, earthy aroma. The Heiress had waited years to open this incredibly rare bottle of burgundy. For The Heiress, her big plans were finally coming together, and she wanted a wine worthy of the moment!

Rheingold was trying to focus, but his eyes couldn't leave her eyes. The woman was just plain intoxicating.

To pour the now-open bottle of red wine, The Heiress shimmied up to Rheingold, almost on his lap. She handed him a glass and poured his. Then she poured hers and handed her glass to Rheingold to hold as she spun to set the bottle in the wine-holder. She took back her glass and lightly tapped his glass with an elegant and reverberating ping. She smiled and said, "Cheers," as their eyes stayed locked. Instantly, he knew it was the most divine red wine that ever touched his lips. "Ah yes, such a great year," she murmured. They both took another big sip. The wine and the moment were indescribable.

Little did he know it was one of the most coveted bottles of red wine in the free world. Ha, with Springsteen singing prove it all night.

Rheingold proclaimed, "This is really good!"

"Good, I'm glad you like it. Let's do one more, big sip," she implored.

She slowly treasured one more sip of her own, looked at the glass, and marveled. Then she grabbed his glass, turned, and placed both glasses into the extraordinary wine glass holder on the limo wall. In what seemed like one full motion, she turned back, wrapped her right hand around the back of his head, and pulled him into an incredible first kiss.

Wow! Seconds turned into minutes.

On instinct, Rheingold's fingers went into her silky soft hair. He caressed her face and softly traced her lips next to his lips. His hand slid down her back. The Heiress arched her back in pure ecstatic joy as his hand found her perfectly rounded ass. She felt the power of his strong hand send warm quivers up and down her spine. Despite her knowing anticipation, she couldn't help but let out a soft moan.

Months after reading so much about this man, everything she had read and heard about Rheingold was proving true. He was everything they said, and more.

As they pulled away from this sensuous first kiss, their eyes locked again. She whispered, "I knew kissing you was going to be amazing." Little did he know, as his glazed eyes stared into her sparkling eyes, she knew more about him than he could ever imagine. She pulled him back into her lips. She loved this part of the song, about proving it all night. In response, she grinded against his strong body as the limo turned north on the Blue Route.

She looked deep into his eyes and with a sultry, sexy voice, said, "We're going to have one amazing weekend that I know you are never going to forget."

They kissed again.

As she was straddling him, her supple, lean, body grinding against him. She didn't say a word. *Oh, sweet joy of heaven!*

Oh shit, she has the song on repeat...

The Heiress was now experiencing everything she read in the Rheingold memorandums. Her heart was beating out of her body. Every part of her body was on fire. Words she read were becoming alive with unbelievable sensations. Her mind was speed-racing through the words she had read about Rheingold Memorandums that brought her to this exquisite moment.

The Rheingold Memorandums: Mother's Little Helper – Spring Break 1984

Kissing Rheingold, The Heiress was remembering the sexy words and feelings she felt reading the memorandums on Ryan Gold Craven, better known as Rheingold.

On the front of the memorandum file were several yellow post-it notes, written with near-perfect penmanship: "Rheingold only told an abbreviated version of his fabled story that led to his fraternity nickname, 'Mother's Little Helper.' From several interviews and research, this is the full story."

The Heiress opened the file to speed-read it.

During spring break of Rheingold's sophomore year of college, he tagged along with his brother and two other souls from the University of Pennsylvania. One was a clone of a young Ernest Hemingway; he was brilliant, dashing, and charming. When sober, the other dude, the smallest of the bunch, was a bloody good, golden glove boxer. When drunk, he took great joy in taunting guys twice his size into fights, knowing full well that when he wanted, he was going to stop them cold with a flurry of punches.

Nicknamed, "Rock Lobster" Rheingold's brother was valedictorian of his high school class. The dude was capable of solving the most complex mathematics and scientific equations, while also using his brainpower to undertake the most outrageously dangerous and funny stunts you've ever seen a human do. Despite years of "twin-competing" with outrageous stunts and double-dog-dares, by college, even Rheingold got nervous when Lobster announced to a crowd, "Here, hold my beer."

Before traveling with them to Florida, "young Hemingway" insisted Rheingold had to read Hunter S. Thompson's *Fear and Loathing in Las Vegas*, and *Fear and Loathing at the Super Bowl.* Frankly, to prepare for a college spring break, there's no better author than Hunter S. Thompson.

They had a ridiculously fun night of partying at Doc Watson's in West Philly, and Pat's Steaks at 3 am. They didn't leave as planned at 7:30 in the morning. Instead, they rallied around noon. Before departing, "young Hemingway" placed two cheap beers on the stereo turntable and turned it on. Not understanding what was happening or why, "the boxer" insisted it was sacrilegious to do this experiment on top of a Led Zeppelin album. Everyone nodded in a hangover agreement. So "young Hemingway" turned off the player and carefully removed the Led Zeppelin album and replaced it with one of their other roommate's lame-ass albums, *fucking Air Supply*. He turned the record player back on, and they watched two Schafer beer bottles circling the turntable. He announced, "We'll drink these beers when we get back." They paused, watching the bottles rotate, wondering if they were making history, or doing something stupid. Then, they left.

The Florida border is 925 miles from the University of Pennsylvania.

They packed into Lobster's blue Ford Pinto, called the Blue Marlin. In the '80s when Ford Pintos were exploding in rear-end collisions, their parents got a great deal on matching Ford Pintos. Rheingold drove the Red Shark and Lobs drove the Blue Marlin.

While these Pintos were a different model than the exploding version, they still carried the stigma, lower price tag, and hazing rights to anyone that drove them.

After crossing the Florida border, Rheingold insisted on checking the oil. The whole trip Lobster had been ranting that the oil gauge was broken. After dropping five quarts of oil into the Blue Marlin, they all dogpiled Lobster in the parking lot.

As soon as they got to Pompano Beach, they declared victory, bought a 30 pack of cheap-ass beer, and raced to the ocean. After pounding the beers, they passed out on the beach. After driving most of the trip to assure his personal safety, Rheingold slept the longest. He was rewarded with a wicked sunburn where his windbreaker failed to cover his pale, white skin. At some point during the night, they were kicked off Pompano Beach and continued to sleep in and on the Blue Marlin. That morning, they transitioned to a grandparent's massive retirement community, called Palm Aire. Irving and Adelle were awesome people, loving grandparents, and just plain cool. That afternoon, instead of going to the beach, Rheingold stayed to play cards and pinochle with 80-year-old Irving. To Rheingold, a day of playing cards and pinochle sounded a whole lot more fun than getting drunk and sunburned on a beach.

Who knew how brilliant a decision Rheingold had made?

Amused, The Heiress twisted in her chair, enamored with the story, but seriously wondering where this memorandum was headed.

After the three guys left for Pompano Beach, Rheingold walked with Irving to the pool at Palm Aire. With Irving and his fellow card-playing retirees, Rheingold enjoyed a couple of rounds of cards under the shade of the patio. Then suddenly, all the men and women in the pool area turned their heads.

Rheingold looked up to see what had everyone's attention. The scene was like a Hollywood movie, and Rheingold struggled to keep his jaw from hitting the ground. Everyone at the pool had turned to watch the entrance of a petite, voluptuous woman. She was 5'1" and thin, with a white bikini that displayed her abundantly overflowing womanhood. Her tiny hips swayed and her youthful, slightly bronzed skin glowed. She gracefully walked over to her father, who sat on Irving's right, immediately across from 19-year-old Rheingold.

"Hi Daddy, hi boys!" she said, as she lifted her sunglasses over her eyes.

"Hi honey," her father warmly replied, as he gave her a quick hug and kiss on her forehead. "How's my sweet Carol?"

"I'm doing great, Daddy," she responded as she looked over Rheingold. "Who's the baby hanging with the men today?" Carol purred in a sultry voice.

Irving introduced Rheingold and the group exchanged small talk. Then after a few minutes, as if he divinely planned the whole thing, Irving announced, "Gentlemen it's hot, let's take a break and jump in the pool." He winked at Rheingold as he got up, holding his shoulder down, mouthing the words, "Not you." Later, Rheingold would fondly reflect how Irving was so cool in setting things in motion.

At 19 years old, Rheingold was about to receive the experience of a lifetime with Carol Tandy, the recently divorced wife of the keyboard player in the globally famous rock band, Electric Light Orchestra (ELO).

Carol was captivating, cool, and way out of Rheingold's league! But epic stories never start on equal footing.

Despite her tiny body, Carol's voice was deep, enchanting, and smoky. Rheingold soaked it up. He politely listened to her stories and joyfully answered her dozens of questions about his life, dreams, and relationships. After several hours of talking, she declared it was destiny and fate that they'd get cleaned up and go out for dinner!

Back at the apartment and with the guys still at the beach, Irving and Adelle were as excited as Rheingold for the evening ahead. Irving was quick to offer advice, while Adelle playfully scolded Irving for being so fresh.

Rheingold was standing outside the apartment building when Carol drove up in a silver Mercedes convertible. It was a sight to behold. He thought, *oh shit, I'm not in Kansas anymore.*

He laughed to himself, *damn, that always cracks me up!*

After he jumped into the passenger seat, he looked at Carol and she was stunning. The stretch dress she was wearing covered her body perfectly. As she shifted gears the dress slid up her smooth thighs in a sexy game of peek-a-boo. She smiled confidently. Rheingold couldn't stop staring at her.

Carol drove several blocks to a parking area, stopped, and told him to get out of the car. She walked around the Mercedes, paused, posed, and spun around to let Rheingold take in everything about her. He gulped. Before he knew what was happening, she walked up to Rheingold and immediately started kissing him like they were long-lost lovers.

After a couple of minutes of intense kissing, Rheingold got the courage to grab one of her staggering breasts that was held firm in her stretch-wrap dress. He got a loving handful, but his hopes crumbled when she grabbed his hand and pulled it away. She pulled back from the kiss, and whispered in her sultry voice, "Baby, if you really want a woman to love you, grab her ass first." She explained, "The breasts and other goodies will come, but first you have to grab her ass...let her know you are a strong, take-charge man. Only rookies and perverts grab tits first."

With that, she took his hand and placed it firmly against her tight ass. They started kissing again. Then she grabbed his ass firmly, "Baby, this is the same way a woman should love her man."

He was quickly learning she knew the right way. Then, as fast as their kiss started, it stopped, and she declared, "Oh my, we can't be late, we have to pick up Candy!"

She smiled and whispered, "You're going to love Candy."

Carol stepped back and tossed Rheingold the keys to the Mercedes. "You drive."

Rheingold caught the keys and looked in his hands, stunned. His brain was processing, *holy shit, I just drove 14 of the 22 hours in a Ford fucking Pinto.* Until 15 minutes ago, he had never sat in a Mercedes.

Carol laughed and said, "Hey cowboy, you're going to be fine."

She smoothly climbed into the passenger seat. After he shut her car door, he walked around and climbed down into the driver's side of the Mercedes. He sat, wondering where to insert the key. Carol leaned over, pulled his face to her lips, and gave him the softest kiss. As they kissed her hand slowly guided his hand to the car key location. Holding his hand, she was sliding the key in and out, as her breasts pressed against his body. She pulled back, and whispered like satin, "That's where the key goes baby…right... in… there." He gulped while she playfully grinned.

Under the brilliant setting sun of south Florida, they drove across town in the convertible to pick up Candy. As soon as he felt comfortable, Rheingold reached over and grabbed Carol's soft hand. She responded by placing her other hand on top of his. Softly, but firmly she started to rub his fingers and hand. Years later, he told friends that holding her hand on that car ride was one of the best moments of his life.

While they were driving and Rheingold was trying his best to concentrate on the road, Carol casually mentioned, "Oh, by the way baby, Candy was just in Playboy...just in case you recognize her."

Meeting Candy

As they approached Candy's house on the intercoastal, she was jumping and waving like a cheerleader at the end of her driveway. Her incredible Playboy body was bouncing up and down inside a tiny dress. Rheingold almost hit a tree.

As Candy approached the driver's side of the car, she shrieked, "Oh my God! Oh my God, you must be Rheingold!" He jumped out of the car to help Candy get in and was just about to say "hello" when she crashed into him with a great big hug and kiss on his cheeks. As she squeezed against him, she said, "Carol, oh my God, just like you said, he's soooo cute. He's adorable!"

Meanwhile, Carol had gotten out of the car, walked over, pulled Candy away from Rheingold, and gave Candy a big hug and quick kiss. "Keep your sexy hands off the boy, woman. He's all mine," Carol purred. "Unless I decide to share him." The ladies playfully laughed.

Dinner With Carol and Candy

Walking into the restaurant with Carol and Candy, Rheingold felt like a million bucks. With no hesitation, the maître d' escorted them to their table. After some laughs about MD 20/20, 19-year-old Rheingold let Candy order the first bottle of red wine. As they were enjoying their first glass of exquisite red wine, the restaurant owner came to the table and graciously told them everything they ordered was on the house. The owner said he was honored they were visiting his restaurant, and he was pleased to accommodate them. Candy stood up and gave him a big hug. Rheingold thought the guy was going to have a heart attack or stroke.

Hearing about the free bill, Rheingold breathed a quiet sigh of relief. He feared his whole spring break budget of $120 bucks was going to be spent on tonight's dinner and drinks. He had no idea the evening's bill was going to be three times more than that.

The trio sat at a table in the middle of the room, well-positioned so every eye in the restaurant could see them. Since she was famous for Playboy, the owner knew by discretely letting a few people know Candy visiting on Thursday, he would pack his restaurant. With Carol and Candy, it wasn't an exaggeration to say every guest was watching them all night long. Everyone in the place was thinking, *these ladies are gorgeous.* Some of them wondered, *who's that guy at the table?*

When Carol excused herself to go to the ladies' room, Rheingold jumped up to pull out her chair. When she stood, she gave Rheingold a passionate kiss. In the process, her healthy right breast fell completely out of her stretch dress. As her breast bounced free, several older ladies gasped, and two wine glasses crashed to the floor. A quick study on being cool, Rheingold calmly scooped and tucked her perfect breast back into the dress while maintaining their kiss. As their lips parted and eyes met, she smiled and mouthed, "Thanks, baby."

When Carol turned the corner, Candy leaned over and tightly grabbed Rheingold's arm. "Rheingold, I'm so happy to see Carol happy. You have no idea the year she's had." Candy got intensely serious. "Can you promise me one thing?" Rheingold, still processing the fact that he was talking to a Playboy model, nodded his head. "Just promise me, when you go back to school, that you will call her, write to her, and love her." She leaned closer. "Rheingold, promise me you'll keep loving her, cause honey, she's head over heels about you. I've never seen her like this." Candy looked up and saw a man with a magazine getting ready to ask her for an autograph. She stared into Rheingold's eyes and tightly squeezed his arm, and pleaded, "Rheingold, I can't tell you everything. Promise me, you will love her back!"

He never forgot the intensity of her stare or the fingernail imprints on his arm.

The View

As they waited for the car valet in front of the restaurant, Rheingold was holding up two beautiful women from the effects of the wine. Rheingold took control and got both ladies tucked into the car. As they got settled in the front seat of the car, both Rheingold and Carol looked into the back seat to make sure Candy was okay.

It was immediately obvious Candy's dress had slid up her thighs and she wasn't wearing any panties. Carol quipped, "Baby, there's a full moon tonight and you're getting the million-dollar view of Candy." Candy blushed, and all three of them laughed out loud.

They sang to radio songs the whole way back to Candy's house. Ever since, when the song *Good Girls Don't* by The Knack came on the radio, Rheingold smiled, turned up the volume, and remembered.

After they dropped off Candy, Carol took Rheingold's hand and asked him to drive along the intercoastal. It was a beauty of a night. When they drove into Palm Aire, she pointed to a place she wanted to park. She took off her high heels, and they walked along one of the two golf courses, under the Florida moonlight. During their long talk, he confessed that he really didn't know much about love, kissing, or making love. Without her shoes, Carol was so tiny, but she pulled him close and held him tight. To Rheingold, she felt larger than life.

Love, especially when you're young, is different when you think you've got all the time in the world. But love is urgent when you know you don't.

Carol asked Rheingold to kiss her again. She looked up to him and she glowed in the soft moonlight. As they kissed, she gently reinforced some of the pointers she had described earlier. She told him the little things that made her feel good. She had him tell her the little things she did that he liked. With the lingering effects of the wine, it was different, more sensual, and her voice was so raspy. This time she held his hand and slid his hand over her body.

She whispered, "Don't forget to softly touch her face, trace her hair with your fingers. And, when it's good, slide one of your strong hands down her back, all the way down to her ass, and grab her sweet ass firmly." She moaned as her hand squeezed his hand onto her taut ass. "Pull her body into yours, and baby she's never gonna forget you."

Rheingold heard himself pray, *please God, don't ever let me forget this incredible feeling.*

He was nineteen, a sophomore on spring break, kissing the woman of his dreams. They were inseparable the rest of the week. Long walks. Long talks. They enjoyed hanging out at the pool with Irving and Adelle. Rheingold formally met Carol's parents and other friendly retirees.

At the end of the week, Carol Tandy called Rheingold's mother, introduced herself, and praised her for raising such a fine young man. After Carol explained the age difference and strong attraction, she asked his mother if she would mind if she lived with Rheingold at school. He sat there in awe as the woman of his dreams was confidently talking with his mother in the most direct terms.

You couldn't make this shit up.

That evening, with his trip home the next morning, Rheingold and Carol had a long, heart-to-heart talk. In the end, he wasn't sure if he conceded, or if Carol decided it was best for him to finish the spring semester without her. They had an amazing last night, but Carol didn't move back to school and live with him. At the time, he didn't understand her carpe diem.

On Sunday afternoon he got back to school. That night Rheingold started four weeks of fraternity pledging. After innocently telling his fraternity brothers about the amazing experiences he had on spring break, his pledge name was immediately changed to, "Mother's Little Helper."

Keeping his promise to Candy, Rheingold and Carol wrote letters like an old-fashioned couple separated by war or travel. The letters were filled with love, hopes, and dreams. He called her on the phone once a week for months. Then, out of the blue, she called him on the telephone.

"Baby, sit down, I need to tell you something serious."

Over the phone they cried together as she explained her advanced breast cancer, how it spread, and the few weeks, or maybe a month, she had to live. She described her tiredness, her fear, and her desire to get her parents prepared for her early departure.

He begged to come visit and take care of her, but she told him, "No. I don't want you to see me like this. Rheingold, I want you to remember me under the Florida moonlight when my body was still amazing and whole. That's the way I want you to always remember me."

Six weeks later he got the letter he dreaded in his school post office box.

As soon as he saw it, he knew it was from her, even though the handwriting was shaky, most likely from her chemo. Following her instructions, her father had mailed the letter to Rheingold the day she died.

Ryan Gold Craven

> *Baby,*
>
> *You're reading this letter after I've gone. I know our time was short and it came on so fast. But I want you to know how much I loved you, our time, and our moments.*
>
> *You are my love.*
>
> *My love for you, and your future is endless.*
>
> *Hey cowboy, you're going to be fine.*

I want you to find a good woman that deserves you, and I want you to make her feel amazing. I know if you find a good woman, baby you're going to be Governor someday.

Promise me, you'll be a great father. How I wish I could have made babies with you.

Promise me, you'll remember me, and always love me. Because I am going to love you, forever!

xoxo,

Carol

And, just like that, his Carol was gone.

Feeling The Emotion

After years of withholding so many emotions, The Heiress wiped tears from her eyes as she finished reading the Mother's Little Helper Memorandum. She thought *that poor kid, 19 years old, and to have that much thrown at you.*

She, too, knew about unbelievable loss.

It was the first of many dozens of files she would read about Ryan Gold Craven.

The Rest of the Limo Ride

Back in the limo, The Heiress and Rheingold were still locked in passionate kisses. Instead of a third repeat of "Prove It All Night," Rheingold immediately recognized the next song, "Not Dark Yet," by Bob Dylan from his stellar album, *Time Out of Mind.*

Dang, he thought, *this woman's choice of music is so cool...these are two of my favorite songs of all time.*

Even as these passionate kisses were exploding her senses, The Heiress was defiantly holding back a reservoir of tears and emotions. Way beyond the words, The Heiress had been deeply affected when she read the Mother's Little Helper Memorandum and she was experiencing it again now. It ripped her soul. Despite herself, she felt overcome by the memories of Carol Tandy, as her trembling lips were kissing this dear, sweet man. Feeling what it must have been like to hold and share that much love, only to have it cruelly stolen away by breast cancer.

The Heiress knew the feelings of love and loss all too well. And for the first time since her husband and children were taken from her, she felt overwhelmed by love.

Dude, Wake Up.

Rheingold was so hot and heavy into his kisses with The Heiress, his mind was spinning. He was having a wild, out-of-body experience he couldn't explain. He was bouncing in and out of reality. Every time he squeezed her The Heiress moaned like she was feeling everything he wanted her to feel. His touches were fire to her skin. Everything was so electric. The urgency and passion were so powerful and real.

He felt she was almost crying; it was so intense.

Slowly, The Heiress leaned back, with her eyes still locked into his. She wiped her eyes and sat up.

She whispered in her sultry voice, "Rheingold it's so wonderful someone special took the time to teach you how to kiss so well. I bet she was one special girl." She caringly smiled, softly caressing his cheek.

He gazed at her in awe.

His body was shaking. He was still processing her passionate kisses, feeling out of body. He felt transported, feeling something with The Heiress that he hadn't felt in over 30 years. Buried deep in the recesses of his mind a strong thought sprang forward, *I haven't felt feelings like this since...since Carol.*

They held each other, in the silence of their bodies quivering together.

Rheingold had no idea that she could know his past, or feel what he was feeling, but she knew.

She knew.

Two Beating Hearts

The Heiress didn't mind her kisses rechanneling Rheingold's hurting passion for Carol Tandy onto her lips, skin, and body. If she was channeling Carol Tandy after all these years, truth be told, Carol Tandy really did teach him well. Her body was so appreciative. She knew Rheingold had no idea it was the first time she let another man touch her, since her husband last touched her skin. But he was so gentle, so loving, so sensual.

Deep down, The Heiress knew it had to be that kind of love and that kind of passion after tremendous, unexplainable loss, to get everyone through the next weeks, months, and years ahead.

More than ever, she knew she had made the right choice in Ryan Gold Craven.

But right now, she knew she had to gather herself, and get back to the game plan!

"Rheingold," she said sternly. "That was amazing. But 'that' is just between us - you and me. No one else can know. I mean no one. Do you hear me? No one!"

She paused for effect. "And, absolutely, no epic storytelling!" she declared with emphasis, grabbing his strong bicep, and squeezing it until it hurt.

"Are we understood?" She spoke in an urgent tone and sharply squeezed his thigh to make sure he got it.

Ryan Gold Craven was 50 something and felt like he was the graduate with Mrs. Robinson. He slowly nodded his passion-charged head up and down, nodding in agreement.

Dang, she just plain had gravity.

He held her exquisite body tighter, looking out the window. It was almost unimaginable, how this woman had so quickly unlocked the deepest parts of his soul. It seemed he should feel sadness, but it wasn't sadness. No, he was feeling warmer and bigger.

His hard-wired brain was chanting, *please God, don't ever let me forget this incredible feeling.*

She slowly moved away from him as they both tidied up. As he looked out the limo windows, he saw the large, elegant mansions they were passing.

Dude, you ain't in Kansas anymore.

Her Tiny House

Shit. Her tiny, little house.

He imagined they were near Villanova. But nothing prepared him for her house. They slowed and turned to drive past a magnificent house that turned out to be the guest/guardhouse on her property.

His eyes widened. *If that's the guesthouse…*

They were riding along a tree-lined, manicured driveway that opened to an expansive open plaza with a huge three-story mansion at the end of a big circle.

The Heiress confidently said, "Rheingold, I can tell already, we're going to be friends for life."

"Now, listen very closely," she held his hand in hers, with swollen eyes as she started her gathering her speech.

"Tonight, I'm going to introduce you to the woman of your dreams. You will fall in love with her, and she will adore you. Tonight, you are my guest. I am your host. I know it's hard to believe but trust me on this one!"

She grabbed his muscular arms, "Look, you need to know. I can't be with you, tonight, period, end of story. I can't be with you! So tonight, I am going to introduce you to a very special woman. In my heart, she is the perfect woman for you. The moment you see her, you will know exactly what I mean."

She paused, with the ache of her mission of faith. "So, I don't want you to hesitate. Don't hesitate one moment. I don't know if it's destiny or fate, but tonight you are going to meet the woman of your dreams!"

"Are we clear?" She looked at him with his deep misunderstanding eyes, "Are we perfectly clear?"

He nodded, trying to comprehend her words and everything else that was happening to him at lightning speed. It was so bizarre.

What the hell was she telling him? It didn't make any sense.

Walking Into The Heiress's Mansion

Jack parked the limo next to the side entrance of the mansion. Rheingold got out of the limo, stood up, and quickly adjusted his trousers. He was hoping his arousal wasn't too obvious in the front of his dress pants. Luckily the cool Friday night air was taking his breath away. He nodded to Jack then he followed The Heiress up the terraced stairs into her tiny, little house.

Tiny house, my ass, he thought.

Some of the events that weekend were a blur, but several moments would be etched in Rheingold's brain for life. No one ever forgets a limousine ride like that.

Walking into the sparkling mansion, The Heiress quickly introduced Rheingold to dozens of friends, and just like on the plane, they were all very polite, polished, and kind. And the ladies! My oh my. They were like Charlie's Angels and Victoria's Secret models-all dressed-up, alluring, receptive, and kind.

Rheingold kept asking himself, *Am I really in Philly? How am I supposed to meet the woman of my dreams? What's going on here?*

As they walked through the crowd, Rheingold awaited the inevitable meeting of the husband, boyfriend, or man of the house. Suddenly the place erupted into shouts and cheers.

He scratched his head, hearing something familiar, and thought, *what the heck?*

Then he realized he was hearing cheers for, "RRRRReeeeeeeeeeeeeeddddd!"

Reed? There he was grinning from ear to ear, walking in with a bottle of red wine in each hand, happy as shit. And he walked right up to The Heiress and kissed her like he was returning from a long business trip.

Shit.

Rheingold's mind raced. There's no fucking way, The Heiress and Reed are a thing! No way, it can't be!

What the fuck!

Just then, the wait staff began handing out selections of Scotch, whiskey, Cognac, or Champagne to the few guests that didn't have fresh drinks. Reed was always creating a big build-up so he could get in a great toast. In less than 20 seconds, everyone was holding drinks.

As the waiter approached Rheingold, he quickly calculated the timing of the number of drinks in his increasingly cloudy brain. The Champagne on the jet. The red wine, *damn that wine was amazing*!

He was trying to measure the first drink impacts. But with Reed any reasonable alcohol calculations were thrown out the window. Reed always shared the best of the best. A rare single malt Scotch, a French Cognac you can't buy in the states, a special case of Champagne, or an Italian red wine he found and loves.

Damn. There just ain't math for that.

Mindful of the Champagne and red wine already caressing his mind, Rheingold asked for a dram of the Scotch. One sniff and he knew he made a great choice. This Scotch was beyond worthy! The waiter smiled and whispered, "Very good choice."

At the grand foyer entrance of the house, Reed stood up on the first step of the spectacular stairway and triumphantly lifted his glass.

"Old and new friends, it's Friday night! You may not fully appreciate this fact, but we are about to engage in an extraordinary weekend. Stories will happen this weekend that you'll want to tell your grandchildren, but I'm confident that all of the memorable moments we are about to ignite tonight will stay safely within these walls."

Reed paused with great effect.

"Tonight, I want to introduce my great friend, a great lawyer, and patriot, Ryan Gold Craven!" Shouts and cheers erupted from the crowd.

Rheingold was shocked and embarrassed.

Reed continued, "And as you know, we've lined up a repeat performance by Shannon!" A louder roar ensured.

"So, enjoy, and remember: No. Fucking. Pictures!"

Reed's toast finished with even louder cheers and whistles from the party.

Fucking Reed. Rheingold paused, *Why the fuck is Reed here? What is happening?*

His eyes caught the beautiful eyes of The Heiress twinkling under the room lights. She was beauty personified and it was clear she was beloved and revered.

Rheingold asked himself, *who was she? And what is this all about?*

Meeting Shannon

Unlike some of the drinks more attune to shots, Rheingold didn't chug this magical Scotch. No way. He could tell it was too good for that. Instead, he savored every sip. He eagerly nodded yes when the waiter asked if he wanted another pour. Who was he to just say no?

Six sips in, other guests were still arriving, often in groups of couples arriving at the same time. He looked around and realized everyone in this place was attractive, fit, well-dressed, and articulate. They all seemed like they were part of the same team. As he was admiring the views, he realized the background music was slightly louder. Then a beloved fraternity song by The Clash started playing much louder. "I'm Not Down" was rocking the room and his mind was in overdrive. *How am I in a big-ass mansion in Villanova, at an incredible gathering...with the hottest hostess in the world and the music is The Clash – the only band that mattered?*

Dude. Get a grip.

Then, as he looked past The Heiress at the front door, she hit his brain like a ton of bricks.

Shannon.

Like lightning striking, Rheingold was stunned!

Dang. She was the real deal. He didn't know how to say it, but she exceeded every category in his definition of dream girl.

Regrettably, Rheingold thought, *Dude, you're too fucking old. She's out of your league!*

But he couldn't stop himself from staring.

Damn. She was fine!

The way she held the red wine glass was classy and elegant. And he couldn't look away as her luscious lips softly touched the tip of the crystal wine glass.

Legends never need liquid courage.

Epic Nights

When everyone else is sitting back in their comfort zones, legends move forward. Instead of waiting, they plunge ahead, eyes wide open. They know epic nights only start when they let go of the brakes.

Shit, that's why they're fucking epic.

Look, you don't get epic sitting at home with two cats on your fucking lap. No. Epic nights start when someone proclaims, "Hold my fucking beer!"

He started walking toward her. Talk about passing the distance test. The closer Rheingold got to her; the more radiant Shannon's beauty became.

Shannon

She applied to Penn State for aeronautical engineering and a week later got her early admission acceptance letter.

Like the trend with football scholarship athletes, Shannon started at Penn State in the spring of her senior year of high school, so she could try out for the fall football cheerleading squad. She never knew it, but her cheerleading score was the second-highest tryout score since they started scoring tryouts. Until then, the highest score was recorded by a PSU senior captain who later made the US Olympic Gymnastics Team. Remarkably, Shannon was a walk-on freshman with only four weeks of team training. Technically, Shannon made the PSU cheerleading team before her original high school graduation date. By the time Shannon left Penn State, she reset the highest tryout score in her sophomore, junior, and senior years.

In the 3.5 years she attended Penn State, she shined. Because of the anticipated travel and training demands of a football season, and through peer pressure from her cheerleading squad, Shannon acquiesced and switched her major to marketing. They were right, she loved the marketing classes. They were also right about the travel and training demands of cheerleading. But Shannon was determined. In the end, Shannon finished Penn State with a dual degree in marketing as well as aeronautical engineering. Her GPA was 3.96. One prick professor in Marketing-400 gave her an A-minus, even though Shannon had the highest grade on every test and paper. She never told anyone, but she also refused his repeated requests for dinner and drinks.

More responsible Penn State professors raved about Shannon as a student. She was kind and curious. She spoke respectfully in class and was never condescending to anyone. She helped other students, even though they had a quarter of the coarse-load and schedule she had. Anywhere she went on campus, Shannon made positive impressions.

Her YouTube videos raving about her Penn State experiences were so popular, the University started using them as their official admissions videos. Often in a Penn State cheerleader outfit, her videos featured incredible gymnastics moves, cheers, smiles, and gushing testimonials enthusiastically praising everything great about Penn State. After her first TV interview with a local station went viral, she appeared on TV shows across Pennsylvania. As they exploded around the internet, she made the rounds on all the nationally-broadcast talk shows, and twice on Good Morning America. On TV, her beauty, energy, and lovely voice radiated. Audiences young and old adored her vitality, perkiness, and sparkle.

By her senior year, Shannon was so well-known and popular, they named an ice cream flavor after her at the world-famous Penn State Berkey Creamery.

After graduation, she grew her social media presence to celebrity status on YouTube, Twitter, Facebook, and TikTok. Now, at 28 years old, Shannon was already one of the most successful realtors on the Main Line. She was living the dream in Villanova with everything clicking, except her man situation.

After a drama-filled relationship with a Penn State All-American football star that every hot chick in Happy Valley was chasing, Shannon decided it was easier to take a break on dating.

But many Penn State grads would acknowledge with a smile that on football and alumni weekends, Shannon usually got two to three marriage proposals from quick-rich alumni made brave by too many brews.

____

Rheingold had a sixth sense about people.

He knew there were a few kinds of men in the game. To him, there were the Stud Watsons, the boy-toy stud muffins that look so GQ-good to some ladies that they just want to get drunk and ride them. These boys know it, and to them, it's a never-ending carousel of willing and available women. Usually, after a few days, the Stud Watsons forget the names of the week's joyrides, and their girlfriend or wife gets pissed when they get another prescription of antibiotics to stun yet another STD.

Rheingold played things much differently.

He loved women and acknowledged they were the greatest gifts on planet earth.

Invisible to most of his ladies; like Candy's haunting words, Rheingold never stopped loving his lady friends. Often without their knowledge or awareness, he helped his former loves for years after their time together ended. In job applications, connections, introductions to men he thought were matches, kids applying to colleges and internships - he loved them stealthily. In many ways, it just worked better that way. No matter how the relationship ended, he never stopped loving them.

On the other hand, sometimes Rheingold's loving dalliances and sexual talents got him into trouble.

Too often, a lady would fall head over heels in love with him. She might even forget the technicalities of her marriage license to fall in love with him. Rheingold was engaging, intellectually interesting, good-looking, and fun. He not only listened but acted on conversations. He sent notes, paid attention to details. With growing intensity, they couldn't get enough. Even years later, long after they weren't together full-time, he might send some of them love letters. "Hi baby, hope you are well. I was in Key West, thinking of you and jotted down a few thoughts." In his way, he wrote them like it was a perfectly normal and natural thing to do. He never realized how carefully and slowly they opened these letters. Often, with trembling hands, they would read his written words bringing tears of joy, loss, and love, a love only they could love and know.

When asked or challenged on why he never settled down or devoted himself to one woman, he would deflect or say it was deeply personal, and never really explain it. Few people heard the intense discussions he had with the women he loved. When he explained his never-ending love for them, as well as his love of the law, and his work. That, even if they weren't together, even if he was miles away in distance or physicality, he was still going to love them, no matter what.

Greeting Shannon

Truthfully, Shannon was optimized.

Through the best food, trainers, and situations, she oozed perfection. She wore the best designer clothes, especially the latest fashions from Philly's designer shops. She had a presence few forgot. And she could spot a Stud Watson from miles away. Besides her gay friends, who fiercely protected her. Shannon knew it was only those kinds of guys that were brave enough to approach her. Up until tonight, she had never met a man like Rheingold.

On a normal night, Rheingold knew he didn't have a chance with a woman like Shannon.

Regrettably, most women in Shannon's category were going to wait for a Stud Watson to grow up and finally listen to his family that marrying a woman like Shannon was a darn good move. But most Shannons didn't know a Rheingold existed.

Tonight, Rheingold thought he knew one thing that Shannon was soon to learn: That it was never a normal night when Reed and Rheingold got together. Then again, as the evening and weekend unfolded, it was self-evident that Rheingold didn't know shit.

As Rheingold was working his way to Shannon to boldly say hello to her sensual lips, Reed was making his way to Rheingold.

“What the fuck, man!”

Reed and Rheingold exchanged the obligatory Italian double-cheek kiss thing, and then Reed shouted, “Shit man, I’m here to get my awesome wines from The Heiress and your sweet ass is sitting here. What the fuck, what are the chances?”

Reed yelled louder over the crowd noise, “Dude, The Heiress said you were cool as shit on the plane and the ride over from the airport. Ride on bro!”

They high fived.

Reed shouted. “The Heiress and Kelby have been friends for 35-years since summer camp together. What a small world!”

Rheingold shouted, “Dude, this place is heaven! This Scotch is incredible!”

Then, as Reed and Rheingold finally reached Shannon, Rheingold placed his hand on her delicate shoulder, “Is she fate, heaven, or what?”

Reed laughed and roared, “Definitely fate, my man!”

Reed raised his hands. “Shannon is heaven on earth, and she's the one asking me about you!”

He turned towards Rheingold. “Shannon I'm so pleased to introduce you to the Honorable Ryan Gold Craven. You gotta meet this dude, everyone calls him Rheingold. His family's been in real estate for four generations. His great-great-grandfather started the Philadelphia Board of Realtors! He’s a real estate lawyer, lobbyist, and civil rights advocate!”

“Wow, four generations in real estate - wow! This sounds like a man I need to know better,” Shannon smiled and without really thinking about it, she took Rheingold’s strong hand into hers and held it. Much like The Heiress, after reading so much about

Rheingold, Shannon felt she knew him, liked him - maybe even loved him - before she ever met him.

Of course, Rheingold had no idea.

Also converging on the scene, The Heiress grabbed Rheingold's well-defined triceps, “Damn Rheingold, your arms are so stiff! What do you do to make your arms so strong?”

It was always the same. Reed unleashes Rheingold, Rheingold unleashes Reed, and legendary nights begin. Now The Heiress was going to play along and join sides with the men.

“Honey, give me your hands,” The Heiress placed Shannon’s tiny hands-on Rheingold’s biceps. “I want you to feel a real man instead of those sissies that keep trying to touch your perfection.”

As The Heiress slid Shannon's hands from Rheingold’s bicep to his triceps, she stealthily reached around and grabbed Rheingold's ass. In her earthy, sultry voice whispered in his ear, “Oh I’ve heard some of the stories about you, Mr. Rheingold.” Then she added loud enough for all to hear, “Come on, Rheingold, flex those pipes for Shannon!”

With that, Rheingold straightened and twisted his triceps as Shannon's deep brown eyes looked into The Heiress’s eyes, then to his triceps, and then into Rheingold's eyes.

Smiling, The Heiress intently whispered to Shannon, “Remember what I told you.”

Reed interrupted the trio’s sexy dialogue by yelling out, “It's time for my special whiskey!” With that, The Heiress winked at Oscar, the bartender, who quickly grabbed four whiskey glasses.

Rheingold proclaimed, “Dude, I’ve got no idea what you are distilling, but your whiskies always kick-off great nights!”

In the middle of the crowd now approaching 60 guests, the four of them tipped a dram of whiskey.

The Heiress and Reed shared a knowing smile. Only they knew the powerful forces at work, which they were so sublimely setting in motion.

Rheingold heard The Rolling Stones song in the background, "Blinded by Rainbows" shook his head and smiled.

Still mesmerized by Shannon, Rheingold watched her slowly raise her whiskey glass to her lips.

Here he was standing in the omnipresence of The Heiress, who 25 minutes ago was passionately kissing him with her luscious lips, and now Rheingold couldn't take his eyes off gorgeous Shannon.

His mind was spinning, *how did The Heiress know Shannon would trigger such an immediate response in me?*

He paused, took a deep inhale of Shannon's essence, and glanced at Reed and The Heiress. His eyes returned to Shannon's eyes and they both smiled. Blinded by Rainbows.

Sometimes life is so perfect.

The music continued to play into a Keith Richard's guitar solo.

The sweetness of fine whiskey lingers on your tongue…almost oily. The sensory overload wicks around your mouth to ignite your soul. It's glorious and earthy. It tingles and awakens. From fields of grain to unlocked liquid courage. Few human creations have resulted in something so raw, pure, and delicious.

Rheingold marveled, *Who the hell is playing this song list?* He pondered as John Stewart started singing "Lost Her in the Sun," and his brain started doing mental backflips. For Rheingold, music was soul-deep, capable of instantly transporting him into memories, feelings, and love.

Recognizing Rheingold was starting to drift again, The Heiress interrupted his musical sojourn by squeezing his shoulder. Then she loudly said across him, “Shannon, it’s time for you to get ready for your performance! Oscar, can you help Shannon get ready in the gymnasium?”

Oscar quickly stepped out from behind the bar. This dude looked like he was fresh off the front page of a military junkie magazine. Even in a fitted Tuxedo, he looked ready to rip off anyone’s head that pissed him off. And yet, he was so calm and serene.

Regardless, Rheingold made sure his feet were balanced underneath him.

“Lost Her in the Sun” continued to play.

Was it him, or was the earth moving under him? Was all of this really happening? He thought he saw The Heiress nod to Reed when she was hugging Shannon? As Shannon and Oscar walked away, he didn’t let his eyes avert from that perfection until Reed grabbed his shoulder, and yelled in his ear, “You fuckin’ old hound dog!”

They laughed the laugh of ancient warriors. Maybe they didn’t carry weapons and bombs. Maybe they didn’t kill or maim to become legends. But over the years, and in different worlds of law, they both had won major battles against bullshit.

Respect.

Whether with swords, pens, or speeches, warriors of every age train, battle, lose, learn, get crushed, and get back up to fight again and again. And then against all odds, when they finally win a big fight, they know.

They just know.

The Performance

The Heiress nodded. On cue, the wait staff started efficiently herding the rambunctious crowd through the grand hall entrance, down an elegant hallway accented with paintings of a bygone era hanging on the walls, to the gymnasium. Walking there, the sound system was blasting, "Wait a Million Years" by The Grass Roots. Like a classic 70's video, Rheingold felt like the hallway was changing colors like a kaleidoscope, it was surreal.

Everyone was grooving and dancing as they happily made their way down the crowded hallway.

Then another Song blasted by The Grass Roots: "Sooner or Later."

When they said "gymnasium," Rheingold had thought to himself, what *do they mean by a gymnasium in a house?*

But surprises kept repeating - and it was only Friday night!

Sure enough, the hallway turned and led to a doorway that opened up into a three-story gymnasium with awesome hardwood floors. On the far end of the gym, there was a basketball hoop cranked up toward the ceiling. The waiters gathered the crowd at midcourt into an almost perfect half-circle. Like earlier in the evening, the waiters made sure everyone had their favorite drink.

Everyone was in a great mood, tapping their feet, laughing and talking wildly. The ladies were swaying to the lyrics.

The lights flickered.

The lights flickered again. A few people were getting uncomfortable as the crowd got quiet. The music stopped.

There was a loud clap, and instantly everyone got silent! It got darker. It was so quiet you could hear people breathing. It went black. Then without any warning, the place exploded with sound and light.

The loudest version of "Love Removal Machine" by The Cult started blasting like a sonic boom over the sound system. *Dang!*

Immediately, concert lights and a bright spotlight lit up Shannon as she leaped onto the gymnasium floor with a triple somersault burst, wearing a very modified Penn State cheerleading outfit.

My oh my! Rheingold liked what he saw. The crowd was enthralled, everyone was awestruck. How the hell did she physically turn all those flips into rolls and leap four feet in the air to then land on her feet, and never seem to stop dancing?

She looked into the audience and once she spotted him, Shannon didn't break her gaze from Rheingold's eyes. She did everything she could to make it seem like she was dancing just for him.

Shannon was smoking hot, a world-class gymnast, and boy, could she shake it. And as she did this kind of leap into a full split, there were gasps from the crowd and then a glass shattered on the ground. Normally when a glass breaks in a crowd people look and instinctively make an "ohhhh" sound. But at the moment, no one flinched, no one moved - not even the guy that dropped his drink.

Despite dropping his drink and getting splashed, this guy remained fixated on Shannon. His hand and fingers were parallel to the ground as if he was still holding the glass. He was hypnotized.

Shannon never flinched. In fact, the whole episode was pure energy to her, as she spun into a headstand, walked on her hands closer to the half-circle, and turned the handstand into a seductive mid-air split. Somehow, she pranced while doing handstands. And yet, through it all, she maintained a powerful gaze directly into Rheingold's eyes.

When she did a handstand her cheerleading outfit revealed her undies were just barely undies, and two more glasses hit the ground. As the song got more intense. she was just getting started. She ran through a series of somersaults, jolted, marched, and she even did a walking-forward version of the Michael Jackson moonwalk in a fashion all her own.

Collectively, the crowd gulped.

Look out.

Shannon had been holding back.

Now as the song peaked, she was simply unbelievable in her raw beauty, sexuality, and athleticism. She was dancing, shaking, flipping, and leaping in ways that defined athleticism and art while defying gravity.

Another round of glasses hit the ground. Two of them belonged to women. And as the song ended, he wasn't sure if the audience was close to breathless, heart-attack, or orgasm but, either way, it was incredible.

Rheingold was breathing deep like he had been on a Stairmaster for 20 minutes. Who knew what would come next? Her entire five-minute, nine-second performance was like a four-hour Springsteen concert that hit every sensory nerve of their bodies.

It was like everyone needed a cigarette. Flushed women were holding onto their men for balance. Even mild-mannered Reed was flushed. And just like that, it was over. The lights turned on.

Slowly, the waiters guided everyone back to the reception hall. No one was walking steadily. Rheingold overheard astonished exclamations:

"Oh, my God, that was incredible."

"Where did she learn to do all that?"

"I've never witnessed anything like that before."

Rheingold finally realized Reed was speechless or couldn't physically speak.

Rheingold laughed, "Dude, do I need to get you an oxygen tank?"

All Reed could say was, "Holy shit!"

The Heiress approached them and coyly said, "Rheingold, I hope you liked it!"

She paused for effect.

"That was all for you!"

Almost on cue, diminutive Shannon pranced into the hallway with the widest smile and glistening eyes. When she caught up to Rheingold, she leaped up and wrapped her arms around his neck and legs around his thighs.

"Rheingold, what did you think? What did you think? Did you like it?"

She was still wearing her ultra-sexy cheerleading outfit when she jumped onto Rheingold, and his hand naturally reached around to grab her ass to hold her up. Another two glasses smashed against the floor.

His brain was processing, like, *wow...*

She's talking to me...I'm holding this dream woman in my arms!

Then Rheingold proclaimed, "Woman! Are you kidding me, you are amazing." He exclaimed as he squeezed her in a big hug. "I mean - You are incredible!"

I'm a believer.

Shannon looked and felt so relieved. She kissed Rheingold on the cheek, then plunged her head and shoulders against Rheingold's chest taking in his lingering cologne and perspiration.

Reed and The Heiress looked at each other and smiled. Like fate, no words or expressions were needed.

In minutes, the crowd was back to the main banquet room. Now packed with around 70 people, most of the guests were feeling fine, visibly energized by the sexy aftereffects of Shannon's dancing, and their libations.

Returning to the main banquet room and back on her feet, Shannon was still fondly snuggling under Rheingold's shoulder with her beautiful head leaning into Rheingold's chest. They stayed there momentarily until Rheingold felt intrusive eyes upon him.

Rheingold looked up to see a perplexed young man staring at him in a bow tie with a young lawyer's gaze. He was positioning himself like he wanted to ask Rheingold a question. Sensing he had to be diplomatic, Rheingold nodded at him as Shannon's body sensually slid against his strong body. But Shannon stayed connected, slightly ruffled that their moment together was interrupted.

The young man gawked, "Rheingold, I don't get it. Why did you call the boys, 'Stud Watsons'?"

Rheingold paused. Then he shook his head as he pondered, *what the fuck?*

It was almost like Rheingold didn't hear the question, so Reed interjected, "Holy shit." A few more people leaned in to hear the conversation and Rheingold very slowly started turning his head to answer the inquiring young lawyer.

"Are you really asking me that?" he said in a low, political growl.

The kid gulped and paused momentarily.

Then the young guy's head hesitantly nodded yes. As a few more guests got within ear-range, Rheingold seized the moment to pontificate a little tale.

"My good friend, have you ever heard of Alexander Graham Bell?"

"Of course! He invented the telephone," This kid responded with glee noticeably pleased that he knew the answer. Rheingold imagined this guy must have read all the answers on the back of the Trivial Pursuit cards as a kid.

"Okay, my friend. Think carefully," Rheingold answered. "What were the very first words that Alexander Graham Bell said?"

The kid hesitated and a puzzled look crossed over his face. He appeared to be sweating over the damn question. Then the awkward moment was broken when an older gentleman in the circle yelled out with a shrieking voice, “Watson, come quickly!”

Watson, come quickly!

Rheingold grinned and Reed beamed, as other men in the know roared and acted like freshman pledge brothers imitating a man undertaking several pelvic thrusts and prematurely ejaculating way too soon. “Oh no, oh no! Aaaahhh.”

Just then, The Heiress timely returned to the circle, smiled, and winked at the rookie lawyer. Her slender fingers traced Shannon's perfect shoulders and she whispered, “Now, now gentlemen. Let’s be kind to the young boys.”

The group laughed while the young lawyer gulped and shrugged. As everyone slapped him on the shoulder, he stood there and wondered, *Wait, are they hazing me?*

Rheingold laughed, “Like Little Stevie Orbit said, “if you gotta ask, you’ll never know.””

Reed started gathering a group for another toast, or speech tied to a new round of drinks served by the finely dressed wait staff. As the guests were circling closer to Reed and Rheingold was stepping backward to accommodate the growing crowd, Shannon leaned into Rheingold’s arms, and on her tippy toes whispered into Rheingold's ear, “Before you get two wines in you, can you quietly follow me. I've got something I want to show you.”

A lady never had to ask Rheingold twice but his mind flashed. *Wait, how does she know about the two-wine thing?*

As Rheingold was turning toward Shannon, he noticed Shannon was glancing at The Heiress.

Reed had retreated to the other side of the room with a large group of the crowd. And soon, Reed was holding court, regaling a past legal victory. Then Reed declared, "A fucking toast!" Lifting his glass he said, "To the old, the bold, and the restless - may they find peace, love, and understanding as they discover true happiness this evening!"

Rheingold smiled and thought, *damn, Reed's halfway to shit-faced and I'm being asked to follow the most beautiful woman on the planet. Yeah, this is already one extraordinary evening!*

The cheers from Reed's toasts were echoing throughout the house as Shannon and Rheingold walked around the palatial house.

In a wild Deja-vu, Rheingold heard 1980 Steve Forbet's song, Lonely Girl, echoing around the house.

Alone

Upstairs, at the end of a hallway, Shannon pulled Rheingold into what had to be one of the significant guest bedrooms. She turned, locked the door behind him, and slowly walked up to him reaching out her hand as if to shake hands.

Instantly his eyes must have betrayed his bummed reaction. But Shannon energetically stepped closer to Rheingold bringing his hands into both of her hands. Her eyes were gleaming and energized as she lowered Rheingold's hands around her lithe body.

"Oh my God, Rheingold, I couldn't wait to feel your strong hands on me."

And as she delicately placed Rheingold's fingers on her exquisitely strong bottom, Rheingold had no idea she had been waiting and hoping for this moment for weeks.

In the intensity of looking into each other's eyes within seconds, Shannon and Rheingold were locked in a passionate kiss. She felt every moment of his lips and hands. Soon, instinctively, Rheingold slid his fingers to her face, softly tracing her cheek and lips as her body felt every sensation. Her anticipation within these moments was excruciating. Slowly his strong fingers slid down her arching back, her mind racing again until his strong hands returned to her exquisite bottom.

Shannon let out a soft moan. From the moment he held her, and the way she moved, moaned, and arched her back, he knew she never had a real kiss, a real man, or experienced real intimacy. Gently, he lifted her onto the bed, slid off her cheerleader outfit, and softly removed the lovely designer shoes she had slipped on after her performance.

Almost on instinct, his hands raced to her panties, and he quickly realized Shannon wasn't clean-shaven. She grabbed his hand and averted it from her tiny little panties, smiled, and kissed him passionately. After a bit, he excused himself.

She lay there softly panting, her mind racing, heart beating, and body trembling, as Rheingold walked to the bathroom. She rolled her eyes as she heard his long-anguished pee splash into the toilet. She thought she heard him sigh. Then she heard him scuffling around a drawer or two and wondered *what the heck is he doing?* He then returned to the bed carrying a towel, a wet washcloth, a brand-new razor, and women's shaving cream. She gulped. While one of her hottest fantasies was getting shaved by her man, she immediately tensed at the very thought of it. And as the full force of her emotions ripped her soul, she melted and started uncontrollably crying. Long painful tears.

Rheingold was visibly shaken. One moment he was golden and in seconds, it was a total meltdown. He reached to hold her and brought her closer into his arms, against his strong chest. She was still sobbing, shaking uncontrollably, but holding him. Slowly he rubbed her neck and whispered, "Shannon, it's going to be okay. No matter what it is, it's going to be okay."

In a few moments, her lower lip stiffened, and in between her sobs, she cried, "The Heiress said you'd understand. She said you'd do something, and you would know how to help me!"

Confused, he didn't know what she meant. Still shaking, she pulled his body closer and whispered, "I know we just met, but like The Heiress said I would, I feel instantly safe with you, like nothing I've felt since this happened." She grabbed Rheingold's hand and they gently slid to the middle of the bed.

"Rheingold, I've never been able to show this to anyone. I'm so mortified, devastated, and afraid but The Heiress said I should show you this, and you might know how to help me." Totally perplexed, Rheingold felt enormously drained. From all his experiences and tragedies, he knew something very tragic was about to happen.

Clearly shaking, Shannon slowly pulled her legs apart to reveal her panties. Just as Rheingold was beginning to think she was just shy and wanted to show him her unshaven womanhood, she slid off her panties and revealed the horror of devastating horrors.

It was obvious the moment it hit him, and it hit him like a ton of bricks. He was staring at one of the oldest and most cruel traditions left in civilization.

Female Genital Mutilation (FGM).

FGM.

While he held her sobbing body, his mind immediately raced to another brutal statistic he had just read a week earlier about FGM. That 200 million women on the planet had been forced to undergo this dreadful practice. He was mortified and angry when he read that statistic, and now in real life, FGM was staring at him right in his face.

He carefully placed his head on her tummy, as her hands instinctively pulled his him closer to her. For moments she sobbed, he held her, and they listened to each other breathing.

"Shannon, you are the bravest woman I've ever met," he painfully murmured. "You are beautiful, you are so smart, and you are so brave. And now I want to honor you."

Shannon didn't know exactly what he meant, but slowly Rheingold kissed his way to her swollen breasts, where he carefully and tenderly started touching them with the softness of his lips. Shannon reactively trembled. With her fear and embarrassment, she never let a boy or man touch her body. She couldn't get past the trauma of potentially revealing her innermost secret or being "found-out."

All this was spinning around her head, as she realized her nipples were aching and she was lost in arousal. While her mind raced, Rheingold was slowly, carefully, and diligently caressing her aching breasts.

She whispered, "Oh my Rheingold, thank you. You are amazing." His hands and fingers started to softly move across her incredible body. His touches were so soft, she could barely feel his touch, her skin was crawling with anticipation and goosebumps. He was playing her skin like he knew everything he was supposed to do. "Oh my God Rheingold, I've never had so many goosebumps in my life."

His lips were now barely touching, almost nibbling her ear, and she could feel and hear him breathing. "You are so beautiful and precious. I'm going to do everything I know to make you feel good." She beamed. She already felt so good and already she was beyond anything she ever experienced. For sure, she had never let anyone touch her like this.

Her gentle brown eyes were wide with anticipation as Rheingold caressed her face and lovingly kissed her soft lips. She had never been kissed like this. She never knew a kiss could feel so good, so wanting. With him, she felt time stand still, like she truly was the center of his universe. Without a conscious thought, she felt herself moan and instinctively part her legs. She was floating on air. *My gosh,* she thought, *what have I been missing...*

She was so turned on, she barely felt the warmth of the shaving cream covering her softness. She felt like passing out as Rheingold's razor slowly trimmed her, leaving behind a perfect tiny heart above her scarred delicateness. He was so gentle and loving. When she least expected it, his warm lips circled her aching breasts which sent more quivers up and down her spine. And still, Rheingold's left hand was softly caressing her skin, giving her more goosebumps across her legs, sides, back and belly. All new sensations. When Rheingold used a warm washcloth to clean her off, it felt so good she felt her body trying to explode. Her lips released another soft, gentle moan.

Her highly trained and logical mind was whirling, seeking answers, *My God, how is he doing this to me? How am I feeling all these sensations when I've been stripped of all my womanhood?*

And just as her mind was starting to curse her tragedy and missing clitoris, she felt Rheingold circling his tongue around the location of what should have been her most sensitive parts with his lips, tongue, and whiskers of his beard. She was letting him passionately kiss her barrenness.

Shannon felt like she was going to pass out as his lips kissed circles around her scarred wounds and then his tongue slid in and out of her tenderness.

Another soft moan effortlessly left her pursed lips. She tensed, not really knowing what to feel. Feelings of shame started to fill her mind. She may have tried to pull him away, but he reached up, and grasped her hand, tenderly kissed her fingers, and whispered, "It's okay, Shannon, it's all good, it's gonna be okay."

As his lips left her fingers, he replaced his lips with his strong fingers and as their fingers intertwined. So softly his lips and kisses returned to kiss across her body. She started to feel okay again, maybe even good. Her taut leg muscles went soft, and unconsciously she felt her legs spread further to receive more of him.

Oh my God, this man knows how to touch every sensation in my body. She felt her whole soul relax, she felt his lips on her neck, back, legs, and belly. She thought*, my skin is so on fire and all these goosebumps. Am I going to have an orgasm just from him touching my skin?*

Then he slightly lifted her and slid his hand underneath her. She felt his hand and breathing was close to her warmth. Agonizingly slowly, she could feel his wet finger touch her, graze her tenderness, tease her. She ached for more of his tender touches. She felt her body lean into his touches. Instead of shame and pain he was so gentle and strong, like he knew exactly what to do. She shifted slightly and ever so slowly, she relaxed more. Without warning, she felt herself let out a long, drawn-out moan. Her stomach knotted as she felt these new and growing sensations.

What the heck is he doing to me? How is he doing this to me? I'm supposed to be barren, ripped and torn, but he is giving me the most glorious feelings I've ever known.

Again, without warning, she let out a loud, outward moan as his finger pressed firmer on the G-spot inside her. Rheingold's whole being was so turned on and her moans were the reinforcements he was seeking to make sure he was touching and loving her the right way.

Her brain was racing. She was truly feeling every second of this, "Oh my God, oh my God, Rheingold." Her back arched, her hips were gyrating uncontrollably to some ancient tantric rhythm. Her moans and gyrations were taking over her body, happening without her control. She gasped, "Oh my God. Rheingold! Rheingold…"

And with that crescendo, she felt the most overwhelming tidal wave of sensations, feelings, and passions - overflowing her mind and rolling over her, coming again and again. "Oh my God, Rheingold. You did it, you did it! Oh my God."

Her body tossed and twisted until he pulled her into him, holding her close, with his head resting subtly on her left thigh as the last spasms overtook her lithe, tiny body. She lay still, breathing loudly in total bliss, pure joy, every definition of happiness.

He took his palm and pressed it firmly over the remnants of her womanhood. He had learned by firmly pressing the palm of his hand against her womanhood it was a special way of maintaining her glowing vestiges of orgasm and bliss. And even though her clitoris was no longer present, she felt the most overwhelming feeling of wholeness.

The world stood still.

He spoke with a deep guttural voice. A voice that would echo in her mind and soul for eternity.

"No one," his voice edged and almost emotionally cracked. "No one can take away your pleasure. No one can steal your 'you', your mind, your essence, your soul. No one!"

Despite the party downstairs, their room was quiet, and they could hear each other breathing.

"How did you know?" she whispered.

He breathed.

"I didn't." He assuredly replied.

"How did you do that?"

"I just wanted to make you feel as good as I could make you feel. And I wanted to help you feel trust, and appreciate it was okay to let a man touch and kiss you all over," he added.

Rheingold slid up her quivering body, and softly touched her face and ran his fingers through her hair. "What happened to you is so tragic." He looked deeply in her wanting eyes. "Years ago, I was asked to prevent a 10-year-old girl from getting FGM. I tried everything, but I couldn't help her, and it's haunted me ever since. Emotionally, it destroyed me."

He paused, "FGM ripped my soul," verbalizing for the first time something that had wrecked his spirit and cast him at odds questioning modern civilization and his God.

Rheingold's voice was shaking. "But tonight, you're like an angel sent by God to me. I'm trembling. Can you feel me trembling?"

She touched his quivering lips, and whispered, “Rheingold, I don’t know how to explain everything,” she started. “But there are things in motion I can’t begin to know or understand. You have no idea how much I love you...and I don’t care if it comes out odd or you don’t understand. You just gotta know – you, this, it's the most spiritual moment of my life.”

Now his voice was shaking, “I felt the same thing. Everything about learning about you, meeting you, seeing you, and these past moments – it’s like an angel delivered you to me. After so many years, right now I feel God’s presence, and it’s truly amazing.”

As her words trailed off, Shannon started kissing Rheingold’s head, face, neck, and shoulders, sliding herself down his strong body.

“You’re so amazing to me,” she said as she got closer to his manhood. “And now it’s my turn to do the pleasing...and you can’t say no.”

And with that Shannon took control. Whatever she lacked in experience she felt her imagination could make up the difference from the movies and Pornhub she enjoyed. Now it was Rheingold’s time to exclaim, “Oh my…wow.” And with that affirmation, Shannon increased her pace and energies.

She wasn’t holding back, slowing down, or teasing. His body twitched. He slowly breathed and moaned her name, “Shannon,” and with that she took him over the edge and shifted her strong arms and hands to firmly hold his arching, recoiling body so she could keep her mouth and movements on him.

He moaned louder from the tremendous pleasures she was unleashing and exploding into his brain. His body quivered every time she reasserted herself. When she softly traced her fingernails over his trembling skin, he seemed to twitch and quiver out of his skin. She inwardly smiled, so pleased to know she could so quickly connect with him and find a way to please this amazing man. She playfully purred her happiness at pleasing him. With that, his body quaked, and she smiled even more.

"Oh baby, I'm going to really love pleasing you." Then she sexily climbed up his body to give Rheingold a long, sloppy kiss.

She licked his lips, relishing in the imaginations that he loved the taste of her. They curled up, snuggled, and satisfied. She loved his breathing, loved his warmth, and shimmied into him even more. She felt him drift off first. His firm grip on her body softened as every muscle in his body sensuously relaxed. She loved feeling his deep, long breaths against her neck.

With a sense of joy she thought, *so this is how it feels. This is what the poets try to describe,* as she took the deepest breath of her life.

____

Then, she smiled like she hadn't smiled in twenty years.

____

Oh my God, I love this. I really love this. He's so amazing, I feel so amazing. How did he do that to me?

As she reveled in these glorious thoughts and feelings, they were perfectly spooning. With his arms warmly around her, she drifted into her first sex-coma sleep.

____

In the weirdest way it seemed like Steve Forbert's song, Lonely Girl was still playing. And, as if on cue, "Angels" by Robbie Williams lightly played over the mansion's sound system.

____

In the middle of the most beautiful dream, she felt him sensuously move his hips against her. She shifted and started a slow tantric wiggle, trying to get him hard. She was determined and arched her back. He responded with firm hands on her hips. They slid closer together and softly groaned. Urgently, they both rhythmically shifted their bodies to maximize the sensations.

A knock on the door brought them back to reality. But Rheingold didn't let her go, and they both playfully giggled like finally found soulmates. He grabbed her hips to reassure her he wasn't letting her go. He quickly repositioned his hips, slid his left-hand underneath her, grabbed both her love handles and pulled her onto him as deep as he could slide. She turned her head so they could look deep into each other's eyes as they both climaxed together. Then he pulled her close to share the trembling.

When she started to move, he quipped, "You're not getting away from me that easy!"

She smiled a smile he would never forget, smacked his ass, jumped off the bed with a gymnastics' move, and announced, "Well cowboy, now I'm the one who has to pee."

With that, she slowly walked to the bathroom, and without closing the door, took a long-awaited pee. She looked down, shaking her head, appreciating she was now shaven. Her whole body tingled. She paused and thought, *how in the world did The Heiress know he'd know what to do?*

Intense in her thoughts, she stood in front of the mirror and played with her disheveled hair in the mirror. She hadn't noticed Rheingold entering the bathroom. He held her, stared at her beauty in the mirror and whispered, "Know, I'm not done with you. We're just getting started."

They got dressed, smiling those knowing smiles. After a passionate kiss they unlocked the door and started walking back toward the party. Unconsciously they reached out and held hands like high school sweethearts. With each step toward the party, the noise level and pulse of the crowd steadily increased. Right before they turned the corner to rejoin the crowd, Rheingold pulled her into him and gave her a sweet, powerful kiss. Just as their lips were parting, The Heiress turned the corner. Unconsciously the three of them quickly hugged.

"My goodness, we've all been wondering where the two of you have been. It's been 55 minutes and we've missed you terribly. You must have gotten lost on your tour of this tiny house," she exclaimed almost triumphantly. He thought he saw Shannon winking at The Heiress.

Then, certainly loud enough for Rheingold to hear, she whispered. "I'm so glad for you honey. I prayed, hoping you would trust him, believing he would know what to do. By the looks of things, you both figured it out quite well." Shannon blushed as her mind was unraveling the intensities of the past 55 minutes. Then the Heiress proudly proclaimed, "now follow me, we're just about to open the 1961 Bordeaux. I wanted a mythical wine to celebrate my new friends, Shannon and Rheingold, and to kick-off our extraordinary weekend,"

Rejoining The Party

The Heiress squeezed herself between Shannon and Rheingold, wrapping her arms over their shoulders and gracefully walked them back into the gathering. Immediately, well-wishers were praising Shannon's amazing dance routine.

Shannon thought to herself. *Oh, that's right. I was so into Rheingold, I totally forgot I did that dance routine just an hour ago.* She continued saying hello's and thank-you's as she pondered. *Oh wait, I still haven't showered, I'm covered with perspiration and sex. Oh my God, I must look so frazzled.* Little did she know, she was glowing. Shannon was grinning from ear-to-ear, radiant and angelic. If she said she was the happiest woman in the world, no one would have doubted her.

As the crowd engulfed them, Shannon's curious girlfriends were circling her. All at once, Missy, Laurie, and Nancy were joyfully asking her dozens of rapid-fire questions. It was hard for her to maintain her composure because her body and mind were still so connected to Rheingold. At some point, Shannon looked at Rheingold and instantly felt a warm rush pulse through her body. A love, a longing, a trust... there was just something about him, an energy that was pulling her into him. She was so lost inside her glow she could barely understand anything anyone else was saying. Spellbound, she looked into his eyes. Even though they were packed in the surging crowd, surrounded by Shannon's closest girlfriends, Rheingold, and Shannon twisted together into a long, passionate kiss.

In unison, her girlfriends all mouthed the words, "Oh my God!" Then someone near them shouted, "Woo hoo!" Quickly, the whole crowd erupted into hoots and hollers like you'd hear at a high school dance.

When you let it fly and release it, love has a radiance that warms any room. Within seconds of the hooting, one by one the couples around the room started kissing their partner. Shannon's girlfriends grabbed The Heiress, and they gave each other a big group hug. As Shannon and Rheingold parted with a sweet sunny smile, her girlfriends interrupted them by pulling on Shannon to join them for a hundred questions. Sensing it was time to let go for the moment, Rheingold smiled and whispered, "Shannon, I'll be back."

Their eyes still locked, Rheingold slowly turned his body and then his head toward the bar. And with his second step away, he heard the girls howl, "SHANNON!" As his hand reached the bar, Reed intercepted him with a bellicose, well lubricated roar, "Rheingold, my man, my man!"

Respect

Euphoric with alcohol, joy, and his special zest for life, it was obvious Reed was owning the party. Hearing his glorious lamentations, the lads were tilted, leaning on walls and tables, and their ladies were leaning on their men like teetering totem poles. Their highly tuned bodies not accustomed to celebratory levels of wine and drinks.

Over the crowd noise Reed proclaimed, "Dude, I knew you were going to impress The Heiress and Shannon. I knew it." Reed stood taller, "I mean you're fucked up, just like the rest of us. But you're like a prophet, man. You have no fear, fighting for what you believe in. You don't care about the money. You just go forward and lead. I mean, who does that shit? You're like a soldier of God. You're like David versus Goliath. And like David, you have all your bloody faults and sins, but despite it all, despite it all - you just stay focused on being fucking righteous."

He paused and quickly looked around but then intensely focused back on Rheingold. "And you know I don't use this word often, but I respect you. I respect you!" At that moment, some old and new friends crowded them and interrupted into new conversations. As this was happening, a few political people at the gathering approached Rheingold, and he endured several conversations about the state budget and situation in Harrisburg and Washington. Inwardly, he groaned at the reality of everything about Harrisburg and Washington.

All the while his mind was rattling. *What did Reed mean when he said that he knew I was going to impress The Heiress and Shannon?* He thought deeper, *what is going on here?*

As "*Take Me Home*" by Jess Glynne started pounding around the room.

Speed Drifting into a Memory of Miami Beach

Rheingold was pleased to run into a former staffer who was now hugely successful running a growing non-profit. Rheingold expressed how happy he was that he had hired so many interns to help light their professional fires and help inspire them to do cool things in life. Like the gift his mentors had given him, he loved to plunge his new hires into big, crazy projects and let them figure it out.

Truly, he was blessed. Standing there he remembered his first big-job boss from telling him at age 24, "I want you to fly to Miami Beach, and sell the International Hotel, across from the Fontainebleau for $4 million." He said, "it's not in operation, so you can easily do showings. Here's a list of ten people to call." Rheingold was two-years out of college and had only flown once. While his family was in real estate, he wasn't a realtor, had never sold a house, and most definitely had never sold a hotel. But he flew down and had some interesting nights on South Beach. While he was out, he shared his story with everyone he met, including some amazingly attractive German flight attendants. They shared his story with others, which led to an introduction to elegant Cynthia, the first Asian businesswoman Rheingold ever met. Cynthia had a Grace Kelly air about her. She seemed to politely adore Rheingold - so much so that they enjoyed a sequence of business lunches and happy hours together. She told him many things about life, business, and businessmen. She told him about China, and Japan. It turned out her father led an Asian airline, searching for a hub hotel on Miami Beach. So, at 24 years old Rheingold sold a $4 million hotel on Miami Beach to an Asian airline in less than six months.

You can't make this shit up.

Back to Shannon

More than occasionally, he'd look up to see her to feel the great inner joy that just rushed into his life. Watching Shannon was so captivating. Every time he glanced her way it was difficult to look away from her essence. She was gracious, beautiful, and kind. She encapsulated everything in his dreams. Truly, she was glowing! Everyone seemed to know her.

As the conversations around him turned to another guest bragging about their role in government and industry, his mind started to drift...

What kind of person would order the mutilation of his daughter's precious body? Why are 4 million young girls being mutilated every year, and we do nothing?

As he was listening to the chatter of the gathering, his blood was beginning to boil.

What the fuck! What the gawd damn fuck!

Painfully, in the middle of all this chatter, he felt long-closed brain cells that he had agonizingly cauterized, beginning to reconnect and resurrect the anger and infuriation of his first brush with Female Genital Mutilation (FGM). It was hitting him hard. His mind was sparking. No one near him could tell, but a long-caged emotional rage was brewing against his calm karma. Under his breath in a savage guttural roar, he swore, *it's time to stop this bullshit.*

Meeting FGM – Summer 2001

Approaching six months into public office, Rheingold had no idea the brutal practice of FGM existed on planet earth until a constituent persistently begged to have a private meeting with him. Then, he was a young state legislator strictly following a recommended caucus rule to never meet alone with a woman in his office or in public.

His district and Harrisburg offices were fierce in enforcing this golden rule, to the point of circumventing meetings because of it. One afternoon he heard commotion at the front door lobby of his district office. He heard this woman's recognizable voice. He walked out, listened to her request. Quietly he nodded to his unbelieving staff that it would be okay to meet with this woman in private. Leading her back to his office, he knew this wasn't going to be good. In fact, he was absolutely dreading whatever she was going to tell him.

Visibly shaken, she walked behind him into the office and closed the door behind her. Her emotional demeanor collapsed just as she was about to speak. Choked-up, she proceeded to tell Rheingold some of the most horrible stories he ever imagined. His mind went numb.

Young girls. Hotel banquet rooms in Houston. A makeshift throne with dozens of linen sheets. Doors locked, armed security, no women allowed. Except one young girl. A ceremony. A religious ceremony surgically removing the clitoris from an innocent young girl. Female Genital Mutilation. FGM. In America. In 2001.

Fuck this shit.

Now, in the middle of The Heiress party, his blood was boiling with the raw anger he remembered all too well. There he stood, revulsed and angry, nodding his head at distracting conversations.

His brain cells wire tripped as he remembered his confrontation with the County District Attorney and State Attorney General. Rheingold pleaded with them to file some kind of emergency injunction preventing any girls under 16 from flying or travelling from Pennsylvania specifically to Houston. He asked them to push any possible court action to prevent young girls from leaving the state, and specifically this little girl's travel plans to Houston.

In the end, the County District Attorney did nothing. The State Attorney General did nothing. Fucking Nothing!

Fucking. Nothing.

Then, a handwritten letter was slipped under his office door threatening his life if he did anything further. He shared this letter with law enforcement, the County District Attorney, and State Attorney General. And still, fucking nothing!

No, no - wait. Through his numerous sources, he found out the Attorney General yelled at his staff, "If that Representative Craven doesn't shut his fucking mouth, arrest him, and charge him with obstruction of justice."

Are you fucking kidding me?! Rheingold's emotions burst inside him as he remembered his soul burning because he couldn't do anything to help this little girl. Instantaneously, he turned away from the crowd and intensely growled under his breath at the wall.

"THAT MOTHERFUCKING MILK TOAST."

Rheingold - The FGM Memorandum

In 2001, FGM was a new issue and so unknown that it was difficult to prove it was happening every weekend across America. Even though it was blatantly practiced around the world for generations, most Americans didn't know a thing about FGM. Elected officials and those that knew, denied it, ignored it, or worse, allowed it.

Then 9-11 happened.

Despite the passage of 18 years, in 2021 FGM was still impacting 4 million girls every year. 4 million girls - every year!

Of course, the issue then and now was bigger than any one Attorney General, but back in 2001 in Pennsylvania - for one little girl – the inability to stop FGM was all that mattered in her life.

Back to The Heiress Party

As his mind raced with anger, he hadn't noticed The Heiress gingerly walk up to him. "How you holding up there, cowboy?"

Rheingold winced, shook his head, almost if he was trying to shake the negative karma out of his brain, and weakly smiled. He declared, "You know, nothing can prepare you for what this life throws at you," he replied trying to be funny or even ironic, but from Rheingold it sounded more like his anthem.

After reading so much about him, The Heiress knowingly responded, "But how you respond is what defines you, Rheingold. That's makes you who you are!"

Rheingold quipped, “Well you certainly threw me a curveball today.”

The Heiress answered, “If someone told you the script, would you have come?

She continued. “And here we are, Rheingold.” She beamed confidently, “And Rheingold, don’t think that everything can’t have a purpose or destiny. What if everything you’ve ever done, everything you’ve ever learned and experienced was all designed to lead up to these moments?!” She stood taller, “What if your list of past accomplishments pales in comparison to what you are about to do?”

The Heiress paused, wondering if it was too soon to reveal too much. But she continued, “It’s always been love, Rheingold. It’s always been love that’s driven you, and that makes you different from everyone else.”

Rheingold was trying to decipher the direct and indirect meanings she was throwing at him when Shannon emerged next to The Heiress with the biggest smile of the evening.

Shannon was giddy and happy, looking at The Heiress while she was reaching for Rheingold, she declared, “When you told me he was going to be amazing. You never told me it was going to be love-at-first-sight, amazing.”

Rheingold, trying to be cool in front of The Heiress but failing miserably in Shannon’s presence, felt his mind and mouth form these words, “I can definitely say, nothing prepared me for falling in love tonight.”

The Heiress calmly responded over the crowd noise, “But here we are my friends, like a destiny, like fate, with a purpose.”

She touched their faces, “In love, right where you need to be.”

The Heiress took a few steps back excusing herself. “And, we all have more things to do!”

Shannon was standing on her tippy toes, looking up at Rheingold as he was leaning down to kiss her.

Her body rubbing against him brought him back from his inner rage.

As the music switched to the song, "*I Like Me Better*" by Lauv, recorded at Spotify Studios.

He whispered to himself, *Shape up, dude. You've done your public service. The past is past! Now, you've got a gift, a beautiful woman to mend, heal, and pleasure.*

Ah yes, he smiled, as the tingling sensations gave way to the more elegant visualizations of this beautifully virtuous girl - tiny little Shannon, the incredible gymnast climbing all over *his* body. And as those deep passionate images were lingering in his steam-filled brain, he smelled her. He felt her hand, her warmth, and her sexy, overwhelming purr, as she stood on her tippy toes to whisper, "Before you have two wines, can you follow me."

She exuberantly grabbed his hand and led him to the most striking couple in the crowd. "Roz and Dance, I want you to meet Rheingold!" Shannon lovingly sang out on her tippy toes.

"He doesn't know it yet, but I'm not letting this man get out of my sight for the rest of my life."

Roz and Dance nodded and smiled knowingly.

"Well, wow, that's something big, unexpected, and worthy of an equally-great toast." Rheingold proclaimed.

"But before I do, Roz and Dance, great to meet you," he shouted over the crowd noise. "How do you know Shannon?"

Roz didn't hesitate. "Well, first off we love Shannon. Second, we hear great things about you. Third, like Shannon, Dance and I are realtors, and fourth, we try to keep up with Shannon on her crazy-ass workout routines."

Dance added, "It's an honor to meet you, Rheingold. I appreciate what you tried to do for women's sports in Harrisburg. That's great stuff, and it's ridiculous the high school in our capital city dropped women's soccer and field hockey! I'm glad you did something about it!"

Rheingold was amazed someone from Philadelphia knew about Harrisburg women's sports!

"Wow, thanks so much. I was so glad to work with some great leaders to start to make that happen," Rheingold added. Just then, the sound system got loud, and one of Philly's most memorable anthem songs, "*Love Train*" by The O'Jays started blasting on the dance floor. The whole place started dancing.

Dancing with Shannon and Roz was extraordinary, and it was obvious why Dance was called Dance. The dude could move. The crowd was grooving. The room was like a modern Studio 54, with amazing video screens, pounding sound, and dozens of coordinating light shows.

As that great song was ending, the beginning of another Philly classic by The Stylistics got everyone snuggling up with their partner on the dance floor. **You Make Me Feel Brand New**

After the slow song ended, the DJ cajoled, "It's not like Philly can't listen to the rest of the world. We had a request from Roz and Dance to this old classic for Shannon and Rheingold." Then the DJ stretched their names like the Rocky V Movie announcer, Mike Buffer.

"Ladies and gentlemen, the next song is for Shhhhhaaannnnnoooonnnn and Rhheeeeinnggoooooollllddd!!"

"Everlasting Love" by Love Affair

Energized by slow dancing with their partners, the place erupted like this song was the best song ever recorded. Everyone was dancing! A circle started to form, and Dance did a flip into a split, into another flip. Soon men and women were trying to outdo each other with dance moves inside a big circle. The athleticism was extraordinary.

As the song was ending, Shannon flashed a sexy smile, stood on her tippy toes, and whispered in his ear again. "Let's quietly get out of here, I want to show you something else in the house."

This time, Rheingold was quick to grab a full bottle of the quintessential 1961 Bordeaux, two wine glasses, and gladly followed his little angel through the crowd of well-wishers and envious stares. Instead of the original path, Shannon walked him to a new corner of the house where she found a convenient back staircase right up to the bedroom, locked the door, and announced, "Rheingold, I've been staring at you all night."

"It was torture," she purred, "not to be naked next to you."

He poured the wine. He found Boz Scaggs live on his phone, and replayed the best live version ever recorded of "Love, Look What You've Done to Me." He programmed this song and another song to play on repeat, "I Need You" by LeAnn Rimes. Rheingold knew he had all night to savor Shannon and this exquisite wine. The Heiress truly knew her wines. She had chosen a mythical wine for this magical night, as the first memorable chords of Boz Scaggs lit up their room.

Like ancient souls, they sat up in bed, naked, intertwined, and happy. She told him stories of her real estate listings, and dreams of renovating old homes on the mainline. Eventually the touches led to kisses and hugging, until they fell asleep in each other's arms. Then, as the sunlight starred in their massive guest bedroom, they woke, curled up like kittens.

Sweet sunshine, he thought, as his eyes tried to comprehend where he was, and what time it was. The first thing saw was Shannon smiling at him, and he thanked God that she wasn't a dream. He chuckled when he heard Boz Staggs still singing in the background. The ornateness of the room reminded Rheingold he was in an exquisite mansion next to the most amazing woman. He thought, w*ow, what kind of blessing on earth got me to land here, next to her?*

Without warning, a stern bell sounded, reminding Shannon to look on the nightstand. Her firm breasts swayed as she found a note, grabbed it, and was preparing to read it out loud. Rheingold couldn't help but notice her radiance in the morning sunlight. He quickly studied her beauty, her voice, and their surroundings and thought, *how did this all happen?* Shannon pretended to cough and started to formally speak as she read the note out loud, "Ahem, please wake, shower, and join us for breakfast by 0900 with the robes you have been provided." They playfully smiled, urgently grabbing each other, knowing there wasn't a schedule on the planet that was going to prevent them from making love. With the sunlight sparkling around the room, looking deep into each other's eyes, they hurriedly found their perfect rhythm and quickly came together. He pulled her onto his chest and whispered, "You are the gift of my life, and I can't wait to spend the day with you, if you let me!"

She exuberantly rejoiced, "Rheingold, you have no idea. Everything is planned. Today is going to be amazing," as she leaped off the bed and did a cartwheel. "You have no idea how much I love you already!" They showered together, and soon followed the written instructions they were provided. Unbeknownst to Rheingold his day was already mapped well in advance. Stored on the warming racks, the robes were soft and warm. Like hours before, they walked downstairs holding hands like school kids. Unexpectedly, as they walked downstairs everything was spotless, polished, and glowing. There were no signs of any party!

Wow!

As they approached the kitchen, they heard morning chatter. As soon as they walked into the palatial kitchen, a female voice shouted, "Oh my God, Rheingold! What, what, Rheingold, what are you doing here?"

Amazingly, in another similar robe, jumping off Reed's lap, and skipping towards Rheingold and Shannon was Reed's stunning wife, Kelby.

"Oh my God, oh my God. I can't believe you're here. And who's this lucky little lady...oh my God, Rheingold, she's gorgeous!"

And soon Shannon was getting the famous Kelby hugs, and smiles, and a dozen of the nicest compliments, and adoring salutations a human being can give another human. Reed was sitting on the kitchen counter, smiling at Rheingold in his half-open robe, and then with the biggest shit-eating grin, he blurted out, "Rheingold you're fucking awesome!"

"You're fucking awesome, man!"

Breakfast

The kitchen table was adorned with a fabulous assortment of fruits, and vegetables. Oscar, the main waiter from last night was smiling, and kindly asked if Shannon and Rheingold wanted any coffee. Even the coffee was extraordinary. As they were talking with Reed and Kelby, the back door swung open, and The Heiress quickly walked in the kitchen wearing the tightest riding outfit Rheingold had ever seen. She was stunning!

Kelby jumped up, "I can't believe you know Rheingold, too. He's amazing and Shannon is more gorgeous than I ever imagined. You guys must have had a blast last night and I'm so sad I missed it to attend a township board meeting." Friends since the sixth grade, The Heiress gave Kelby a kiss, and a long, loving hug. "Kelby, I'm so glad you got here at midnight and surprised Reed in his bed. I'm sure he wasn't a rock star last night, but I bet he was happy to see you in the morning."

Kelby smiled one of her famous mischievous smiles. "I'm not saying a thing," as she leaned back against Reed, and he pulled her closer to him. The Heiress proclaimed, "Well, it turns out,

Rheingold Craven lived up to everyone's predictions." She proudly added. "Reed, just like you thought, he was quite fond of Shannon's little dance routine."

Kelby smiled and squeezed Reed. "Oh my God, how many glasses did she break this time?" Kelby inquired.

"Oh, with Rheingold in the room, she set a new record of nine broken glasses." The Heiress proclaimed.

Oscar, the waiter gleefully but calmly added, "Actually ma'am, your beautiful friend, Miss McNaughton was holding two glasses that she dropped, so the official tally was ten broken glasses." They all laughed, and Shannon blushed.

Reed barked, "Holy mackerel, Shannon was teasing Rheingold from the moment he laid eyes on her." He added, "You weren't kidding when you said she had a thing for strong bald guys with beards."

Everyone was talking around Rheingold, and he started to ask, "What do you mean I'm meeting everyone's predictions?" When The Heiress interrupted.

"Top, top," she popped. "My friends, we have a busy little day before our busy evening so let's get ready for our ride into town and get ready for the festivities."

"I want Shannon to try on that dress she liked at Sophy Curson, and the men have a 11:20 appointment at Holt's."

Kelby interjected, "No, No. We definitely need to go to Joan Shepp. Shannon definitely needs Joan Shepp."

The Heiress jested, "Kelby can't I ever set the schedule with you?"

Kelby brazenly wisecracked, "Look, I'm the only one on the planet crazy enough to question you, and yes, yes, we are definitely taking Shannon to Joan Shepp."

Changing topics, Reed kidded, “That's right dude. Shannon's your date tonight. And shut the fuck up, you can thank me in 20 years, brother…”

With that, Shannon jumped up, hugging Rheingold with her arms wrapped inside his robe. “I had no idea you were going to be my blind date. I thought I was going with some dumb-ass, rich kid. Oh, Ryan Gold Craven, this is going to be so awesome!”

Rheingold, not understanding, looked at The Heiress. “That’s right, Rheingold. You get the grand prize, and I get the dumb-ass, rich kid.”

Responding to The Heiress’s nod, Kelby kissed Reed. Shannon kissed Rheingold and the two ladies ran off like schoolgirls to get dressed.

The Heiress walked around her kitchen, dressed in her stunning horse-riding gear. She was perfect in form and figure with the most elegant stride and walk. She nicely said to Oscar, “Can you have the team serve Reed and Rheingold that incredible power breakfast we prepared for them. This weekend, they’re going to need all the strength and energy they can muster!”

As “Lord Is It Mine” by Supertramp started softly elevating in the kitchen.

And just like that, the most aromatic, country breakfast was sitting in front of them. Reed and Rheingold sat down and ate like kings. As they ate, Oscar, announced in his thick Scottish accent, “Gentlemen, I took the liberty of noting your clothing sizes last evening. In the next room, we have gathered a fresh pair of clothes for your festivities.” He smiled, “As soon as you are ready, you may try them on at your convenience.”

After they finished breakfast, they slipped into the coolest set of suburban gear, complete with black Italian loafers, and navy-blue cashmere blazers. Finally, alone with Reed for the first time since his arrival Rheingold exclaimed, “Dude, holy shit. I’m at a total loss for words. Dude, Shannon is amazing!”

"Brother, it's all you man. You're the one who's fucking amazing!" Reed pointed out and continued raving.

As they were bantering, the ladies and The Heiress were walking back into the kitchen, and The Heiress announced,

"Jack has the limo ready outside, so let's go! We've got a full day ahead of us, gentlemen."

Reed barked, "Upward and onward."

And within moments, they were comfortably seated in a black Lincoln Navigator limousine speeding into center city, Philadelphia. During the ride, Rheingold couldn't take his eyes off Shannon. If he had, he might have seen the four other Lincoln Navigators surrounding the limo.

As "Just Another Nervous Wreck," by Supertramp ranted down the Schuylkill.

The Day in Philadelphia

As they rode into the city Rheingold was genuflecting. Last night, about 45 minutes into the evening it hit Rheingold hard. Everyone at the party was beautiful. He remembered looking around, recalling the greetings and observations. Everyone was in good shape, posh, and in sync. While Rheingold wasn't ready to run a marathon (shit - he hated running), he was still strong. He could still leg press reps at 700 and do his age in unassisted dips. But what caught his eye was none of the men were fat shits. A few of the gentlemen, while finely dressed and articulate, seemed a bit out of shape. But most of the men looked like chiseled cornerbacks, wide-receivers, linebackers, and fullbacks.

In college Rheingold worked out with a Marine called Mr. Delbaugh, who was pound-for-pound the strongest shitshow he ever met. Then, at his part-time job in law school as a strength-trainer, Rheingold had trained several more Marines. He respected their no-nonsense strength, grit, and steadfastness. Pound for pound Marines were the strongest guys he had ever met. He'd laugh to himself when skinny-ass lawyer dudes would revel in their stories of athletic prowess, and he'd think, *these dudes don't know shit.*

Try to train with a USMC gunnery sergeant. Try to train with Navy Seals - they politely play along; let you think you are keeping up with them when they're just playing with you! The truth is, once you've seen the best of the best, you should acknowledge it, admire it, and be damn sure to thank them for it. It's their blood, sweat and tears that keep us free. *Most whiny weak asses don't know shit.*

Driving Down the Schuylkill

Rheingold thought he could feel a vibe for an evening, quickly assess situations and scope-out the talent. Sometimes it's booze or a good cigar. Some nights when you least expect it, a beautiful woman walks through the door. And every now and then, the door opens, and in walks Reed Caputo.

As they passed boat house row, Rheingold was recalling flashbacks from last night. *What was Reed doing there? What was I doing there?* Rheingold was trying to remember the sequences. He arrives, in walks Reed, the crowd roars, "Rrreeeeeeddd." Until then, calm, cool and collected, The Heiress rushed over and gave Reed a big, long kiss in front of the whole crowd. Then Shannon. And in the world where things just flip, he didn't know shit.

"Ouch."

Rheingold felt a sharp pain as he realized Shannon was squeezing his hand with her fingernails. "Yo dude, you're thinking too much. Enjoy the moments, baby." For a moment, Rheingold thought to himself, *Shit, was she reading my mind?*

As the Supertramp song was jamming!

Holts

Since 1898, Holt's has sold cigars. In 1985, Holts created the Ashton cigar brand, now one of the most famous cigar brands sold in more than 60 countries. As they passed the houses of Boathouse Row and approached the Philadelphia Art Museum, everyone was soaking it in.

Looking out the window Rheingold pondered again, *Dang, I'm holding hands with the most beautiful woman I've ever seen. She's fallen in love with me, and I can't get enough. She's amazing. I'm sitting next to Reed, my brother from another mother, with his awesome wife, Kelby. And directly across from me is the mysterious Heiress, the most interesting, powerful, and intriguing woman I ever met. That yes, I've also just kissed like a rock star.* Rheingold paused, *Dang, looking at her, she's in the category of the most amazing woman that planet earth has ever produced, and she correctly predicted I was going to fall madly in love with Shannon. Really, what is going on?*

Rheingold didn't know the half of it. Not even close. He didn't know shit. But in the moment, mind-bending as it was, he was hanging, enjoying the ride of his life, and feeling like he was in heaven on earth. He was riding in a limo with amazing humans, driving to world-famous Holt's, apparently to get fitted for tuxedos, and enjoy a cool lunch with cigars. Who the hell was he to file a complaint?

Reed blurted out, "Brother, we are going to have a blast at Holt's. You have no idea, dude. You don't know shit my man."

The ladies, previously transfixed in a discussion on evening gowns and shoes, shouted in unison.

"Reed...please!"

As they approached Holt's on Walnut, Shannon gave Rheingold a big, long kiss. "Rheingold, I'm going to miss you."

Reed grabbed his shoulder, "Let's go, Romeo."

They jumped out of the limo and walked toward Holt's. The Heiress lowered her window and winked at the gentlemen outside the front door. Almost like he was stung by a bee, he hustled across the sidewalk, completely ignoring Reed and Rheingold.

"Yes, yes, I assure you everything will be spectacular," the gentlemen hurriedly said to The Heiress, as the limo started moving.

Rheingold looked back to see the limo speeding off, to the booming sounds of, "Beggin'" by Maneskin. The guy at the door rushed back toward them, "Gentlemen, gentlemen, yes, yes, let me show you the way."

Reed had been walking toward the front door, but the gentleman altered their course. He walked them to the side door for Ashton's Cigar Bar. The sign said it wasn't open until 4 pm. But they walked upstairs to an unseen side door, down a hallway, down a flight of stairs to an elevator. Rheingold noticed there were four buttons in the elevator, 1, 2, 3 and HOLT. The gentleman pushed the HOLT button. Without the usual wait of normal elevators, the doors swiftly opened and immediately after they walked in the doors shut. The elevator quickly whisked-them to the floor labeled, HOLT.

Man, the cigar smoke aroma was overwhelmingly grand when the elevator door opened. As they walked off the elevator the atmosphere was nothing short of wow. The hallway expressed the most ornate, gold-gilded walls and doorways. The carpets were spectacular. The hallway led to a room fit for kings and captains of industry. In fact, that's exactly what it was. Even Reed was speechless.

They followed the gentleman, past a couple of guys clearly enjoying fine cigars, past an equally ornate bar to a room you could only call extraordinary. Clearly, they weren't in Kansas anymore. As they walked in, another door opened and a man from Boyd's carrying two tuxedos was frantically walking towards them. "Gentlemen, gentlemen, step right this way. I have your two tuxedos and I want to make sure they are perfect. Yes, you stand here, and you stand here."

Moments later they were wearing different, but exquisitely designed black tuxedos that fit perfectly. The man declared, "Super." He continued. "As you know The Heiress demands nothing short of excellence. Yes, I'm confident you will be pleased. If you please, thank you for removing them so I can wrap them for your departure."

The original gentleman that brought them to the room, interjected. "Gentleman, The Heiress has arranged a wonderful lunch for you. Joining you, she has requested your indulgence for two quick briefings with the most recognized experts, well-versed in two topics of interest to both of you." The gentlemen retraced their path and soon they were seated with the two well-dressed men, that were definitely enjoying their cigars.

The maître de announced, "Gentlemen, before lunch we recommend you enjoy the fine cigars these two gentlemen have already commenced." Nodding, toward their two cigars that smelled divine. Despite their 50 years on earth, both Reed and Rheingold seemed to hesitate about enjoying a cigar at 11:15 am and before eating lunch. But as soon as they tasted these fine cigars, they knew they didn't know shit.

FGM

The older man spoke first. He mentioned he was lead counsel for the recent STOP FGM Act, signed into law on January 5, 2021, by President Trump. Rheingold thought, *wait, I didn't know Trump signed a FGM Act.*

Female Genital Mutilation is an international horror. On this planet, in 2020, there are over 200 million women that have been scarred for life, ripped of their womanhood. In 1996, the Female Genital Mutilation Act was passed in the United States. In 2018, the act was struck down in Michigan as unconstitutional by US federal district judge Bernard A Friedman. The Department of Justice decided not to appeal the ruling. However, the US House of Representatives appealed the ruling. As of September 2020, 39 US states have enacted laws that prohibit FGM. At the same time, 11 states in America have failed to enact legislation prohibiting FGM.

In 2013, Congress enacted the Transport for Female Genital Mutilation Act which specifically prohibited "vacation-cutting," a practice to transport girls outside of the United States to perform FGM. Today, as many as 227,987 young girls are at-risk in America. With immigration and reduced public awareness, FGM is on the rise in the United States.

On September 21, 2020, the US House of Representatives passed the STOP FGM Act, 2020. On December 15, 2020, the Act passed the Senate without amendment by Unanimous Consent. Then, on January 5, 2021, President Trump signed The STOP FGM Act, now Public Law No. 116-309.

According to a 2016 survey by the UN Children's Fund (UNICEF) nearly 90 percent of Egyptian women and girls between 15 and 49 have undergone FGM, as the ritual is widely practiced by both Muslim and Christians despite the 2008 Egyptian law banning FGM. In the State of World Population 2020 report, 200 million women and girls alive today have undergone some form of genital mutilation in 31 countries. In 2021, 4.1 million girls are at risk of being subjected to FGM. *Four million.*

Somalia has the world's highest FGM prevalence at **98 percent**, with tragically 68% of women undergoing the most extreme Stage 4 FGM called infibulation. Egypt has the highest number of women that have had FGM (27.2 million), but Somalia has the highest percentage rate.

On February 2, 2021, Egypt arrested a father and retired nurse for carrying out FGM on a 15-year-old girl, as the country announced plans to increase enforcement. On February 6, 2021, two UN agencies urged Somalia to commit to ending FGM. **Worldwide,**

more than 8,000 girls endure FGM worldwide, every single day!

Legislators, activists, political leaders around the world have been assassinated for speaking out against FGM. For centuries, governments and kingdoms have turned a blind eye to FGM. All the European powers with African colonies knew. The slave trading nations knew. All the famous Kings and Queens of Britain, France, Spain, the Middle East, and Asia, they all knew. They all knew and did nothing!

Nothing.

Both Rheingold and Reed were pale and shaking their heads in horror. *How the hell can this shit still be happening on this planet? It's so barbaric, awful, and cruel.*

Sex Trafficking

The second man spoke next. He mentioned he was one of lead counsel inside the FBI's human trafficking division.

Human trafficking is the business of stealing freedom for profit. In many cases, traffickers' trick, defraud or physically force victims into selling sex. In others, victims are lied to, assaulted, threatened, or manipulated into working under inhumane, illegal, or otherwise unacceptable conditions. It is a multi-billion-dollar criminal industry that denies freedom to **24.9 million people** around the world. Sex trafficking occurs when one person manipulates another person into sex acts in exchange for something of value, such as money, food, shelter, or drugs.

In cases of sex trafficking involving adults aged 18 and older, the law requires evidence that the victim was forced, coerced, or defrauded. However, in cases involving people under the age of 18, sexual exploitation is always illegal, regardless of whether there is evidence of force, fraud, or coercion [1]

"Human trafficking is a crime that occurs in every corner of the globe, including the United States, and disproportionately affects the most vulnerable populations among us. At its core, human trafficking is the coercive exploitation of another person for commercial gain," Lindsey N. Roberson, the senior legal counsel at the Human Trafficking Institute, the Virginia-based organization behind the report, writes in an introduction to the document.

"Because it is an economically motivated crime that often hides behind a hierarchy of power and control that is difficult to understand, unravel, and prosecute, an effective public justice system is essential to holding traffickers accountable. In the United States, federal law known as the Trafficking Victims Protection Act (TVPA) provides a comprehensive legal framework that criminalizes human trafficking and encourages a victim-centered and trauma-informed approach when handling these complex cases," Roberson observed.

In 2019, a total of 606 criminal human trafficking cases were moving through U.S. district courts. That tally included new cases, pending cases and cases on appeal, the report reads. The Human Trafficking Institute. In 2018, according to hotline data, 199 human trafficking cases had been reported in Pennsylvania. Like many crimes against women and children, Human trafficking is widely underreported.

Rheingold and Reed were speechless. Really what could you say, what could anyone say. Bullshit organized crime, and no one is going for the jugular to stop it.

Lunch at Holts

After the awful intensity of the topics, the lunch they enjoyed was spectacular. Course after course of two tapas plates for the four men. To finish, they enjoyed plates of the most tender lamb chops that just kept coming out, until they all begged for mercy. Their post-lunch cigars and the rare Macallan 1940 scotch were equally indescribable, as was the conversation with these two brilliant men. As their cigars and second Scotches were almost finished, the maître d reemerged and announced, "Gentlemen, in a few moments, your limo is arriving. We have wrapped together several gift packages we're confident you most definitely will enjoy. And please don't forget your tuxedos."

Shellshocked, they thanked the two lawyers, the bartender, and staff. They followed the maître d to the front door. Within seconds the limo arrived. Entering the limo there were gleeful shouts and happiness. Shannon jumped on Rheingold's lap for the ride back to Villanova. As they were approaching The Heiress's mansion, everyone was talking about the greatness of afternoon naps, and it was agreed they'd reemerge at 5:30 for the ride to the US Constitution Center.

Rheingold and Shannon almost raced back to their bedroom. And with the zest of their prior encounters, they hastily ripped off their clothes. Their bodies hit the soft sheets and their kisses were passionate and hot. In the moment, he held her body next to his and the body warmth was sublime. Shannon was rubbing Rheingold's magnificently bald head and Rheingold's fingers were deep in Shannon's soft luxurious hair. 50 minutes later Rheingold woke up from the most intense dreams of his life. As his sleep was subsiding, her eyes were watching for his eyes to open. As soon as she saw his eyes, she slid up and down his body until she could climb onto him. She smiled as his still awakening eyes were displaying so much passion, lust, surprise, and ecstasy. She didn't look away as she increased her pace, and his strong hands found her love handles. He couldn't hold back when she let out a moan, he was sure the whole house heard.

The limo ride to Philly was exciting and the Champagne was exquisite. The only difference with this trip into Philadelphia was Rheingold saw the half-dozen large Black Navigators loaded with extra people, equipment, and weaponry.

The Schuylkill lit up to the sounds of "Sunday Morning" by The Outfield.

The National Constitution Center

On September 16, 1988, President Ronald Reagan signed the Constitution Heritage Act of 1988 which established the National Constitution Center. The act called for a national center "within or in close proximity to the Independence National Historical Park" that "shall disseminate information about the United States Constitution on a nonpartisan basis to increase awareness and understanding of the Constitution among the American people."

Warren Buffett wrote in 2016, "If a statue is ever erected to honor the person who has done the most for American investors, the hands-down choice should be Jack Bogle."

Jack Bogle ensured that the dream of a National Constitution Center became a reality. He was Chair of our Board of Trustees from 1999 to 2007 and presided over the opening of the Center in 2003. He worked tirelessly with the leadership of the Center to secure $60 million in federal funding and the remaining $120 million in public and private funding to open the Constitution Center.[1]

Inventor of the index mutual fund and founder of The Vanguard Group, Blair Board of Trustees Chairman Emeritus John C. Bogle '47 was a titan of the financial industry and an extraordinarily dedicated, favorite son of Blair Academy. His spirit of innovation and drive to excel, and vision for a better future led Vanguard to become the world's largest mutual fund organization. He brought those same sterling qualities to 47 years of unparalleled leadership, philanthropy, and service to his beloved alma mater, Blair Academy.

Bogle entered Blair as a junior in 1945, together with his twin, David '47, and following in the footsteps of his older brother,

William '45. A scholarship recipient, Mr. Bogle worked as a headwaiter in the dining hall and distinguished himself as a high honor roll student, editor of *The Blair Breeze* and *ACTA*, and class treasurer. He was known for his "ready wit and smile," and his classmates elected him "best student" and "most likely to succeed" as he graduated *cum laude* in 1947.

Mr. Bogle credited his Blair teachers with having made a tremendous difference in his life, and his Blair experience propelled him to Princeton University, where he studied economics and wrote his senior thesis, "*The Economic Role of the Investment Company*." That pivotal work launched his career in the investment industry, and his ingenuity and dedication to business integrity and hard work brought him to its pinnacle.

Hired at the Wellington Fund upon his *magna cum laude* graduation from Princeton in 1951, Mr. Bogle rose to become the company's chairman in 1970. An "extremely unwise" merger—that Mr. Bogle considered his "biggest mistake"—led to his dismissal from Wellington in 1974. However, from there, he founded Vanguard and, in 1975, created the world's first index mutual fund. His insistence on the superiority of the index fund and his concern for the individual investor were radical departures for the investment industry, but his wisdom has been borne out in Vanguard's success.

Mr. Bogle served as Vanguard's chairman and chief executive officer from 1974 to 1996. He retired as chairman in 1999 and then became head of the firm's affiliate, Bogle Financial Markets Research Center. A prolific writer, he authored 12 books and countless articles, op-eds and features on investing, financial markets, and the investment world.

Recognition for his contributions to the financial industry came from many quarters over the past several decades; among the most notable were his designation by *Fortune* magazine as one of the investment industry's four "*Giants of the 20th Century*" in 1999 and his being named one of the world's 100 most powerful and influential people by *Time* magazine in 2004. In 2016, the Pennsylvania Society awarded Mr. Bogle its 108th-annual Gold Medal for Distinguished Achievement, an award that recognizes leadership, citizenship and contributions to the arts, science, education, and industry. Later, business magnate Warren Buffett described Mr. Bogle, a man who, "helped millions of investors realize far better returns on their savings than they otherwise would have earned," as "a hero to them and to me."

Even as he invested himself fully in his career and his growing family, Mr. Bogle gave generously of his time, talent, and treasure to the institutions he held dear, especially Blair Academy. He is a benefactor of faculty support and teaching excellence through the John C. and Eve S. Bogle Teaching Prize, and his many gifts include those that have generously supported the construction of Bogle Hall, Blair's science building; Armstrong-Hipkins Center for the Arts; Hardwick Hall, the school's athletic and activity center; and the tournament squash court. Especially dedicated to the support of scholarship aid for deserving students, Mr. Bogle established the Bogle Brothers Scholars Program in 1968, which has since provided the gift of a Blair education to nearly 200 students. Mr. Bogle delighted in meeting his scholars at an annual luncheon and kept in touch with many of them long after graduation.

Beyond his involvement at Blair, Mr. Bogle also gave of himself as chairman of the board of the National Constitution Center from 1999 to 2007; as a generous supporter of Princeton University; as a trustee of the American Indian College Fund from 1996 to 2002; and as a leader and member of numerous organizations, including the American Philosophical Society and the American Academy of Arts and Sciences. He received honorary doctorate degrees from more than a dozen colleges and universities. Source: Blair Academy.

Rheingold often said his solo dinner with Jack Bogle in Washington DC, was one of the highlights of his professional career.

Raising the Funds for the National Convention Center

After years of selling a dream — raising funds for something that didn't even exist yet — the folks at the National Constitution Center in Philadelphia weren't about to be stymied by a couple dozen dead Presbyterians.

The former Philadelphians surfaced, so to speak, in 2001, on the first day of construction on the museum and education center dedicated to enlightening the public about the Constitution of the United States of America. It seems that part of the center's parking garage was being built on an 18th-century cemetery that had been moved in the 1950s — most of it, anyway.

Once a spade unearthed the first body, construction screeched to a halt while archeologists sifted through mounds of dirt and retrieved a million artifacts: bones — both human and chicken — nails, shards of glass and pottery, and other pieces of 18th-century life in Philadelphia. The discovery of the bodies — people from various ethnic backgrounds who, according to city records, lived and worked in the area surrounding the NCC in Philadelphia's historic district — lead to the largest and fastest urban archeological dig ever.

One year, 37 corpses and $5 million later, construction continued.

The NCC was founded in 1988, after the bicentennial of the Constitution, when Congress issued a charter for it to 1.) form a program of outreach and education about the Constitution and 2.) build a museum dedicated to the country's most important document.

The challenge: to get people from around the country to invest in something that, at the time, was nothing more than a paper model and some flashy graphics. And the graphics were, indeed, flashy.

Creative agency AEI Digital, whose offices overlook the NCC, took the blueprints for the museum and used video-game technology to create a 3D "fly-through" of the center that put viewers right in the middle of the action.

Then, in 1996, then-Mayor Ed Rendell (later governor of Pennsylvania) came on as the chairman of the board of the National Constitution Center.

Out There on its Own

The original fundraising campaign, which began in 1988 and picked up speed with Rendell's involvement. The campaign goal was $185 million; the actual take: $185,000,216.

Of that, $108 million came from the federal government (U.S. Department of Education and U.S. Department of Transportation), the state of Pennsylvania, the Delaware River Port Authority, and the city of Philadelphia. The remaining $77,000,216 came from the private sector. The original $185 million development goal included $40 million for the NCC's endowment, as well as $6 million to cover the first year's operating budget (Building costs ate up the other $139 million).

Source: The Archives of the National Constitution Center[2]

The Gala for the National Constitution Center

Rheingold and Shannon's First Date

The Constitutional Gala was designed to be the biggest fundraiser in the history of the National Constitution Center. Remnants of Tropic Storm Gordon had washed out the 20th anniversary celebration, leading to the build-up for this year's massive event. For this gala, three former Presidents were featured speakers and guests included 35 current and former heads of state of the leading nations in the world. With a theme for International Freedom, the week-long build-up for the Saturday gala included several days highlighting global Constitutions ensuring freedoms found in our

Bill of Rights. The Thursday program was dedicated to global freedom.

As their magnificent limousines arrived, paparazzi swarmed toward the car doors. Jack gracefully swung around to carefully open the door. As Rheingold and Shannon stepped out, cameras lit up the crisp September evening. Camera flashes optimized Shannon's natural beauty and the elegant dress she was wearing that simply amplified her glow.

Amidst the glamorous entrance, something or more distinctly someone caught his trained eye. While most of the paparazzi were dressed casually, two tall statuesque Nubian gentlemen dressed in crisp tuxedos disturbed his thoughts. Rheingold made mental notes while he stared in the dark eyes on the larger of the two, as he moved forward.

Why were they staring at him?

Besides those two clowns, Rheingold and Shannon were impressed as they walked in the pageantry of the Gala through a covered walkway. Roz and Dance were immediately behind them, along with another 24 elegantly dressed guests of The Heiress arriving from the other six Navigators. The Heiress's limo with Reed and Kelby didn't stop but continued toward a barrier that two Philly police officers moved without pause under the building. Rheingold rolled his eyes, and thought, *there you go!*

Months later, Rheingold would learn that The Heiress, Reed and Kelby attended an invitation only reception with the three attending former US Presidents and other heads of state.

Rheingold and Shannon were quickly surrounded by twelve flawlessly elegant couples he recognized from Friday evening's gatherings. It crossed his mind that even the ladies were ripped, as well as the guys. He remembered some of them from Friday's party. With their form-fitting European-cut Tux pants, Rheingold easily noticed a couple of these guys had massive, bulging biceps and thighs. All the men were wearing tinted sunglasses with security earpieces. Roz and Dance were holding arms with

Rheingold and Shannon like they were walking into a wedding reception.

As they walked-in, paparazzi cameras were flashing wildly. He kept rehearing The Heiress's stern warning before they'd left the mansion, "Look Rheingold, you can't fully understand, I can't tell you everything, but you listen to me. You stay together, stay with the group, stay with Roz and Dance, there's a lot of bullshit in this city, and powerful forces at this event. Stay next to Roz and Dance. Drink with them, sit with them, laugh with them. I know you are used to walking around a crowd, shaking hands, but this is not the night, Rheingold. You don't know me, but I hope I've impressed you with a clear vision since we've met that I don't bullshit."

What the fuck? he thought to himself. *It's a fancy fundraiser, there's three former Presidents and billionaires in the crowd, this place is going to be swarming with secret service studs, and private security forces.* Shutting down his brain, he beamed as his eyes turned toward Shannon in her amazing black dress.

"Oh shit, Johnny G... dude, what have you been doing?" Rheingold blurted out to Johnny Gurgin as they reached out to shake hands.

"Rheingold, what the hell are you doing in Philly, man?" Johnny said as he slapped Rheingold hard on his shoulder.

"Hold on, hold on. Excuse me, Rheingold aren't you going to introduce me to your daughter?" he shouted as he was bellowing out an overwhelming laugh and grin.

"Nice try, Grandpa." Rheingold laughed. "Shannon, please meet the biggest asshole in Harrisburg, Johnny Gurgin. When he's in Harrisburg the sewer authority works overtime for all the bullshit he's laying down."

Shannon mischievously smiled as she squeezed Rheingold biceps. "Pleased to meet you, Mr. Gurgin. I can assure you Rheingold was definitely my Daddy last night. This man's amazing!!!"

As Gurgin's jaw dropped to the ground, Rheingold slapped him back, "Dude, it's okay, grandpa," he said. "You would have had a heart attack just watching the lady dance, my friend."

"You're too much, Rheingold, you're too much." And, just as they met, they hit each other on their shoulders, and passed into the night.

Rheingold said to Shannon, "He's the best. He's the best. The man's always happy, always glad to see you, and he gets things done! They just don't make men like him anymore."

Shannon squeezed his bicep harder again. "Anything you say, Daddy. But as far as I'm concerned, they don't make anyone like you!" she purred. Rheingold, not one to hesitate, slid his hand down her back, cupped her perfect ass cheek, strongly squeezed a handful, and whispered, "Little lady, you make me smile."

With that Roz caught up to them, wiggled into between them, with her arms grabbing their shoulders. "Yo, Yo, sweet things. Did you get the memo? This is a black-tie event and PDA is not allowed before midnight?" She joked and jabbed Rheingold in the ribs with enough jab Rheingold noticed the lithe strength of this Italian Irish beauty. "How about we see what kind of juicy wine this shindig has to offer?" Everyone's head nodded.

"Sounds great," as Dance joined the three of them firmly smacking Roz's tight ass. "It's about time, Roz-baby, that Champagne is definitely starting to wear-off." Roz gave him a quick, intense warrior look.

In the background, Alison Moyet was performing her famous song, "Only You*"* with the Philadelphia Orchestra to the swelling crowd adjoining the Constitution Center in Independence Park, in front of the famous State House, where the Declaration of Independence had started it all.

"Well, if it isn't, Mr. Ryan Gold Craven. Give me a hug, you, big beef," smiled a radiant Sydney Cadwalader Lodestone.

"Holy wow, Syd. I was hoping you were going to be here. I'm so glad I get the glory of seeing you," Rheingold fired back. They gigantically hugged. As they parted, Rheingold pulled Shannon closer to his side, "Shannon, this is, the Sydney Cadwalader Lodestone, my great friend, who lives in Philadelphia."

In the push of the crowd, they grasped each other's arms, each of the ladies staring into Rheingold's sparkling green-blue eyes. Shannon instantly knew this woman loved Rheingold as much as she did, and for decades.

Sydney nearly shouted, "Oh my God, Rheingold, she's so gorgeous, and so young, and so you!" her voice trailed off in genuine deflection.

Catching herself, "Oh my, Rheingold and Shannon, I'm so sorry, this is David, David Smith of the University of Pennsylvania. David, this is Ryan Gold Craven. Well, everyone just calls him Rheingold." She smiled proudly radiant again.

Rheingold shook his hand. "David, pleased to meet you. Whatever you do, you better treat Syd right, or I'll come back and beat on you!" He laughed, as David flinched.

Seeing Dance failing in his mission for wine, Roz had made eye contact with the wine servers and soon red and white wines were in everyone's hands.

Sydney Cadwalader Lodestone was one of Rheingold's soul keepers. At least twice in forty years, they had tried to spark-up the college-summer magic between them and make it more. Yet, each time it got powerful and real, Rheingold panicked. But like all good loves, they were never really over each other.

David rolled his eyes. Of the 3,500 anticipated guests, all week long he heard Sydney wonder aloud, if Rheingold would be attending with the other Pennsylvania dignitaries. Earlier in the week, she had shared with David another round of Rheingold news after her high school/college friend had secured a first step victory toward restoring women's soccer and field hockey at Harrisburg school district.

"Shannon, I am so pleased to meet you in advance of your speech tomorrow," Sydney kindly remarked. "You are truly brave, and it's my great honor to meet you," she jabbed Rheingold in the ribs and told him. "You've definitely met your match here, sir."

Shannon was thanking Sydney and David, smiling and equally frightened to finally face the scale of the audience she would be speaking in front of tomorrow before a global audience. To his great surprise for the first time, Rheingold learned Shannon was speaking tomorrow. Puzzled, he wondered how Sydney knew, and he didn't know. Rheingold thought he heard something whiz by his face, but he passed it off as crowd noise.

But Roz and Dance were alert and looking left, then right. In an instant, Rheingold could tell Dance's earpiece was lighting up, but he couldn't hear the urgency. "Father FGM, entering. Stage left." Then static. "Stage left 100 yards. 75 yards, 60 yards. Dance, he's headed right for you, he's walking to A2, 50 yards to A-2."

Static. The crowd was starting to notice what was happening and they were pushing, shoving, and scrambling as fast as a crowd could move backwards and out-of-the-way. Soon, the crowd's voices and noises reached a fever pitch.

"I'm seeing six soldiers with the father!" static, "Three more soldiers at stage right. Make it four more soldiers at stage right." Static. "Teams converge! Teams converge!"

"Oh shit, it's my father," and with that surprise announcement from Shannon, Rheingold was staring at a tall, slender, sheik glaring mad-red into his eyeballs. Rheingold was totally unprepared for what happened next.

Father FGM

"Fatima Hafsa. Fatima Hafsa," he yelled at his only daughter. "You must come home. You must leave this place before it is too late."

Instinctively Rheingold reacted, shifting his body forward, in-between this Islamic cleric and his Shannon. He thought, *who the hell is Fatima Hafsa? And what the fuck is going on?*

"Fatima Hafsa, Fatima Hafsa," the man yelled. "You must renounce your lifestyle, tonight, and come home before it is too late!"

Amir al-Mu'minin (Arabic: أَمِير ٱلْمُؤْمِنِين, ʾAmīr al-Muʾminīn) is an Arabic title that is usually translated "Commander of the Faithful" or "Leader of the Faithful."

Omar ibn Khattab, the second Rashidun Caliph of Sunni Islam, was reportedly the first individual to have the title attributed to him. Ali ibn Abu Talib, the fourth Rashidun Caliph of Sunni Islam, and the first Imam of Shia Islam, had the title attributed to him, and is synonymous with his name in Shia discourse.

The term was frequently used by the leaders of the Islamic Empires of Rashidun, Ummayad and Abbasid. Leaders who uphold Islamic customs and values and fight for its cause and are devoted to the ummah are rewarded the title.

The use of the title does not necessarily signify a claim to caliphate as it is usually taken to be, but describes a certain form of activist leadership, which may have been attached to a caliph but also could signify a level of authority beneath that. The Ottoman sultans, in particular, made scant use of it. Moreover, the term was used by men who made no claim to be caliphs.

"Father, you have no right!" Shannon yelled back. "You have destroyed me in every way, and now, I follow the direction of Allah to be away from you, always."

Shannon yelled, "No God would do this to me. You did this to me. You did this to me!"

In Islam Muhammad is considered the last of a series of prophets (including Adam, Noah, Abraham, Moses, Solomon, and Jesus), and his message simultaneously consummates and completes the "revelations" attributed to earlier prophets.

Regarding this matter, the Qur'ānic criticisms of human nature become very sharp: "Man is by nature timid; when evil befalls him, he panics, but when good things come to him, he prevents them from reaching others." It is Satan who whispers into a person's ears that by spending for others he will become poor. God, on the contrary, promises prosperity in exchange for such expenditure, which constitutes a credit with God and grows much more than the money people invest in usury. Hoarding of wealth without recognizing the rights of the poor is threatened with the direst punishment in the hereafter and is declared to be one of the main causes of the decay of societies in this world. The practice of usury is forbidden.

"Father, I am never going back, I am going forward," Shannon yelled emphatically.

"If you do not come with me, right now, there is no hope for you, her father's voices tailed off, as the crowd was now reacting and pushing away from the confrontation. Rheingold intensely looked around, sizing-up the situation to realize he and Shannon were encircled by two groups of fierce warriors.

It was quickly evident, the guests at The Heiress's mansion for the past 24 hours were no strangers to combat, as 24 of them were now brandishing black conical batons, 30 inches in length, of a newly crafted alloy unrecognizable by x-ray machine protocols. Likewise, in some kind of similar fashion the 30 followers of Amir al-Mu'minin ripped-out similar technology with bronze-colored baton sticks.

On the Gala stage it seemed like a modern West Side Story confrontation. As these tense moments ticked-off, police sirens and whistles were blaring with officers racing toward the confrontation as the crowd was trying to run away.

Rheingold barked, "Why don't we all relax! No one needs to get hurt. Let's all stand-down."

As fast as this circle had developed with menacing precision, a kind of parting of the sea was occurring. At first unexplained, then The Heiress emerged, gliding elegantly in a regal white dress gown, toward Shannon. The Heiress was glowing. As she approached the fiery circle, her body and stature were further amplified as a now circling SWAT team helicopter's spotlight focused on her. With the powerful aura she clearly possessed, the once menacing opponents faded backwards like melting Kerry gold butter.

"Iman Abdul. We come in peace, and we wish to leave in peace." The Heiress commanded in a stern voice worthy of a Marine Gunnery Sergeant.

Was she speaking through a microphone?

"If we leave in peace, we will all live. If we leave in battle, few will survive."

Inside this crowd of humanity, with guests scurrying for safety, The Heiress kept walking toward the Iman, while each side of warriors stepped aside as if they were controlled by a mystical power or force. The Heiress raised her hands, seeming to push back the batons with an invisible force.

"Give us peace today. Iman Abdul. Give us peace!" she harkened.

His penetrating glare slowly switched from Shannon to The Heiress. Almost as if knocked from amnesia, the Iman quickly assessed the fast-evolving situation. He looked at his number two for assurance, then he commanded with an equally bellowing bark to his intent warriors.

He yelled, "Stand-down. In the name of Allah, stand-down, and walk backwards with me."

With that, as if practiced for years, the entire group of elite Islamic warriors surrounded the Iman. Despite the chaos and crowd, they slid backwards in a perfect rhythm to where they had entered the stage, each one of them never dropping their intense staring at Shannon.

Iman Abdul yelled, "Today was not the start. Today was the warning.

"Fatima Hafsa, you are no longer my daughter. I can no longer protect you. I can no longer protect any of you."

Rheingold grabbed his neck and thought he threw off what he thought was an insect or mosquito. Little did he know it was far from an insect, but was the latest bug technology, smaller than a mosquito. But it wasn't Islamic or foreign. In that millisecond, in the same motion, Rheingold whipped his arms around Shannon, just as he thought her feet were giving way. Instead, Shannon was repositioning her athletic body as she was also hit by the same kind of bug.

Unlike Rheingold, Shannon knew this moment was destined. She knew it had come to this. He watched as Shannon and The Heiress nodded in unison. For a split second, Rheingold thought, *was this whole thing orchestrated and known beforehand, too?*

His mind screamed, *what the fuck is going on?*

The side effect of the encounter had revealed a moment of solidarity and truth. While last evening Rheingold wasn't really paying attention to the crowd around him. Tonight, it was evident 24-highly trained and gifted individuals were not only party guests, but they were part of something bigger, arranged, and focused.

Roz and Dance had acted on instinct, and immediately surrounded Shannon and Rheingold in a protective zone. The pushes and guiding hands Rheingold had felt weren't the crowd or Islamic warriors but Roz, Dance and 24 others packing tightly together worthy of a Roman phalanx. Then Rheingold grabbed his belt wondering what just hit him. He looked back at The Heiress and despite her glowing radiance, he saw The Heiress wince.

"Everyone to the cars. Plan B. Plan B," The Heiress instantly commanded!

Rheingold and Shannon both gasped at the same time. The Heiress was bleeding profusely. Her left leg and left side of her white dress were turning bright red with blood.

The Heiress barked. "Roz, Dance, don't let Shannon and Rheingold out of your sight. Complete Plan B. Nothing is to change our plans. Tomorrow must go on. Do you hear me! Tomorrow must go on."

"Jimmy D, Teri-Lynn, Missy, and Petrizzo, get me to the heliport landing, as soon as possible."

She commanded, "Carry me, fast. Carry me!" they all looked shocked but reacted with speed.

She looked intensely at her steadfast loyal team, and spoke clearly into her microphone, "Kimberly, get the medical copter here immediately, and then call Dr. Ash, be fast. I've been slashed and poisoned."

Everyone except Rheingold and Shannon knew Dr. Ash was the preeminent doctor in Philadelphia. They also knew Ash was a close friend, confidante, and business partner of The Heiress. They also knew, he knew, she wouldn't call unless it was an emergency and time was of the essence. All the contingency planning, all the tactics and strategies, months of training and counter-training, the one thing that hadn't been staged was an injury or death of The Heiress.

Shannon watched as her head wilted down, from so strong, so worldly and powerful, to dangling. Just as Shannon was ready to scream about her father, her world started to radically change again.

Out of the corner of her eye, Shannon saw Sydney in total shock, only standing because David was standing behind her, holding her shoulders - half for manners and half because he had shat his pants. In shock, the rest of the crowd was screaming, in shock, and reacting to the lightning-fast evolution of the Shannon confrontation to the bluntness of the blood-stained Heiress.

With one fluid motion, Roz and Dance whisked Rheingold and Shannon across the stage platform with 20 other compatriots clearing the way. They quickly passed through the covered security gates and bewildered city police. As they were approaching their Navigators, Bad Dave was lofting assault weapons to each soldier. As soon as the limousines and Navigators had perimeter check-outs, Roz signaled, "Let's get out of here, Plan B, people, Plan B."

As Roz joined the perimeter, they all saw the AH-64 modified Apache lifting off at great speed to the west. Every single one of them silently prayed.

Rheingold's mind was racing a million miles a second. *What the fuck just happened? Holy shit, who was that Iman, dude? Who is Shannon and what's up with him calling her, "Fatima Hafsa?" Why is Shannon giving a speech tomorrow? How did The Heiress get sliced and poisoned?*

He hesitated to speak his mind, but then these emotional words poured out of him.

"Shannon are you okay?" were the first words his lips produced, and he reacted in reflex. Shannon grabbed him closer and curled-up even more under his arm.

He finally heard her whispering, maybe chanting, "I knew it. I knew it. I knew it. I knew he wouldn't just let this fly," she revealed with increasing intensity. "I can't believe he wants to make this a war. But if it's a war he wants, then he's going to feel every aspect of total war!"

The Conference on Global Women's Rights – Summer in Philadelphia – Months earlier

Because three US Presidents and multiple foreign leaders were already scheduled to speak at the global conference, the global media was ready to register, reserve flights, and book hotel rooms to converge on Philadelphia. Six-months before the conference the conference announced the registration system would be activated on a Sunday. 122 guests registered.

Twelve weeks ago, event organizers were notified the registration system had crashed. Several emergency calls and budget authorizations later the IT department refreshed the registration system, only to witness a gigantic surge in registrations for the 10:00 am Saturday timeslot, called Women's Global Awareness. In fact, 99% of registrations were for the 10:00 am time slot. The IT team ordered more bandwidth and support. At 7:48 pm the following Tuesday, the event registration system crashed again. When IT leaders started to address the situation, they discovered 182,344 users tried to register at 7:48:12 pm, crashing the server and related spam-filters. At first IT leaders thought a trojan or Russian computer virus was crashing into the registration data center. But soon Help Desk emails in a near-equal amount were slamming their system with requests for the Shannon speech.

The IT Director issued this report.

At 7:48 pm on Tuesday, a TikTok user named Shannon made an emotional appeal asking her TikTok followers to attend her 10:00 am speech at the Global Conference on Women's Rights. Within 12 seconds over 182,000 users tried to register for the event. These extraordinary numbers escalated. After this surge, our system was reconfigured to handle 300,000 single-moment users at any given time. Prior to Sunday, the record single-moment load surge was 50,000 users a minute when the 2019 Rolling Stones concert dates were announced for North America. After Sunday, we should have an updated capacity to handle a surge of 400,000 users per minute.

Event organizers were excited, dumb-founded, and scared. Their homerun projection for the event was 180,000 guests over the whole of the three-day conference. Now, they had over 400,000 registered guests for the 10:00 am time slot on Global Women's Rights.

The next day, a hastily arranged conference call was scheduled for noon with the Philadelphia Convention & Visitors Bureau. Stunned, they announced over 40,000 hotel rooms and Air BnB reservations had been booked in the last 24 hours in the greater Philadelphia region. According to their website, there were only 37,000 hotel rooms in the greater Philadelphia region. The Philadelphia Airport called in a panic to tell the CEO of the PCVB, their Thursday and Friday flights into Philadelphia were overbooked and they didn't know what to do. The requests for daily flights were greater than the airport ever handled during the busiest week of Thanksgiving or Christmas.

Boardroom – Pennsylvania Convention Center Headquarters Philadelphia, Pennsylvania

"Who the fuck is Shannon? And what the fuck is TikTok?" demanded Kevin Christopher Brandon, II, the CEO of Philadelphia Convention & Visitors Bureau. Mr. Brandon, a CMU, and Penn Law graduate, served in Iraq and Afghanistan as a USMC Colonel. He had been a County Commissioner in nearby Delaware County before his unusual appointment to the PCVB the year beforehand.

"I have no idea!" stammered Michael David "Wally" Ray, the President of the Philadelphia Parking Authority. "What the hell are we going to do?"

"TikTok is the new Facebook," stated Bernadine Kristof. "Shannon was the first user to reach 10 million followers," she added. "On Tuesday, at 7:48 pm she posted she was speaking at 10 am at the Conference for Global Women's Rights. Even though our system crashed, apparently 1 million users hit our registration system in the next ten minutes. Our initial review indicates there were 2 million distinct hits for hotel rooms in the next 45 minutes, and 25,000 hotel rooms were booked within an hour, 10,000 booked in two hours. Literally, there are no open hotel rooms or Air BnB within 100-miles of Philadelphia. "

Bernadine added, "The same kind of thing happened with airline tickets. The airport flights are booked from Wednesday to Tuesday flights– it's going to be a shitshow. There's never been anything like this!"

"I am sharing a handout with a series of TikTok posts Shannon made over the last 72 hours," she said.

Sunday 9:37 pm: #DreamTeamQueens - Big Announcement on Tuesday night. It's my #comingout. It's the biggest thing I've ever done!

Monday: a series of quirky videos and lip-synching songs with Shannon dancing

Tuesday morning: a video of Shannon doing gymnastics (she's very talented)

Tuesday 7:48 pm: Shannon posted a very emotional video that's already been shared over 47 million times. The TikTok video was her life history. She was an exceptional student, dual aeronautical engineering, and marketing degree from Penn State, a four-year Penn State football cheerleader. The TikTok video builds up to her announcing she was a victim of FGM, and she will be speaking at 10:00 am at the Conference for Global Woman's Rights. She asked if anyone could attend to support her.

This morning there were more than 4 million comments on her TikTok post, from all over the world. For perspective, prior to this post, 10,000 comments were an extraordinary number of comments.

On Wednesday at 8:20 pm, Shannon's TikTok post: #DreamTeamQueens, OMG, you are Amazing. You are Amazing! I understand there's 37,000 hotel rooms in greater Philadelphia and you all booked 40,000 hotel rooms. Amazing! Amazing! I'm in tears. I love you all.

"What does all of this mean? What is FGM?" barked Michael David "Wally" Ray.

"Sir, FGM – means Female Genital Mutilation," Bernadine quietly added. "It's an awful thing."

"I don't even know what you mean. People actually do this to themselves?" Wally asked?

"It's much worse."

"Religions. Parents. Cultures. They do this to their daughters. It usually happens to pre-teenagers" replied Bernadine. "The UN estimates there are more than 200 million women victims of forced FGM."

"Holy shit, 200 million women," yelled Kevin Christopher Brandon, "I heard about this in Iraq, but I had no idea. We thought it was make-believe."

"Who would do that? What does it have to do with Philadelphia?"

Bernadine spoke, "In America as many as 513,000 young women are at-risk. 11 states have no criminal bills against FGM."

"But how, why Philadelphia?" Wally asked.

Bernadine added, "Sir, for perspective #DiscoverPhiladelphia has 58,000 followers, mostly in the tri-state area. Shannon has over 30 million followers. She has made fighting FGM a global cause and more than 30 million people are following her messages to end FGM in America and around the world." Bernadine continued, "And now Shannon is bringing her message to Philadelphia, and the Conference on Global Women's Rights."

"You have to appreciate with almost 30 million followers, some of the most famous women in the world are following Shannon."

Bernadine quipped, "I'm not sure you can understand Shannon or what is happening until you watch this TikTok video. It won't take a moment."

Without hesitation, she pulled-up the TikTok video on their state-of-the-art videoconferencing equipment… pressed play, and she dimmed the room lights.

They couldn't notice Bernadine was shaking.

The Shannon TikTok Video

The song, "A Moment Like This" by Kelly Clarkson started playing and building up.

Guitar lead-in starts with baby pictures of Shannon…

When Kelly Clarkson's glorious voice starts exploding into the song, the screen splits. 30% of the screen is Shannon lip-synching the lyrics to the song, while the other 70% of the screen continues with Shannon baby pictures and young girl pictures.

As the song and Clarkson reach a crescendo! The graphics change to the small screen showing Shannon performing junior gymnastics while the larger split screen starts tragically revealing details of FGM and what happened to Shannon when she was only eight years old.

Clarkson voice rips into the heart-tugging song.

As the facts and figures popped on the larger screen, Shannon was performing flips and spins at Beaver Stadium.

The graphics described the awful impacts of Female General Mutilation as Shannon's gymnastics reached world-class levels. Then the video shifts as Shannon is featured as a Penn State cheerleader running onto the football field, and she leaps off a pyramid of ladies to the lyrics.

Graphics continuously appeared on the screen describing legislation and global efforts to end Female General Mutilation with pictures of Shannon testifying before the US Congress…As Kelly Clarkson sings about people waiting for a moment like this.

Then the screen turns white.

A few seconds later, Shannon appeared on the screen, and announced her speech at 10:00 am at the Conference for Global Women's Rights in Philadelphia. She asked if her friends would support and attend with her. The screen showed Shannon and 3-other women thumbs-up, lip-synching, "I will" to the screen quickly showing 8-women with the thumbs-up, then 16, 16, 32, 64, 128…256.

Then, as the emotional Kelly Clarkson song started to end, the screen slightly blurred into a scene of Shannon, alone, crying outside of the Congressional hearing.

As the Kelly Clarkson song slowly faded. The room was silent except for outright weeping. Everyone was sniffling. There wasn't a dry eye. Everyone was unabashedly wiping tears from their faces. As one of the men was wiping the tears from his eyes, he let out nothing short of a wailing groan.

Finally, the USMC Colonel (Ret.) Brandon tried to speak. "Maggie, I want," his voice cracked. He slowly gathered himself. He looked at his watch, trying to gain his ability to speak.

"Maggie, I want to call a press conference for 2:00 pm. And I want you to get everyone that works here in this room, and I want all of our live feeds working." His voice strengthened. "I heard about this FGM in Iraq. At first, we thought it was make-believe. I had no idea it was 200 million women. I wish," his voice cracked again.

"I wish... I wish we did more, I'm so sorry." He buried his head into his big hands. He regained his composure. "Right now, right here, we're changing the entire theme of this event. Get the marketing people in here and get them. No- get the whole office in here to watch this. I want everyone to know what this is all about. No more sweeping this issue under the rug."

Bernadine spoke, "Sir, I don't understand. The brochures are already printed. Three US Presidents and a dozen foreign leaders are attending to speak on world peace and global warming. It's a four-day conference on Thursday, Friday, Saturday, and Sunday." Her voice trailed as she was cut off.

Colonel Brandon barked. "Yes, you're right. That's all going to happen, just as planned. But more than 500,000 people are going to come to Philadelphia to see and hear Shannon speak. And we are going to make this the greatest day for Philadelphia and the world." His eyes were sparkling with an energy he hadn't felt since combat.

"Look, I've got a daughter. And, like that song just said, we've waited our lifetime to make this the greatest moment in our lives. We must work together. We need to end this bullshit."

Racing Back to Villanova

Rheingold still had no idea.

He knew nothing about any of this.

As they sped out the Vine Street Expressway, up the Schuylkill to Villanova, Roz told Rheingold the whole story. Shannon was shaking underneath him as Rheingold held her firmly. It was like he was keeping her from shivering despite the summer temperatures. Roz explained Shannon's powerful and courageous TikTok videos, and the millions of followers she had. Now, 43 million followers. The first TikTok video with Shannon mentioning FGM was Shannon performing to the American Idol version of "*Piece by Piece*" by Kelly Clarkson. That TikTok set every record on TikTok, for views, comments, shares. The TikTok that shook the world to the song, *A Moment Like This*, when Shannon revealed her FGM campaign, and her pledge to dedicate her life to eradicating FGM.

Then Roz explained a few things Shannon didn't know. With her vast fortune held in funds, foundations, and trusts she controlled, The Heiress was a significant investor in TikTok, (and many other prominent start-ups). Months ago, she was briefed by the TikTok leadership team about Shannon. At the meeting they showed Shannon's FGM video. The Heiress was openly moved to tears, an occurrence no one had ever witnessed.

Within a week, since Shannon lived near Villanova, The Heiress arranged an elegant lunch meeting, and immediately a special friendship was struck. Shannon playfully told The Heiress she'd love to perform and dance at one of the famous Friday night Heiress gatherings of her leadership teams. That was just a few weeks ago and already that dance routine had produced legendary stories, and the broken glasses.

Rheingold paused and asked, "Hold on, when was your first TikTok video on FGM?"

Shannon whispered, "Less than two months ago."

Rheingold ran his fingers through her soft hair, "Oh Shannon, 41 million followers in a few months. I don't even know what that means. But I want you to know, I love you no matter what, even if I never heard of this Tik-Clock thing. I'll do anything to protect you," he asserted.

For the first time, Rheingold was beginning to appreciate the gravity and magnitude of what was happening around him. "Shannon, I'm still trying to understand everything. But what the heck happened tonight?" He studied her eyes, and asked, "Was that really your father?"

Shannon sat up. "Rheingold, I love you. I know I just met you. But- but The Heiress has been right about so many things, and she said she knew I'd love you." In an increasingly animated state she started, "Yes, that was my father. He's a very powerful man. Since I decided to speak-out against FGM, my life- I've basically been on the run. They've threatened to kill me, all over the world. I've lost track of the death threats. I was on the run. And then like destiny, I met The Heiress. It was a miracle. She's protecting me. And now you've seen her elite team in action. She's training an army to change the world. She runs so many things, does so many good things it's difficult to imagine."

"I met The Heiress, we had an amazing lunch, then The Heiress said she'd help me make the 'A Moment Like This', Kelly Clarkson video. It was so amazing, I mean, in days Kelly Clarkson helped me produce the second FGM video and Kelly Clarkson guest-stars in a portion of it. Kelly Clarkson brought together her favorite music videographers, and they were amazing. This morning, we had over 69 million followers on TikTok."

"Tomorrow, they are expecting 750,000 guests across Independence Mall and surrounding streets and tens of millions of viewers on live broadcast," Roz remarked.

"I guess that's why my father had to act tonight," Shannon added. "No question, the powerful forces defending FGM don't want me to speak tomorrow. To silence me, they want me dead. And, if I'm not dead soon, they will probably kill my father. They are threatening the lives of everyone I know. I love my family, and everyone is at-risk," she explained as her soft eyes turned red and moist.

"But tomorrow, the show's going on," she said sternly. "I told my mother and The Heiress I'm taking this to the goal line. I will help end FGM in my lifetime, so my daughters and granddaughters, are forever FGM-free, or I'll die trying to end FGM."

"I won't stop."

Rheingold squeezed her shoulder, hoping she felt the growing love he felt for her.

"Shannon, you are the most amazing woman I've ever met," Rheingold proclaimed.

"The Heiress told me that you would love me and take care of me," Shannon whispered. "The Heiress told me, instead of running away, we'd turn, and run full speed into this mess to fix it."

Quietly, she added as she squeezed even closer to Rheingold, softly biting on his ear, "And somehow she knew you were going to make me feel alive. She told me I would fall in love with you and feel things I never felt before."

The song, "Piece by Piece," hauntingly echoed on their ride to Villanova.

The Heiress and The Oikos Center

Three years earlier, several prominent physicians, investors, and the University of Pennsylvania Medical Center, quietly developed a special triage center for the ultra-wealthy and connected. Patient-accessible only by helicopter, the Oikos Center was elite, family-driven medical care. The Heiress was one of the leading forces in the creation, funding, and crafting of the Oikos Center. The helicopters used by The Heiress and the Oikos Center were the most advanced medical copters in the world, equipped with the most advanced medical triage equipment available anywhere on the planet. Through her incredible foresight, by treating The Heiress on the way to the Oikos Center, these elite helicopters saved her life.

Whoever or whatever sliced The Heiress knew exactly what they were doing. Fortunately, by hitting Rheingold's belt they missed her internal organs by inches. The medevac team immediately appreciated the severity of the wounds locations and expertly reduced her bleeding, shock, and blood pressure so she could safely transport to the Oikos ER. With so many billionaires and world leaders in attendance for the US Constitutional Center gala, the Oikos ER was staffed with its best ER rotations.

Before she went under anesthesia, The Heiress called Kimberly and asked her to lead a meeting, with all the team leaders to update their security plans based on these new developments. Then she said something prescient. "Kimberly, tell Petrizzo to make sure they put up the bullet-proof glass around the speaker's platform,"

The Heiress ordered. "I don't think I was stabbed; I'm pretty sure I was shot by something."

By the time Shannon and Rheingold walked into The Heiress's mansion, The Heiress was already in surgery.

While The Heiress and her leadership team hadn't anticipated any injury or death of The Heiress, this elite leadership group had hundreds of hours of intense War College-level leadership training to plan for every possible nuance, and battle chaos.

In minutes, the leadership team sent an elite force back to the US Constitution Center with a specific mission. They drove down the Schuylkill Expressway in the military-equipped, Black Lincoln Navigators. As they approached Independence Mall, the leadership team had already coordinated with the FBI and City of Philadelphia for a limited 20-minute search of the stage.

On a hunch shared by an Oikos ER doctor, The Heiress' elite team brought two state-of-the-art metal detectors they used for minefield training sessions. The elite team moved quickly through the yellow security tape to the gala stage. From there, it only took 25-seconds to find what they were seeking.

The FBI and Philly police never saw the metal detectors go off. Four of the soldiers quickly turned and used advanced cell phones to take hundreds of pictures in all four directions from the metal detector's find.

None of this was a normal crime scene. None of the technologies were available to any retail shopper. This crime scene was going to be the most advanced investigation the world had ever seen.

Disc Guns

One of the side-benefits of US ultimate frisbee manufacturing, was the extreme study of manufacturing plastic, cylindrical objects that could be tossed in a spinning motion for ultimate frisbee. With several of the top ultimate frisbee players from MIT, Harvard, Caltech, and Stanford, it wasn't a surprise to see some of the players in the military-industrial complex surrounding those engineering schools. As drone innovation got increasingly miniature, in deep DARPA labs, the concept of mini-razor-disk bullets emerged (MRDBs). The lethality in the early reports led to further innovations, trying to prove MRDBs could bend on purpose, in-flight, much like ultimate frisbees.

The metal detector team quickly reloaded their equipment in the Navigators. As they sped from Independence mall with the three discretely recovered MRDBs, hundreds of pictures were being uploaded to The Heiress organization's super-computers. Within seconds The Heiress organization's HPC^6 Dell supercomputers confirmed The Heiress hadn't been sliced by a knife or sword, she had been shot by a disc-gun, and sliced by an advanced MRDB.

Another team using the HPC^6 Dell supercomputers was studying all the available video footage. Soon they concluded the intended target of the three MRDBs was not The Heiress, but Shannon. In the split seconds that the MRDBs were approaching Shannon, Rheingold had moved quickly to place Shannon behind him, and away from her father. In doing so, Rheingold had moved Shannon 18 inches to his left, thereby opening the trajectory pathway to The Heiress and the other two errant shots that missed The Heiress by millimeters. Through Rheingold's torso-twisting motion, the MRDB that had struck The Heiress grazed Rheingold's metal belt buckle, altering the MRDB pathway to miss her liver, pancreas, spleen, and kidney by millimeters. In other words, a boatload of luck had kept Shannon and Rheingold safe and The Heiress alive, as sunrise started to hit the Philadelphia skyline.

Sunday Morning, The National Constitution Center

"Sunday Morning" by the Velvet Underground reverberated around the city on a 3-repeat song pack through Philly's best rock n roll radio station. The set-up crew and security completed their walk-throughs. Everything appeared as safe as they could imagine. Everyone prayed they were right.

By 0745 on Sunday morning, Independence Mall was standing room only. But I-95, the Schuylkill, and Broad Street were overloaded with incoming traffic. By 09:20 am, Philly police estimated 750,000 people were within six city blocks of Independence Mall. Outside of the 2018 victory parade for the Philadelphia Eagles, and the 2015 Pope visit, the City of Brotherly Love had never experienced anything close to this magnitude. Some reports indicated another 75,000 people were never able to find parking, so they listened on their car radios.

Because he was ridiculously stubborn, Rheingold insisted on being as close to Shannon as possible. He kept insisting he could take a bullet better than anyone, which didn't score him any points with combat veterans. He later regretted his boasting when Kimberly made him wear a Kevlar vest under his suit jacket. Shannon was glad he was close. She held his hand tightly from the moment they left Villanova. Rheingold's mind was swimming as he soaked-in everything happening around him. While the world was waiting for Shannon to speak, Rheingold had his first alone moment as he stood off-stage. Ridiculously, his first thought was, *I guess we're not in Kansas anymore.* But his second thought was deeper. *Of all the men in the free world, why am I the man standing here?*

Shannon Speaks on Sunday

While everyone knew the crowd was attending to listen to Shannon, Shannon insisted that her remarks remain as originally planned as part of a panel discussion on Global Women's Rights. So, as originally planned, of the three panel speakers, Shannon spoke last.

The crowd groaned when the second speaker was announced and it wasn't Shannon, but the crowd listened respectfully to her remarks. As the second speaker finished her remarks, the crowd noise swelled to a low roar with anticipation and excitement.

Appreciating this event would define Philadelphia for years to come, Colonel Brandon invested heavily in the sound and video systems for the event. As Shannon was announced and walked toward the podium, more than 750,000 center city guests would hear her remarks with crystal clear sound, while millions on mobile apps, TV, internet and radio would see and hear Shannon with high-definition video and sound. Most of the crowd could watch the program on hi-tech video screens throughout Independence Park and downtown Philadelphia. He knew with high-quality sound and video, the program would be broadcast on video screens in Times Square, London, Paris, Tokyo, Rome, and thousands of downtowns around the globe.

Dressed in an exquisite purple velvet dress designed by Nicole Miller, Shannon shook hands with the other two speakers and approached the middle of the stage. She waved as the crescendo of cheers reached a deafening roar.

To her great surprise, off-script, as Shannon was almost center stage, Colonel Brandon's team played Shannon's TikTok video featuring the song, **A Moment Like This**, by Kelly Clarkson.

The impact was stunning. Hundreds of thousands moving in unison, waving their hands above their heads. As the song reached parts where Shannon revealed her FGM, you could feel the tears and weeping of thousands. Colonel Brandon stood proudly between his wife and daughter. His strong arms around each of them as tears streamed down his face.

In the middle of the stage Shannon stood alone, in front of the 700,000. She was so proud, so honored, weeping tears of joy and relief, weeping for the 200 million. She looked up, petrified. She knew full-well a sniper's bullet could greet her before she spoke. She turned and looked at Rheingold. It was a smile that filled her soul. She wanted to run to him, but her feet were frozen. She stood transfixed until he mouthed the words, "I love you." Like sparks, the words, the thoughts, the feelings exploded inside her. Yes, she thought, *yes, this is my destiny. This is what I wanted. I was born to do this.*

Slowly but with magnetic energy she turned and walked to the podium. She held up her hand and surprisingly the weeping crowd quickly quieted.

Then Shannon spoke confidently,

"Good morning, Philadelphia! My name is Shannon."

With that the crowd of 750,000 roared to life, emitting the loudest noise in the history of Philadelphia. After 20-seconds of deafening roar, Shannon raised her hand and the crowd quickly quieted.

"I am deeply honored to be with you this morning. I am Shannon. I am a woman. I am here today on behalf of the 200 million women that are victims of Female Genital Mutilation. FGM is real. FGM happens in the United States. FGM happened to me. A few months ago, I told my story. Thank you for listening and caring!"

"As much as FGM hurt when it happened to me. As much as it hurt living with FGM, and as much as it hurts retelling my FGM story; nothing has hurt me more than reading the thousands upon thousands of other FGM stories. My heart," she paused as her voice and emotions collided. "My heart goes out to all of you. We are sisters for life! For centuries no one lifted a finger to help women facing FGM. *No one!"*

"Over the past 25 years, with the transparency and awareness created by the internet, FGM has been made known to the entire free world, and despite that knowledge and despite this crime against young, innocent girls; FGM still happens to 14,000 young women every single day on this planet,

14,000 girls. Every single day!

For 25 years we have waited for governments and religions to end FGM. For 25 years nothing has changed. But this year, through the help of so many of you, we will fight FGM on every street in the world. We are going to eradicate FGM in our lifetime."

Shannon's voice reached a fevered, out-of-body pitch.

"Together, we will eradicate FGM in every village on every continent on this planet. Together, we will win this war. Can you join me when I say: we will win this war! We will win this war!"

"Can you join me when I say: we will win this war! We will win this war!"

The crowd roared.

"Can you join me when I say: we will win this war! We will win this war!"

The booming crowd noise echoed up and down Independence mall, east and west across Market Street.

Shannon caught her breath. She raised her hand and the crowd quieted.

"My friends, thank you for coming to Philadelphia to tell the world, we will win this war! Thank you for watching on television and the internet to tell the world, we will win this war! Everyone listening, can you join me when I say: we will win this war! We will win this war. We will win this war!"

Shannon let this chant reverberate around the world. When she raised her hand, the crowd quieted.

"Six weeks ago, we started The Shannon Fund to eradicate FGM in our lifetime. In six weeks, we have raised almost $500 million dollars!"

"We are working together with every organization in the world that is trying to eradicate FGM. We are working together with every religion and government to eradicate FGM. I wish I started my mission earlier in my life. I'm sorry I didn't start sooner." Shannon paused to collect herself. She continued, "As we speak, this morning we are launching websites and resources in 200 countries to eradicate FGM. Where are my TikTok Friends?" Instantly the crowd of 750,000 people roared. After 20-seconds, when she raised her hand, the crowd got silent almost instantly.

"To the brave women facing the tyranny of FGM, we want you to know we will protect you. From this day forward, every woman on this planet will be protected. Every woman that seeks personal safety, or the safety for her daughter, granddaughter, relatives, or friends will be protected. No one will be turned away. No one will be hurt against their will. No one will be alone. My name is Shannon!"

The crowd roared.

"My name is Shannon."

The crowd roared louder.

"My name is Shannon."

The roar of the crowd swelled to a deafening level.

"My name is Shannon, and we will win the war! Thank you, Philadelphia!" The crowd roars to unprecedented noise levels.

"Can you join me when I say: we will win this war!"

The cacophony of the crowd continued to chant, "We will win this war! We will win this war!" Shannon waved to the crowd. She stepped away from the podium and circled the stage.

Everyone that attended the Shannon speech in Philadelphia, said it was one of the most amazing ten minutes of their life.

Two miles away, The Heiress watched on the TV in her room at the Oikos Center. Despite her injuries as soon as The Heiress woke from her anesthesia meds, she was on the phone with Kimberly. Years later her medical team would recall how fast she recovered, only hours after her extensive surgeries. Watching Shannon, The Heiress glowed with pride. She hadn't prayed in years, but she intensely prayed every moment Shannon spoke.

Returning to Safety

By now, Rheingold was appreciating the depth and skills of The Heiress's Army. Not only did they drive into Independence Mall through an undisclosed route, in vehicles equipped for Afghanistan, but outside of the US Constitution Center, they had constructed temporary bomb-proof roofing over pathways and holding areas. Shannon was shielded from any direct views in case there was an active assassination attempt on her life. Philly police, secret service, and the US Constitution Center had invested heavily in ultra-superior gear and equipment, so guests were protected. With three former US Presidents, and foreign leaders, extreme levels of security were deployed. With Shannon speaking, local and federal law enforcement had no idea how many millions extra that The Heiress invested for security and protection.

Within minutes of her remarks, Roz and Dance escorted Shannon and Rheingold into the backseat of their Caiman MRAP vehicle, part of a fleet of 12 Caiman MRAP vehicles. This morning no one was taking anything for granted. The luxury of bullet-proof, black Lincoln Navigators had passed.

Roz called Kimberly, "We're packed and headed to you," Kimberly responded, "Copy that. Roz. Copy that."

Listening through her tech pack at her hospital room, The Heiress breathed a long sigh of relief.

Back at The Heiress's mansion, with a twinkle in her eye, Shannon asked Rheingold if he could follow her. Rheingold smiled, knowing full well, that following Shannon was something he was always going to enjoy. Soon, they were intertwined in a hot steamy shower without a care in the world.

The Telcon debriefing with The Heiress and Kimberly was quick. Immediately The Heiress thanked everyone for their flawless performance. Roz and Dance did a quick feedback loop on the situations witnessed by the team. Using their facial recognition technology, as 250 members of The Heiress's Army worked their way around the crowds, there were only two sightings of known FGM terrorists, both five blocks from the Constitution Center. After all the training, equipment, and extraordinary security measures The Heiress demanded and negotiated with the city, FBI, and secret service, she and her leadership team remained surprised the FGM terrorists did nothing.

Later that evening, she remarked to Kimberly, unless there was a divine intervention, something didn't add up.

Monday Morning, National Holiday. Banks, Schools, State & Federal Offices Closed

The National Constitution Center

By Monday morning, the record crowds were long gone. It was a national holiday Monday, so downtown Philadelphia was vacant. By 0900 am, a clean-up crew was restoring Independence Mall to the best shape possible. In addition to 42 volunteers, there were 24 city workers, 12 sanitation workers, and 20-members from a private event firm removing the gala stage, platforms, and the roof-covered pathways. The holding areas had another 18 people working on them. City police had already removed most of the armored vehicles that served as protection barriers. At 0930 am, four police officers were communicating with headquarters to get keys for two armored vehicles still parked next to the Constitution Center. Seven families were walking to the Liberty Bell. Three lifelong Philadelphians were out walking their dogs, a beautiful Border Collie, a Scottish Rough Collie, and German Shepard. Two members of the Philadelphia Eagles were doing a photoshoot for

Philadelphia magazine with a team of three from the photography firm.

At 0959 am, the massive explosion rocked Center City, Philadelphia.

At least 380 people were instantly killed. The fact that more people were not killed was a miracle. Surrounded by office buildings, that section of Independence Mall on holiday weekends was nearly vacant. Within an hour, the national and international shock and outrage was as great as 9-11 and Pearl Harbor. Every news station in the free world went live, covering the gruesome news, developments and aftermath.

---

20 blocks away, the explosion jolted the Oikos Center. Immediately, The Heiress was on her cell with Kimberly and Roz from her room at the Oikos Center. As soon as they were live, she asked, "What the hell just happened?"

Roz responded, "We're not exactly sure, but a major explosion just took place at the Constitution Center. We've got drones up, and we're already monitoring metadata from the top 100 TV stations, internet and social media sites around the world for clues."

Roz added sadly, "The death toll is going to pass 500."

Washington, D.C.

In the White House, unannounced the Chief of Staff Anne Frank Murray raced into the Oval Office and interrupted the President. "Mrs. President, there's been a terrible explosion at the National Constitution Center, hundreds are already dead." She quipped without thinking, "it's so awful but if the explosion was yesterday, hundreds of thousands would have died!"

"Wait, what arc you talking about, what?" responded the President.

"Ma'am, we don't know any details but 60 seconds ago there was a massive explosion at the National Constitution Center."

In a panic, The President barked, "let's get in the Situation Room as soon as possible. Is my daughter okay? Is my daughter okay? She was there yesterday with her friends."

How Did They Get There?

Ali Ibn Abdullah was a 50-year-old computer programmer, 1991 graduate of Glassboro State College. Known to friends as Ali, he was a 26-year employee at a defense contractor, working in telecommunications. Ali was a devout family man, not outwardly religious at work or school functions. That he was a member of the Shafi'i version of Sunni Islam was unknown to anyone outside his family. His position didn't require updated security clearances, his religion and family backgrounds were not vigorously checked before the age of Google.

In the 1990s as world awareness and pressures to end FGM increased, the Shafi'I school of Islamic jurisprudence reiterated its position that FGM was obligatory. On the surface Ali wasn't involved in the day-to-day debates of FGM at his mosque. While his father was devoted, Ali was working 60-hours a week, and busy with his family's Americanized lifestyle of the sports, arts, and music interests of his three young boys. On most weekends, Ali and his family weren't unlike other American families following kids to play recreational soccer.

Ali's father and other devotees were increasingly alienated by US federal and state laws to curb the practice of FGM.

---

24 Hours Before in East Camden, New Jersey

Outside Camden, New Jersey the last 24-hours had turned ugly. Everything here was brutal.

Yesterday after Shannon finished speaking, across the Delaware River, in an east Camden basement, 10 of the 11 devotees of the FGM culture stood in shock as the first replay of Shannon's speech reverberated again across the screen on CNN. It was almost as-if, they had to see Shannon's speech twice to fully appreciate their entire mission to kill Shannon had not only failed but that absolutely nothing had happened at all. Almost immediately, the angry men turned to stare and then apprehend Ali. Even though one of the men was Ali's revered father, no one was gentle.

In minutes, Ali lay prostrate across the table, severely beaten to shouts of, "What have you done?", "You are a traitor", "Allah condemns you to a long, painful death."

Two of the men had served for 20 years in almost every major action of the Shafi'I across the globe. They had served under ruthless leaders in some of the fiercest war zone settings. For Ali, these two were going to heighten the pain he was about to experience.

Two hours later at noon on Sunday, they forced Ali to witness the horrible torture of his father. In front of Ali, the leadership had conferred and judged Ali's father equally guilty of the mission's massive failure. 30 minutes later, after another leadership meeting, another man was accused, whipped, and severely beaten. They destroyed this man's back with the whip. Through their yelling and screaming, it was obvious this man was Shannon's father.

Throughout the day and night, the three of them were brutally beaten.

At 0800 am on Monday the Ruthless One started a meeting to discuss the two armored vehicles sitting next to the Constitution Center. One of the experienced assassins voiced his concerns. "Ali may have placed incriminating evidence against the group in the bombs or bomb encasements."

His life almost over, Ali lay prostrate listening to the leaders discuss his fate. As he did, his mind drifted to the beginning of this nightmare.

Destiny or Fate – A Father/Son Dinner

Ali remembered it was a cold Thursday night that Ali's father asked Ali to attend a father/son dinner with him. Since Ali was working so hard, he hadn't seen his father recently. Ali thought it would be a convenient way to spend time with his father. Instead of their mosque, the dinner was going to be held at the house of a member of a neighboring mosque. After decades of his authoritative father handling all aspects of their relationship with the mosque, Ali didn't think twice about his father being vague about the details.

During the 90-minute drive, Ali spoke with his father about upcoming summer vacation plans, his career pathway, and retirement options once the children had graduated college. His father was attentive but distracted.

The property was down a long narrow lane that opened-up in front of an interesting gate. As they got closer, two men emerged from a gate house with submachine guns and walked toward their car. Ali's father answered their question with his full Islamic name. The guard member nodded his head indicating my father could proceed forward. The gates opened quickly. After 25 years in the industry, Ali was quick to notice advanced communications gear and camera systems lining the road and gate area. The moment triggered a statement a college professor used to say, "I guess we're not in Kansas anymore."

The security surrounding the main house seemed excessive for a father/son dinner. Sensing something was happening more than he was told, Ali asked his father, "Why do they have all of this security for a father son dinner?"

His father mumbled, "you'll see soon enough."

Judging by the number of cars, this was going to be a big dinner. As they walked up the front steps, Ali's father was again asked his name. His father repeated his full Islamic name. As they walked inside, the initial greeter nodded to another elderly man, who gave the impression that Ali's father should follow him. For the first time Ali felt a sense of fear and loathing surrounding his father. Looking at his father, Ali got the feeling that whatever was happening, it was larger than his father ever imagined.

The elderly gentleman took the father to two open seats in front of a small speaker's podium. Ali's stomach felt increasingly empty as he didn't observe anything to do with dinner in this large gathering room. Certainly, he thought to himself, it would be impossible to hide the smell of middle eastern food in this house. A feeling of deep dread kept building up inside him.

As they were getting comfortable in their seats, the elderly man that brought them to their seats was handing out a piece of paper to each guest. Ali and his father both received copies. Ali started reading his copy.

U.S. Homeland Security Investigators Are in The Garden State This Week as Part of Operation Limelight USA.

The goal of the initiative is to combat a practice known as Female Genital Mutilation, or FGM.

Brad Breyers, assistant special agent in charge of the U.S. Immigration and Customs Enforcement Homeland Security Investigations Team, says agents have been at Newark Liberty International Airport all week speaking to certain passengers traveling with girls under the age of 18 to countries where FGM is performed. Some of those countries include the Central African Republic, Kenya, Somalia, Egypt, Togo, Chad, Guinea, Sierra Leone, the United Republic of Tanzania, Niger, Ethiopia, Ghana, and Nigeria.

In all, 31 different countries in parts of the Middle East, Asia and Africa have been identified as FGM hotspots. He said passengers traveling with girls to these destinations are identified and investigators will talk with them "about the law and explain the risks and the legal implications and hopefully deter them and deter the parents from doing this practice."

"In those countries it's a cultural practice," he said. "FGM is performed as a rite of passage or a coming-of-age ceremony."

World Health Organization defines Female Genital Mutilation as "all procedures that involve the partial or total removal of the external female genitalia, or other injury to female genital organs for non-medical reasons."

It is against the law on a state, federal, and United Nations level.

He said the Centers for Disease Control estimates 66,000 girls in the New Jersey and New York region may be at risk for FGM, and more than 200 million around the world may be forced into undergoing a procedure that can include cutting, piercing, and in some cases sewing shut most of the vaginal area.

"Usually, a parent will take their child, their girl, their daughter overseas to a country to have FGM performed, that is against the law, it is a federal crime."

He explained it is illegal to take your child out of the United States to have FGM performed, punishable by up to five years in prison. Dreyer noted FGM can have serious medical complications, including death, and may take weeks or months of recovery time, depending on what exactly is done.

He said the age of girls subjected to FGM varies from country to country, culture to culture. Frequently it's done between the ages of six and ten, but also it may involve girls in their teens.

Efforts to crack down on FGM were ramped up after people in different communities brought the issue into the spotlight and increased awareness about it. Dreyer said the goal of the operation is prevention. He added in some cultures there is strong pressure to perform FGM.

"Hopefully, those families on the fence about whether they should do it to their child, this could hopefully affect their decision making."[3]

A chill went up Ali's spine. He dreaded this topic whenever it was broached at the mosque or family discussions. He always thought to himself, *Thank Allah, I have three boys.* Several times other fathers in the mosque tried to get Ali's opinion on FGM, but Ali found ways to avoid direct answers and discussions. Now, in addition to losing his hunger, Ali's sense of fear and loathing returned and doubled.

Ali didn't know the person near the speaker's podium, but his father shook his hand. They exchanged pleasantries. Ali's father introduced Ali to this man using Ali's full Islamic name. Another man, older, more deliberate was slowly approaching the podium. The small talk around the room eerily stopped. The older gentleman was introduced to Ali's father, then to Ali. The man nodded, and slowly moved to the prominent and ornate chair behind the podium on a platform six to ten inches higher than the floor.

Another gentleman started speaking to the crowd of nearly 100 men. Ali recognized four other men from his mosque. While he recognized them, he didn't know them well. He recalled they always seemed militant and angry at the world.

"You know why we are here," he started. Ali immediately noticed everyone in the room nodding their head. "We are grateful and honored to have Iman Muhammad Abu Usman with us tonight." Again, the crowd nodded with their knowing approval.

He reverently said, "Surely to Allah we belong and to Him shall we return."

He paused, before continuing.

"We are also pleased to have a new servant of this group with us tonight, Ali Ibn Abdullah." Again, the crowd nodded. It was only after they started looking at Ali with sharp, blank stares that he realized, *Holy shit, that's me!* "Ali Ibn Abdullah will be a great asset to our cause with the technology he knows so well."

Back to Camden, New Jersey – Sunday 09:59 am

Just as Ali's mind was recalling his name being announced at the dinner, the entire house shook from a tremendous explosion. While everyone else was freaking out, Ali managed to muster the briefest of sighs. He lay silently whimpering at the deaths he had just caused but was eternally grateful to Allah that hundreds of thousands of innocent lives had been spared. As soon as the room settled, the Ruthless One raced toward Ali. "You changed the day! You changed the day!" he shouted at Ali waving a big Arabic knife. Not everyone understood what he was screaming. And he again screamed, "You idiot, you programmed the bombs to explode on the Monday holiday instead of Sunday. You fucking idiot!"

Ali was so battered he barely heard the muffled screams of The Ruthless One. His mind rejoiced at the repeating prayer that kept him alive all night. *Dear Allah, merciful and just. If I must kill and maim, let it be hundreds instead of hundreds of thousands. Through me, make your divine intervention. Lift up my soul. I beg you to protect my wife and children.*

Ali remembered his thoughts after the father/son dinner and subsequent clandestine meetings. What can he do that his wife and children might be spared. True, he knew he would be killed for mission-failure. He also knew his father would be killed, but he prayed to Allah for an answer to his prayers. Late one night, he had a dream-like vision that was crystal clear. Make everything seem like one, big, giant mistake and his prayers could be answered. Of course, he couldn't tell his wife or family about his vision. But twice he got up the courage to quietly whisper in his wife's ear. "Someday many may reject me, but afterwards you may learn, through Allah and his divine intervention, I saved many in hopes of saving you." When she cried and begged him to explain, he only said, "You must promise me you will never say anything about this to anyone. No one. No one. In Allah's name, you must never speak of this! You must say that I never told you anything about my work. You must realize that you and our children will be at great risk. Say nothing of this!"

As the others started realizing how bad Ali had fucked-up, they started walking toward Ali and his father. The Ruthless One shouted, "You fucking idiot! You have written the death sentence for all of us!"

Ali's father grunted, "He should live, he should live, it was only a mistake!"

The group started yelling, pointing fingers, until The Ruthless One pulled out his Sig Sauer P228, aimed it at Ali and fired three rounds into his brain. In the airtight basement, the unexpected shots damaged everyone's eardrums. As the echo blast was fading, The Ruthless One turned and fired another two shots into Ali's father's brain. Again, the stunned group was just about to shout, when The Ruthless One fired another two shots into Shannon's father's brain.

The Ruthless One loudly shouted, "We are exercising Plan C." He yelled to his trusted friend, "Mohammed, go to the car with Ahmad, and bring down the 12 bottles of nitro." He shouted, "We're incinerating this site, and moving." As Mohammed and Ahmad raced to the car, The Ruthless One reloaded his Sig P288, and grabbed another P288. Once he had the guns, he immediately killed the other five devotees, each with bullets to the head. All told, they unloaded two carloads of nitro into the basement.

Within five minutes, the residents of Camden, New Jersey heard another tremendous explosion. Nothing was left, not a trace of the suburban house rented by "Robert Hamilton." With the power of the internet, following his instructions, Ali had gone online and rented the house in East Camden under the most WASP-sounding name he could remember. He fondly remembered his attorney, Robert Hamilton. To Ali, Rob was the kindest, most gracious man he had even met. He thought, Rob will know I was forced to do these dreadful acts. Rob will know. *I pray to Allah,* Rob will tell them.

The white-heat incineration cratered the house with a giant, smoldering hole in the ground. The explosion incinerated the two cars in the driveway, and damaged six nearby properties.

Shannon At the United Nations

As the buildup to the Philadelphia conference ignited, The Heiress had used her international connections to get Shannon scheduled to speak at the United Nations the Wednesday after the Philadelphia speech.

The Heiress had deep connections in New York and the UN, but she was especially leery of the security getting in and out of the facilities. While the security council nations didn't oppose FGM restrictions and clampdown on sex trafficking, many African and Arab nations wanted FGM and sex trafficking off the UN agenda.

The massive Philadelphia explosion shook every civilized nation. The death toll heightened international awareness of FGM, and the demand for action. World leaders were briefed on the factoids of what the death toll would have been if the bombs detonated on Sunday morning. The three former US Presidents acknowledging they were at ground zero, pledged to help lead global FGM eradication efforts.

Late Monday evening Rheingold held a team conference call of his lobbying firm. After explaining the explainable portions of the weekend, he asked the team to cover his schedule for the next few weeks. On Tuesday, Rheingold and Shannon met with the gentlemen experts that Rheingold had met at Holts. This time they met at The Heiress's compound. Roz and Dance also briefed Rheingold on the massive security surrounding the Heiress compound. Unbeknownst to the casual observer, the nearby mansions and properties were long ago purchased by The Heiress and her ancestors to expand their security perimeter. Most of The Heiress's Army leadership lived in the adjacent mansions and farmhouses. In some directions the perimeter extended several miles. Their jamming technology prevented drones from flying-over. Except for lost drivers or scheduled deliveries, there was no reason for an outside visitor to drive or walk anywhere near the core perimeter. Outside of the White House, Camp David, 16 Downing Street, few properties in the world had as much visible and invisible technology securing the perimeter as The Heiress's compound. Recent attacks and earlier bombings of the US Capitol proved Congress leaders should have listened more closely to The Heiress's warnings on the lack of security in most of Washington, DC.

Many leaders in The Heiress's Army were couples, who in former roles would have been compromised or prohibited from dating or marrying a special force's teammate. The Heiress's Army presented an opportunity for elite warriors in the US and foreign military industrial complexes to stay together and raise families. Instead of outcasts of other mercenary Armies, The Heiress's Army contained individuals that wanted to safely marry and raise families.

New York Preparations

With The Heiress unable to travel to New York; Roz, Dance, and The Heiress's Army leadership worked quickly to tighten all aspects of the already rock-solid UN transport plans. The announced approach would be west to east then south down the Harlem River Drive to FDR Drive to get to the United Nations. The diversion route would be a more publicized route up the east side.

Rheingold insisted on being Shannon's extra security willing to block bullets and explosions. Originally, four cars, now the trip would be 8-cars of Heiress warriors with six-crews in Navigators and two-crews in loaded and armor-plated black Lincoln MKZs. By noon on Tuesday nine nations including Egypt immediately protested the inclusion of Shannon on the Wednesday UN Agenda. Despite the Philadelphia massacre, the nations were furious the UN Secretary General had pulled a seldom-used executive privilege to place Shannon on the speaking agenda with less than 24 hours' notice.

Getting to the UN

That morning, everything was going exactly as planned. Shannon appeared ready. Rheingold was anxious. Despite the intensity, Rheingold was soaking in the NYC scenery. In his mind, he remembered the UN was on the east side of 42nd Street, and Times Square was right smack in the middle of Manhattan. His mind drifted to high school field trips to New York City. Ha! It's difficult to imagine a school district letting 40 kids go to NYC with only six chaperones and eight hours of free time. Back in the 1980s, Times Square was crime-infested with prostitutes, drugs, johns, and run-down buildings! As they sat in traffic, he marveled to himself, *dang, this place has really changed.*

It wasn't necessary, but Rheingold took mental notes on the transport route. His mind drifted to Madison Square Garden and amazing trips to Big East basketball tournaments with his father and his friends. The late lunches at Villa Mosconi with their homemade Buffalo Mozzarella, and incredible Osso Bucco. His father zealously loved the Zuppa de Pesce. Oh my, the house red wine, the bread, the desserts, with a ceremonial post-meal Sambuca with the coffee beans. He thought, *I'm so glad I had those times with my father.*

Even in the most intense moments, you can reach a nirvana-like numbness of joy, in those split seconds when the mind races down memory lane. Shannon's soft touch to his cheek immediately brought Rheingold back to reality. He turned to her with glowing affection! They held hands as he gazed out the bullet resistant windows.

Hold on. He wanted to give directions, and mention they seemed off course. Before he could speak, their vehicles jolted and veered into an underground parking lot.

---

15 minutes later, the UN explosions rocked NYC.

Years in the making, the UN technology office now beamed with pride. Unbeknown to the assassins, the entire two block radius around the UN was devoid of humans. Monday's Philadelphia explosion gave them the perfect opportunity to unveil operation *BeTupac2.* Using *BT2* advanced hologram technology around the UN gave the appearance that everything was normal on NYC streets. In the weeks that followed, Hollywood would be amazed at the detail the UN Technology office used to give the appearance of bustling streets. When in fact it was robust holograms complete with fog machines, steam, and other visual obstacles to extend the mirage.

Instead of hundreds or thousands of dead, while there was car, road and building damage, as far as NYPD and FBI investigators could determine, there was no loss of human life.

Yes, the executioners saw and heard Shannon's caravan approach the UN. Yes, they saw Shannon, Rheingold, and bodyguards exit their limousines and walk towards the UN. Yes, they pressed their bomb triggers just like they imagined. But their destruction only impacted pixels.

Rheingold's brain struggled to grasp the innovative technology they deployed. "Wait, by taking a few pictures and videos of us, you were able to transpose us onto a hologram. You made us walk, I opened a car door for Shannon, held her hand, all without us doing anything?"

The arrests were swift and thorough. The UN security team had almost every assailant on high-definition sound and video, arriving, and planting bombs. The micro dust and bug particles they shot in their hair and clothing served as the tracking devices to the safehouses that in the end weren't safe at all.

As scheduled, Shannon's UN speech was delivered in a high-tech TV studio that was ten safe blocks from the UN. Her UN remarks were shown across 200-nations with record-television and web audiences. As she watched Shannon's animated and passionate remarks, The Heiress smiled to herself from her Oikos wellness bed in Philadelphia. The numbers spoke for themselves. Like it was her destiny, instead of the usual UN audience of a few thousand, today's broadcast surpassed the most-watched Super Bowl!

Within an hour, just like East Camden, another safe house in Jersey City was nitro torched. Four more bodies were incinerated in the basement never to be discovered, as The Ruthless One drove away.

Rheingold – Facing Fate

The nice thing about a late morning speech in NYC was the ability to get back to Villanova before dinner. After an intense morning sitting next to Shannon with little opportunity to touch and kiss her, Rheingold was anxious to get back to the safe house. He couldn't wait to let his hands ecstatically touch her skin. As his mind drifted, he marveled at how much pleasure he received from touching and caressing Shannon's skin. How many times had he glanced at his hands, almost in awe, as his hands, fingers and palm simply throbbed from the joy of touching her? Her skin, he couldn't explain it. But her skin gave him a magnetically charged sensation he couldn't explain away. He couldn't get enough of her.

As their caravan crossed the Delaware on I-95, out of view of the others, Rheingold slowly positioned his hand underneath Shannon's perfect bottom. It wasn't long before his movements, and her wiggles had fingers exactly where Shannon wanted them.

She turned her head, out of the view of others, and mouthed, "*You are amazing.*" He smiled as she gracefully closed her eyes.

As sunset approached, The Heiress mansion had an incredible sunset glow against its roofline. Exiting the vehicles, everyone stood in awe, shaking hands over their successful mission. Just as the small talk started to get deep, Shannon and Rheingold politely excused themselves, with well wishes for the evening. Grasping his hand, Shannon felt like a teenager walking away from a crowd with her man. They both grinned as their slow walk turned faster as soon as they were out of everyone's view. Shannon's house was a short walk from The Heiress's mansion.

The door locked as Rheingold shut the door. Shannon was already half out of her clothes. Far from her modesty of a few short days ago, she ripped off her clothes with a reckless abandon only matched by Rheingold ripping off his armored business suit and vest. Next to the bed, their naked bodies met. She arched her back, on her tippy toes to receive his passionate kisses and hands. Her soul ached as her genetically exploding body oozed its sexuality. Both ached with urgency. Like always as the milliseconds of arousal triggered the horror of her mutilation, her mind splashed with worries about her surgically removed femininity and her ability to be sexual, but Rheingold washed away all her worries, fears, and doubts. Already she felt the beginnings of another set of mind-blowing orgasms. Oh, she didn't want to wait or give Rheingold any opportunity to tease her. She pushed him to the bed, motioned for him to lie down in the middle of it, as she climbed above him, trembling with sexual feelings. He watched as she kept moving up his anticipating body. Instead of straddling him Shannon bravely lowered her body onto Rheingold's face. Obviously recognizing her intentions and desires, Rheingold grabbed her sweet ass and hips with his strong hands and guided her onto his face. Even without her womanhood, Rheingold's tongue and fingers magically gave her sensations that she felt from her toes to every neuron in her brain. And when his tongue and fingers touched magic spots, her body convulsed and she moaned, "Oh my God, Rheingold. It's so good, it's so good." Shaking, she quickly slid down Rheingold's body, and after days of practice,

Shannon slid perfectly onto him and immediately started feeling her first orgasm quickly building as she yelled out. Within seconds her contractions, twisting, and moaning brought Rheingold to the point of no return, as the surge lifted his body. His hands squeezed Shannon's perfect hips as their bodies tossed and turned together.

Shannon collapsed onto his powerful chest. Her body was still pulsating and heaving, as she slowly caught her breath. Rheingold's fingers immediately found her soft hair. The room was so quiet, they could hear the clock at the end of the hallway. Almost in harmonic unison they both said, "You're amazing!" They both knew.

They knew.

Rheingold woke first from their nap and was starving. He carefully lifted Shannon off his chest, tucked her under the covers, and whispered, "I'm starving, I'll be right back."

He quickly dressed, soft khaki pants and a brand-new college fraternity sweatsuit. He threw on his Vans instead of loafers, grabbed the key fob for his Lincoln and walked to the garage. He was excited to drive his Lincoln. His fraternity brothers had coordinated a tag team to get Rheingold's new Lincoln MKZ from Harrisburg to Villanova. One of guys threw a brand-new fraternity sweatshirt on the front seat. He pondered, *dang, I haven't driven a car in 15 days.* Ever since he left politics, Rheingold had driven a Lincoln. Even if he was going to be decidedly non-partisan, Rheingold wanted his vehicle to transcend his deep-rooted feelings toward the civil war, ending slavery, and fighting for civil rights for all people, creeds, and lifestyles. Yup, to him, driving a Lincoln said a lot. And he was damn sure in his lifetime he wasn't driving a German or Japanese car no matter how nice they were. At an airport, if the rental car wasn't American, he'd rather drive a South Korean car. Nothing against the people, no. They were hand-working, kind, and considerate people. But as nations, Rheingold wasn't convinced they had done near enough to compensate the world for WWII, after what they did to Hebrews, Chinese, Koreans, Europeans, and Americans, no, not even close.

Another quirky thing with Rheingold was his undying lust for Wawa. Born in Wawa land, living in Harrisburg was like living in exile from Wawa. It was rare for Rheingold to enter Wawa-land without stopping to grab a coffee, a chicken quesadilla, or tastykake. What Rheingold didn't fully appreciate was his desire for a quick visit to Wawa broke every rule The Heiress and Kimberly specifically told him not to do. The other thing he didn't know, was his little escapade hit between two shifts of the video surveillance and personal security assigned to Shannon and Rheingold.

He drove to Wawa without a care in the world.

Just as Rheingold was placing his order inside the Wawa, The Heiress noticed something out of the corner of her eye. Bored, she was watching the video monitors the tech team had installed in her room at the Oikos wellness center. In her hospital bed, she twisted her body so she could use her laptop to manipulate the cameras on the Heiress compound, other properties, and Shannon's house. She deftly reviewed the security cameras to confirm what she thought she saw. Rheingold's Lincoln was missing from Shannon's garage. She speed-dialed Kimberly at the compound, who quickly called the newly on-duty security team. They raced to Shannon's house to confirm the car was missing from the garage, and Shannon was safe inside. Within minutes, the cyber team and PHC^6 Dell had tracked his car in the Wawa parking and within seconds, four black Lincoln SUVs were speeding towards the Wawa on Route 30.

Rheingold had no idea the peril he was facing!

The Race to Wawa

Back at the Oikos wellness center The Heiress was frantic. With Shannon confirmed safe, now the sole focus was Rheingold. Despite real-time updates, surveillance pops, and circling drones, The Heiress had a deepening dread that all this technology and investment had holes and weaknesses that humans could inadvertently puncture or elude.

Why didn't he listen to me?

She kept repeating in her trained mind*, doesn't he fully appreciate the gravity of the situation? We've got the best food in the free world and he's running off to a Wawa? Rheingold what were you thinking?*

As these cascading thoughts were exploding, she started feeling ill, an ache, a dread, something deep, pinging her inner most feelings. *What if I can't protect him, what if we don't get to him in time?*

Of course, she was feeling anxious because one of her own was at great risk. She definitely felt that. But as this was unfolding, and it became obvious to her that the security teams weren't going to get to that Wawa for another ten minutes. Deep down, she knew her feelings about Rheingold were more complex, intense, and real. Her arms were shaking. Instead of verbalizing the intense love she felt for him, she cursed, *My God, Rheingold, why aren't you picking up your phone? Why isn't Wawa picking up their phones?*

Death Approaches

Weeks before the Shannon speech, The Ruthless One had started 24-hour surveillance of The Heiress's compound. Using dark-cloud surveillance systems designed and perfected by Ali, the Ruthless One was able to see every movement to and from the compound. The Heiress and the US government had no idea Ali's surveillance technology matched their technologies. Based on his knowledge of DoD surveillance capabilities, Ali had triggered his encrypted technology to take 12 bursts of pictures on every approaching and departing vehicle. Ali installed small but advanced cameras on a telephone pole that Ali correctly estimated were 25 feet beyond the tracking capabilities of The Heiress compound's cyber security system's perimeter.

Every single vehicle was processed, but this time Ali's AI facial recognition popped up Rheingold's image into the central processing module. In milliseconds an alert was sent to the embedded assassin teams. They quickly reacted with further alerts that Rheingold was travelling alone in a black Lincoln. They quickly phoned The Ruthless One.

Ali's second innovative technology play was six blocks from the first alert system. Here, Ali developed a miniature drone launch on top of a dormant 1950's street light console. Within seconds of the first alert, the mini drone was airborne following Rheingold's black Lincoln and uploading thousands of data points to the systems controlled by The Ruthless One.

The Ruthless One had been instructed to find every opportunity, even if dumb luck, to kill Shannon before the Philadelphia speech.

It was pure coincidence, minutes before Rheingold drove to Wawa, that an assassin team of two brothers sat in the parking lot of a Moroccan restaurant just blocks from the Wawa. Smuggled into the US through the Mexican border, the assassin team was imported to kill Shannon and stop the FGM situation. They were in America a week before the rest of the international team to do advance work and assess opportunities to strike as soon as possible. By dumb luck and zero planning they were two blocks from the Wawa.

The Ruthless One was immediately on the phone, sensing the good fortunes of this unexpected prize. He marveled to the oldest brother, "The whore's infidel paramour has sprung the protection of the castle walls and we're going to crush him like a bug." He shouted, "I don't care where he goes. I don't care what he does. I don't care if you have to kill 20 Americans, I am ordering you to kill this man as soon as you can. Kill him!"

The brothers exchanged a knowing look. They knew they were the best assassins in Islam, but they didn't kill innocents or children.

Despite their absolute lethality and common cause, these brothers despised the act of killing innocents. The terrorist's predictive intelligence software and the drone's real-time photography indicated the Wawa convenience store was the most likely destination. Quickly, the assassins drove to the Wawa.

In a tiny rental car, the assassins parked in the Wawa parking lot. The older brother watched in amazement as one of their primary targets was standing alone, inside a Wawa, unprotected, with no care in the world. Instantly, the older brother used Ali's phone app to kill the phone service in the Wawa store. Then he killed the cell phone service in the 100-yard perimeter surrounding the Wawa. He barked at his younger brother, "Go into the store, follow him, and when he is 12 feet outside of the store, break his leg. I want this dog to feel absolute pain before I drop two bullets in his brain." Without any hesitation, the younger brother jumped out of their rental car and headed into the Wawa. As he was walking, he threw on a Phillies shirt and hat they used as a disguise.

"How many minutes are they out?" The Heiress implored into the phone.

Roz replied, "It looks like five minutes if we don't hit all of the lights!" Roz continued trying to put on a good face, "We're working on getting all of the lights green within the next few seconds."

" No, I don't feel good about this at all." The Heiress interjected. "Tell them to get there as fast as possible."

Rheingold kept cursing his phone. He pondered to himself, *why don't I get cell phone service in Wayne, Pennsylvania? It's the wealthiest, damn place in America?*

After using one of the Wawa computer screens to place his order, Rheingold walked to the check-out counter to pay. He used the restroom. Along with a couple other dudes he was waiting for his order to be placed on the countertop. He smiled to himself when he saw the Arabic man walk past him with the Phillies gear. He thought, *geez, the Phillies sucked this year, but man is their fan base diversifying. Back in the day, when Dad had Sunday season tickets, Phillies fans were white as white could be. Half the city hated Dick Allen just because he was black, despite the MVP numbers the guy produced. In fact, Dick Allen should be in the Hall of Fame. It's all damn racism*, he thought to himself.

His brain was unraveling a plethora of Phillies memories and his father, until the flashpoint when Rheingold saw the assassin's piercing eyes staring back at him. It hit him like a ton of bricks. *Holy shit, what the fuck was I thinking*? His mind whirled. *That guy is definitely here to kill me and I'm not packing heat. Shit, my cell phone's dead! Shit,* he remembered the checkout clerk telling the other cashier that the phones weren't working in the office. He thought, *maybe they cut all the phone lines just to get me.*

Instantly, Rheingold's survival instincts kicked into high gear. Stay calm, asshole. You've seen enough spy movies to know acting stupid gets you killed. Rheingold did a quick look around the store, pretending he was buying a pound bag of Wawa coffee. His mind raced, *if he's got explosives, I'm going to stay on the opposite side of the coffee stand from him. It doesn't look like anyone else is here with him. If he's solo, I can race him to my car and try and make a clean getaway. Shit.* He cursed himself again for defying The Heiress and skipping out of the house without security.

Without waiting for his Wawa order to be called, the moment the assassin looked away to pretend he was picking up a tastykake, Rheingold went low, lower than the countertops to bend and sprint his way to the back door. As his hand hit-the-door, he heard the assassin start to sprint after him, by the yelp of the lady he must have pushed to get out of his way. The race was on.

In the next split seconds, a lot went down.

As soon as Rheingold breached the door he raced toward his car. He felt an explosion burst past his face. There were two reasons the trained assassin's brother missed Rheingold. First, Rheingold tripped on the sidewalk and fell. The second reason was the split-second twitch the shooter made as he realized the loud noise approaching him was a Black Lincoln Navigator barreling toward him at 90 mph. Just as the shooter comprehended what was happening, the Lincoln plowed into his tiny rental car, killing him instantly.

As Rheingold was reacting and trying to get back on his feet, the younger assassin from the store was already in motion, swinging the crowbar he had left at the front door to inflict severe pain on Rheingold.

The assassin's swing hit Rheingold's left shoulder with a crushing blow that knocked Rheingold to the ground. Still in a swinging motion, the assassin spun around with another slam to Rheingold's upper thigh. Everything happened so fast, the young brother stopped to look in horror to see his brother's car smashed full tilt by the Lincoln Navigator. He stood motionless, as Rheingold withered in the parking lot. His horror quickly turned to terror, as he started to walk toward Rheingold, pulling out his Marushin Ruger Mk1 Maxi handgun from his jacket. With each milli-second his brain was registering madness as he processed the reality that his beloved brother was dead. Just as he was raising his arm to shoot Rheingold, bursts of semi-automatic weapons opened fire on him. It looked like he still might fire his weapon until three more guns opened fire, knocking the gun from his hand, puncturing every vital organ in his falling body.

In seconds, the rest of the security team formed a security perimeter around Rheingold. Dance yelled, "Rheingold, we've got to get you to safety. It's going to hurt like Hell when we lift you." With that, another racing Lincoln Navigator sped and stopped right next to Rheingold. Four guys jumped out of the vehicle to help Dance lift Rheingold into the Navigator. With every fiber in his lungs, Rheingold screamed bloody pain as they grabbed his shoulders and legs to lift him quickly into the Navigator.

A second Navigator sped into position so the other teammates could lift the two assassins into that vehicle. Dance reached around Rheingold and coaxed him into giving him his key fob. A second teammate drove Rheingold's Lincoln MKZ back to the compound. Within twenty-four seconds every vehicle was racing out of the Wawa parking lot, except for the crushed rental car, which quickly exploded with white heat the moment they were clear.

For hours, onlookers tried to explain what happened to police, investigators, reporters, with surveillance drones listening from the CIA, FBI, Heiress's Army, and The Ruthless One. Within minutes The Heiress's Army knew the rental car was rented by a fake ID with a credit card linked to an encrypted and untraceable cryptocurrency. Two hours later the CIA and FBI still had no idea there were assassins or an assassin vehicle.

In front of the hi-tech screens Ali had installed, The Ruthless One watched the news clippings and surveillance uploads in total disbelief. He had his best assassins against an unprotected, unarmed nobody, and the result was nothing. He had no knowledge, awareness, or reconnaissance on anything that happened.

The Ruthless One was furious.

Dance was quickly on the phone with The Heiress. "Ma'am the situation is under control. We have Rheingold. He's going to live. But he's going to have injuries to his left shoulder and an awful bruise on his thigh." Dance continued his report, "the two assassins are dead, we've got them in the other Navigator. Petrizzo and Missy torched the assassin's rental car with the new explosives. With this technology there won't be a trace of the vehicle. We used our new data flash technology linked to the HPC^6 Dell to crush video surveillance cameras within a 600-foot perimeter. So, right now there's no evidence or leave-behind."

The Heiress replied, "Dance, I'm so glad you were there. Thank you. Tell everyone I said thank you. I'm so relieved and grateful."

Slowly, The Heiress hung up her cell, turned off all her equipment and monitors, and started to weep. *Thank God.* Decades of non-emotion. Decades of dedication. Decades of insulating her heart and soul from any feelings whatsoever. She breathed deep. She continued weeping and shaking. For the first time in 25 years, she realized she loved again. Yes, she thoroughly adored Shannon, her cause, her being, and her spirit. Shannon was like a daughter to me. But she knew, even with Shannon, she maintained her distant and secretive personal defense mechanisms. But Rheingold. Was he a brother to me, a father to me, a soulmate, a lover? She wept. She felt love in her heart. Shaking her head trying to understand her feelings and emotions, she wiped her face.

Gawd damn woman. Get a hold of yourself. What the heck?

She calmed herself, tried to get out of bed, but the instant shock of pain held her back. She softly fell backwards on the bed. She grabbed her phone and called back Dance. "Dance, thanks, can you put him on the phone?"

Dance looked at the phone, almost double-checking to confirm it was The Heiress on the line. Her voice was different, softer, gentler. Dance nodded. Rheingold winced. He lifted his non-injured arm to take the phone from Dance.

"Hello," he said meekly into the phone, sounding like he was responding to his Kindergarten teacher, Mrs. Tucker, knowing he had done wrong, caught in the act.

"Don't you ever do that to me again," The Heiress shakingly implored. Her voice wilted with physical pain, and the pain only a woman can know.

"I won't," Rheingold groaned into the phone. "I promise I won't."

He thought he heard her whimper. The phone clicked and he just plain gulped. With the adrenaline wearing off, the sound of her voice, and real pain emerging every time he breathed. Dejectedly Rheingold realized he had foolishly put a dozen people in serious harm's way. He was selfish. He was lucky to be alive. He left Shannon alone. All for a Wawa chicken quesadilla.

Minutes later, The Heiress speed-dialed Kimberly. "Kimberly, I seriously need to get back to the compound. After the team safely returns Rheingold, can you have them drive to Philly to bring me home. I've been away too long."

Kimberly wanted to say something motherly about staying put and getting healthier. But she caught herself and place. "No problem, I understand. I'll make all of the arrangements." Kimberly paused, weighing the events of the week, and emotionally said, "It will be good to have you home. I think we all need you home, right now."

The Ruthless One watched three more TV stations give ridiculous and conflicting reports on a shooting at a Wawa on the Main Line. The reports indicated there were no bodies, no vehicles, no plausible explanations, or whereabouts. He called the rest of his implanted team in Villanova into a meeting. He was 20-blocks from the Heiress compound, "I want you to quickly find out what happened tonight and find our men." He demanded. "I don't know what happened. But I want to know everything as soon as possible." He walked out in disgust. In his mind, he deployed two of the best assassins that ever lived. Yet, he still had no idea what happened, where they were, or how they could disappear? He speed-dialed another phone number. "In an hour, I want to be fully briefed on every upcoming presentation of the American whore, Shannon," he shouted. "I want to know everything we know in an hour."

At the compound, "*People Get Ready*," by the Impressions reverberated on-repeat across The Heiress Army internet radio. He was satisfied this was the warrior song everyone needed overnight. Alone, tearing off his gear, Dance felt drained. The 24-seconds kept repeating in his mind. *We were split seconds on-time, split seconds.* The demons of past firefights filled his uneasy mind. I've seen what happens when we're split seconds too late. His mind shifted. He knew his opponents were equal warriors, fighting for a cause they believed. But his mind got stuck on Ulysses S. Grant quotes about southern rebels fighting to protect slavery.

"I felt like anything rather than rejoicing at the downfall of a foe who had fought so long and valiantly, and had suffered so much for a cause, though that cause was, I believe, one of the worst for which a people ever fought, and one for which there was the least excuse." -- Ulysses S. Grant

He winced remembering the savage wound to Rheingold's shoulder. He thought, *where are the men? Where are the warriors that should be appalled by FGM. Where are the chivalrous knights of old? Why aren't they fighting for these women? Why this womanizing lawyer? He doesn't listen. He puts people at-risk. Why has fate brought together a tiny gymnast and a middle-aged lawyer to lead this cause?*

The Heiress Story

Wealth begets wealth.

Some daughters resent their father's humanness and faults. Some daughters, like The Heiress, absolutely adore their fathers. Today, it's difficult to know much about The Heiress. If you google her, you'll find a few society pictures and an occasional article. But for the most part, despite her obvious wealth there is little, if anything on the entire world wide web about her. As a result, that lack of information is usually where most inquiries end.

Through amazing AI technology that gets exponentially better every second of the day, anything about The Heiress is observed, filtered, and reviewed. Years ago, anything she wanted to disappear; disappeared.

In the beginning it was a daily swipe, then they got it down to twice daily. When it was hourly it was difficult for the most experienced hackers to find anything about her. Over the past six-months her IT team was getting it close to "real-time." The intensity of her desire to be anonymous was incomprehensible. But she knew information was power. In a world with information-overload, the lack of information was even greater power.

Rheingold Needs to Know

Not surprisingly, over his career Rheingold had amazed an interesting array of friends, colleagues and drinking buddies. The information his team gathered in three days on The Heiress was a strong as the Mossad file on The Heiress. Yet, the scant details Rheingold and his team compiled were sketchy at-best.

Rheingold just felt he needed to know.

Ironically, it didn't cross-his mind that the Wi-Fi and broadband he used at The Heiress mansion wasn't off the rack Cisco, Comcast, or FiOS. The Heiress smiled to herself when she read the file Rheingold had gathered about her before Rheingold saw it in his in-box. After reading for several minutes, she looked up and mouthed to Kimberly, "Dang, he's good.'

What No Research Could Find

16 years ago, outside of Philadelphia, The Main Line. Wealthy patriarch. White, Anglo-Saxon, Protestant. Business owner. Many interests. Blind trusts. Family roots into the American revolution. Private schools. Foundations. Buildings and libraries named after family members on the campuses at Penn, Princeton, Harvard, Yale. Car accident, explosion. No survivors. Then mysteriously no investigation, no more stories.

A 75-year-old patriarch, his wife, their son-in-law, and three-year-old granddaughter killed. But their daughter, the son-in-law's wife, the mother of the child was missing, not in the wreckage. The Heiress. By a strange twist of fate, she wasn't in the car with her family. Instead, she had driven separately so she could buy a birthday gift for her father.

One of the largest accumulations of information in Rheingold's file on The Heiress was research about the 2005 film, Batman Begins, starring Christian Bale as Batman. The file was packed with sketches of martial arts, Navy Seal training, ancient strength training, diet, health. Not unlike Bale as Batman there's a decade of no information on The Heiress.

She took a year to hike, alone. First the famous hikes in America, then the world. To her she wasn't solo, for unlike most hikers, The Heiress hiked with communication technology not mass-produced, but made solely for the world's special forces. There were instances where she faced death, and serious injury, but through her superior technology she feigned death.

The Heiress didn't serve on boards of directors. Yet, through her controlling trusts, foundations, and holding companies she had significant ownership interests in many prominent companies trading on the NYSE and NASDAQ. Her quiet empire had large ownership stakes in dozens of mutual funds and start-up companies, both in the US, UK, Tokyo, and globally. Discrete white-show lawyers represented her interests around the world. Publicly, she had no office. She appeared on no lists of wealthy individuals. There were few pictures of her. And yet, there are smatterings of references, comments really, of The Heiress with heads of state, leaders of corporate America, entertainment icons, and internet entrepreneurs. Meetings, conversations with Apple's Steve Jobs, especially when he took back control of Apple. She had the most extensive research on global supply chains, oil and gas, narcotics, heroin, poppy fields, as well as FGM and sex trafficking.

Rheingold found several references to 1735 Market Street in Philadelphia. But it was almost like the 50th Floor didn't exist. He discovered the common elevators didn't have a button for the 50th Floor. The fire escapes didn't have doors for the 50th floor. Drones couldn't see inside the 50th floor. How could that be?

The CIA, Mossad, MI6, KGB, Red Army, seemed to respect her desire for privacy, and yet it seemed if and when she wanted access, they were only a phone call away. Or was it, she was a discreet phone call away for them when they were stuck or lost. Maybe her technology was better? Maybe she didn't have the red tape?

After what little his team was able to find, Rheingold paused. They never saw it coming. They underestimated her because she's a woman.

Closing the file, The Heiress smiled. Still, they really didn't know, and now through her advanced AI technology literally programming itself real-time to continuously get better, they'd never catch-up.

The Heiress shook her head and got deep in thought. What the CIA and FBI didn't know or refused to admit, but Mossad had already discovered, was evil and brutal regimes were starting to use AI technology to jump ahead of the West.

America's short-sighted H1B visa and citizenship policies had opened the flood gates for college students from around the world to live, learn and train at the best American universities. Yet ridiculously, after America educated these foreign students, because of caps on citizenship, America exported these talented American-educated minds back to the Middle East, Asia, Africa, and Europe.

A sane American strategy would have given lifetime HB1 visas and citizenship to any student in the world that graduated with a STEM degree and remained and worked in the United States. Instead, despite the global war on terror, increasing Russian and Chinese power struggles, and stalling college enrollments, American public policy kept exporting American-educated scientists, engineers, mathematicians, and information technology graduates back to the Middle East, Africa, Russian and China.

Literally, America was knowingly subsidizing the STEM educations of our enemies and their military industrial complexes.

Rheingold Asks to Meet with The Heiress

The Heiress got a text from Kimberly. "He wants to meet with you. Make sure you are OKAY. I believe he has a hundred questions to ask you. He wants to meet you, alone. I gave him your cell number."

The next text to The Heiress was from Rheingold. "We need to talk. I need to know you are OKAY. Can I visit you, alone?"

Rheingold got a text from The Heiress. "Kimberly will arrange it."

The Heiress and Kimberly Phone Call

The Heiress spoke first. "Kimberly, I need you in this meeting with Rheingold. You've read all the files. You know him and all of the situations as well as I do."

Kimberly wasn't pleased but she chose her words carefully. "I appreciate everything this man has done professionally. But the womanizing I can't reconcile. I don't see how you can admire and love a man that has so much history, so many stories."

The Heiress winced as she tried to sit-up in her bed. "Can't you see and feel what happened to him?" The Heiress paused. "Everyone this man loved either died, lied, or had something terribly tragic happen to them. He's afraid to love believing something bad will happen if he loves too much."

Kimberly quipped, "I just don't see it. I admit after meeting the man, listening to him, I see the magnetic attraction he ignites. Truthfully, I thought there was no way in the world, Shannon would even like him. But wow, she immediately fell in love with this man."

"Kimberly, I read all of those files. At first, I had the same reaction you had. I almost stopped reading. Maybe it was the irony that we liked the same wine that kept me reading. But something remarkable occurred to me reading about his professional successes against all odds and his relationships with women. It was how he treated people. Inadvertently, the files kept casually mentioning he was respectful to staff and workers. That's what's different here. I've met many of the infamous men from the #MeToo movement. Most of them were awful to their staff. Disrespectful and demeaning.

The Heiress stiffened up. "The moment I met Shannon I knew she was going to fall in love with Rheingold. I knew Rheingold would love everything about her. I knew. Everything about Rheingold is a love story."

"I wanted Rheingold for Project Poppy. But he is perfect for Shannon and eradicating FGM."

Kimberly interjected. "It could sound like you set this whole thing up."

"No. No. This is not David, Bathsheba, and Uriah the Hittite. I won't and will never order Shannon to the front of the army. The world knows, by her own free will, Shannon was already front and center before we met. I met her when she was in great danger. No, this is different. Right then, I decided I was going to use all my resources to protect Shannon and help her eradicate FGM. I also decided I was going to give her the one thing she deserves in all the world. Love."

Kimberly spoke softly," there's no doubt we are on a worthy mission. Everyone embraces the decision to help Shannon end FGM, and delay Project Poppy for 6-weeks. It's just. Maybe I don't know how the world will see Rheingold and all his flaws."

The Heiress stared into Kimberly's eyes. "Look, the world wants to believe it's changed, but hasn't changed much at all. Until men decide FGM must end. Until men will fight FGM to end it, FGM will continue unabated across the world. FGM is more community-based, it's not religious in the truest sense. Men have to join us, to end this."

The Heiress's voice cracked, "Here's the one big thing on this planet. Men aren't perfect. But flaws and all, we need men to step forward and declare FGM no more. That's the only way FGM will end quickly and quietly. That's why Rheingold is perfect. Yes, he's human. Yes, he has tremendous flaws, but he's also filled with love. I knew once Rheingold fell in love with Shannon, the two of them would change the world."

Kimberly added, "but isn't Rheingold the one being set up here?"

"Rheingold was born to lead. He walked away. Now it's time for Rheingold to remember why he is here."

Rheingold Texts to The Heiress

"I had a long talk with Shannon. I spoke with Reed and Kelby. I spoke with Roz and Dance. I want you to know, I'm here on my own free will. Nobody owns me."

Rheingold sent a second text, "since you know so much about me, two things. No matter what happens I love you, too. Get healthy we need you back here, asap. No need to meet. And second. Thank you. Thank you for taking a chance on me. Thank you for introducing me to Shannon. More than anyone, you know, I'm in way over my head on all of this, but I'll make sure I don't let anyone down, including you!"

Rheingold Articulates the Daughter's Campaign

He didn't recover. Three Advil didn't do much. At some point, he'd need shoulder surgery. Shannon helped him get dressed, especially his shirt and jacket. But he was there.

In awe, Rheingold was amazed at the power and ability of The Heiress to pull so many resources together at a moment's notice. The twelve women The Heiress had assembled were the best women marketing professionals on four continents. Already the articulation of the grand strategy was in full motion by the time Rheingold got involved. Damn, he thought, I'm the only man on this Zoom meet. He listened. He took notes. He was mesmerized.

He kept mouthing "amazing" to Shannon as they listened and watched together.

At the end, The Heiress quipped in a commanding voice, "Rheingold, what do you think?"

Rheingold carefully measured his words. "Wow this campaign is so thorough and deep. It's comprehensive and impressive," he added. "I can see it; I can feel it," he paused. "It's just..." he collected his words, "for branding, I've listened to everything you want to do to end FGM and sex trafficking. It's strong. It's powerful." He was building up to his pitch, to his signature move that made him famous in his little world of Pennsylvania politics. "Look, I don't want to be disrespectful, dear Lord this strategy is one of the most powerful proposals I've ever seen," he looked up. "But as I'm listening, visualizing the powerful impacts of your proposal. I kept thinking about the most powerful thing we need to do; our objective is to get nations to join together or be forced to join together to ban FGM and sex trafficking. If we- If we could take everything you have proposed and get nations to co-sponsor uniform legislation, that's clear and concise. We'd just need a tweak or two to get to a stronger, more pronounced end result. A global co-sponsorship campaign to get every nation to end FGM and sex trafficking so we can isolate and focus on the remaining holdouts, by exception report!"

He had everyone's attention. He winced but he stood up. This thigh throbbed.

"Look, every issue impacting women is huge. I'm doing a quick gut-check. I believe the branding campaign would be more powerful if we broadened it and titled it, *My Daughters Team.* What I'm poorly trying to articulate is all of you are daughters. I keep it a very private matter, but I have a daughter that I adore. Some of you have daughters. There are 200 million daughters impacted by FGM. There are millions of daughters trapped in sex trafficking. There are other issues impacting our daughters. By using My Daughter's Team branding campaign, it sets the stage for a branding effort that both sexes can understand and support. A broader campaign leaves the door open to fix more things."

He shifted, and grinned, "Think of how many men coach their daughters to play sports. I don't mean the over-the-top dads like mine, running up and down the sidelines, screaming their freaking heads-off…" He paused, trying to wave his uninjured right hand and arm like a lunatic coach. But coming off like a wounded penguin. Everyone laughed.

He just pulled you in.

"I'm talking about the millions of fathers that just plain love their daughters and want to be there for them."

He paused, a little choked up.

"Really, and I mean truly, I believe in Shannon's heart of hearts she wishes and yearns that her father was on her team." His voice cracked, "Just when she needed her father most."

He repositioning himself, wiping his eyes.

"Everything we do is uncharted territory. But everything we are doing is about building the unstoppable team," he leaned in. "I think of these 200 million women, and I believe they wish their parents had stood up for them, just when they needed them most!" He stood up, almost hypnotic, "I'm closing my eyes, picturing your amazing commercials and advertisements all across the world in 200 languages."

He closed his eyes. He opened them wide. In a loud, powerful voice, he said, "I'm on my daughter's team."

"I'm on my daughter's team."

He looked deeper into the camera.

"I'm on my daughter's team."

"I'm on my daughter's team."

The Heiress was wiping her eyes. Rheingold kept repeating in different voices each time.

"I'm on my daughter's team!"

"I'm on my daughter's team!"

She realized Rheingold had stopped talking loudly after the fifth time, but everyone on the call was loudly repeating.

"I'm on my daughter's team!"

"I'm on my daughter's team!"

Shannon's eyes were filled with tears. Just when she didn't believe it was possible, she loved this man more.

Listening together, at the Command Center, their misty eyes immediately met. In the same unison Roz and Dance loudly proclaimed, "I'm on my Daughter's Team." They hugged tighter than they had in years. Dance whispered. "Last night I used that man's name in vain. I had no idea why he was here. He didn't listen. I didn't really like him. But. But he just ripped me." One of the toughest men on the compound and US soil, he gathered his voice. "I sat there listening to *People Get Ready* questioning the Lord. When the Lord was right there telling me all you need is faith. All you need is faith, and you just thank the Lord." Dance stiffened up, "Baby I just want you to know I'm on my Daughter's Team. I'm on Shannon's team. But most importantly, I'm on Your Team. I'm on Your Team." She was an unofficial Navy Seal, one of the best female athletes in the world, trained to exhibit a heart of steel, but now she pulled-in closer to this man she loved with all her heart. "I know baby, I know." *And I thank the Lord every day.*

The Marketing Launch for My Daughter's Team

After Rheingold's My Daughter pitch, the 12-members, Shannon, Rheingold, and The Heiress developed the simplest, most effective marketing plan ever launched globally. The 12-members of the were asked to bring in two of their most trusted leaders. This team of 36 finished every aspect of the global marketing plan in three days. For starters, every member nation of the United Nations would have 12 leaders, sports figures, religious leaders, celebrities, and personalities for each country's "daughter" marketing.

ZOOM WITH THE HEIRESS

With her strong ownership and debt interests in each firm, The Heiress flew in the CEOs of William Morris Endeavor and Creative Artists Agency to her airport hangar at the Philadelphia airport. The almost rundown facade of the hangar was purely for show. Inside, the hangar had the same technology installed at The Heiress's compound. Essentially, the hangar was an iron-reinforced nuclear-bomb proof bunker. Still not ready for regular transport, The Heiress briefed the two fiercely competitive leaders of her ASK over their secure communication system. She appeared on the 12' ultra-high-definition screen and shared 4-minutes of catch-up with both of them. "We want your 24 biggest names for a global marketing campaign. Your biggest names with daughters. Everything about this campaign is unprecedented. Globally, everything, all footage will be shot, edited, approved, and released in less than 24 hours. At the same time, around the world, every participant will see the exact same instructions, the exact same video, and then they will be asked to do two takes. Each take will be the same five words. Participating will be national leaders, global celebrities, and athletes from 200 nations in response to the Philadelphia and UN bombings. Like the We are the World campaign, people will regret missing this. I'm obliged with the strictest confidence to share with you that this same message will be recorded by President Jennings and Queen Elizabeth, as well as Beyonce, Diana Ross, Madonna, and Angela Jolie, as well as Tom Brady, Michael Jordan, Will Smith, Tom Hanks, Bono, Paul McCartney, Bruce Springsteen, Daniel Craig, and their wives. As you may know, Kelly Clarkson is already deeply engaged. Your top talents will be part of the national and global campaigns, respectively."

"I want you to know what I'm about to tell you is a secret designed only for your ears. Frankly, we believe we have the only cybersecurity on the planet that the terrorists can't hack. That is why I am meeting you here in my bunker. Old School. I'm telling you in-person so we can give you the crypto keys for our secure communications portals. You and your artists will receive emails and memos informing you that the recording will take place in 24 hours at 12 noon, Eastern Standard Time, all around the world. No special technology is needed, except this encrypted VPN key code. There will be no exceptions. It can be any internet portal, but they must use our portal VPN technology at 12 noon, or they won't be recorded. Within hours of 12 noon tomorrow, the most recognized faces on the planet will be leading this campaign."

"Most importantly, we want both of you to be in this campaign as well. For many years, I have greatly admired how both of you have balanced motherhood and highly successful careers. I was pleased to be your sponsor as the first female CEOs in each of your organizations. You have made me very proud."

They both awkwardly smiled at her, never knowing The Heiress helped advance their careers.

"Since we don't have a lot of time, I'm going to ask if you have any questions, and then we'll be off. I'm confident you will be impressed by the final product. I want to tell you how much I will appreciate your efforts. I look forward to seeing you both soon."

With a nod, the three of them were moving.

Building The Heiress's Army

After her year(s) of hiking, training, and self-discovery, The Heiress got serious on her mission to change the world for women. In addition to consolidating her financial power, she immediately started recruiting the best special ops leaders in the world. Her strategy was to give real lives to retired members of special forces that wanted to have a spouse and kids. It was an instant attraction, especially with the salary, benefits, perks, and living arrangements. She also knew with international terrorism and their evil use of technology it was increasingly difficult for the members of the world's special forces to have normal lives with spouses and children. For recruiting, every candidate was carefully screened and vetted by the team. If they passed muster, their file was reviewed by The Heiress. Following extensive background tests, an interview took place at one of her mansions on the Villanova compound. They were asked to bring their significant other to the interview. During the interview, the group took a walking tour of the mansion and grounds. At the end of the tour and interview, The Heiress would add, "And this would be your house."

Why Rheingold?

The Heiress knew she was going to need the most powerful lobbying firms to help her win the legislative and budget issues for her causes. Her first interviews were law firms her companies used. They were Philadelphia's famous white-shoe law firms that featured lobbying or government relations expertise. These lawyers were the cream of the Ivy league from pedigree families with generational connections and friendships. Her top law firm had a strong presence in Harrisburg, and they asked The Heiress to visit the state Capitol to meet with the Governor (since they essentially ran his campaign and fundraising efforts).

As The Heiress was getting a tour of the State Capitol, she was standing in the Rotunda with her group as Rheingold walked past them with several uniformed members of the armed forces. As Rheingold was passing, one of the older lawyers said under his breath, "What a fucking asshole." She was shocked. She never heard this 60-year-old lawyer cuss.

She quickly asked, "Peter, I'm shocked, what did that guy do to you?" He immediately blushed.

He paused and disgustingly muttered. “Oh him. That guy kicked my ass so bad three years ago, I almost lost my partnership.”

He continued, “I’m so sorry you heard my comment.”

The Heiress, now intensely curious, asked, “Well, is he an asshole or is he good?”

Peter reflected, and said, “No, he’s more than an asshole and he’s better than good.”

The Heiress was pulled into Peter’s ponderings. She asked, “Good grief Peter, what was the case? What happened?”

Peter turned and sternly lectured, “First of all, he’s a goddamn womanizer. I’m sick and tired of hearing about his antics in bathrooms and rooftops with some of the most attractive women in politics.” The Heiress’s jaw almost hit the ground.

Peter unapologetically continued, “Second, he’s so fucking nice and cool. He drives you nuts when you’re opposing him. He makes your clients and your cause feel so damn important and appreciated. He’s so brilliantly charming, I had a couple female clients settle their cases, terminate my contract, just so they could jump in the sack with the bloody bastard.”

“From all of his bathroom and office shenanigans with the ladies, there’s a not so quiet saying around the Capitol that his name really isn’t Rheingold, it’s, ‘Oh my God, Rheingold.’”

Peter was on a roll. “But that’s it. The man is brilliant, well-read, funny, and engaging. He’s damn good, and he has a fierce determination to only represent the very-best causes and circumstances.” He paused, reflecting in admiration and awe, “You won’t see him represent a tobacco or gaming company. He just won’t do anything for the money, which is ridiculous in this town.”

Peter appeared to almost sputter. “And civil rights!”

“The man is a relentless, tireless advocate for the poor, afflicted, and unfortunate. There are so many instances where he single-handedly won victories and budget authorizations for these hopeless causes, and multinational companies never saw what hit them. Reporters and politicians ask him, 'So Rheingold, who's your client in all of this, how are you getting paid?' And usually he just smiles, laughs, and quips, 'They don't have any money, so I did it for free.'"

Just as it appeared Peter was going to rant even more; they were interrupted to leave for their meeting with the Governor. The Heiress wondered to herself, *What the hell can you do in a bathroom?*

After meeting with the distracted but apologetic Governor, besieged by the media for his comments against raising the minimum wages, The Heiress got another opportunity to speak confidentially with Peter. Before she could speak, Peter interjected, "Look, I know I'm not supposed to share this information with clients, but you're the most unique client we've ever had." He looked around to make sure no one was within ear-range. He got quiet and secretive, "We have an extensive file on the man. He's crushed us so many times, our firm Chairman demanded a no-stone-unturned investigation against Rheingold. He wanted raw ammunition to try and ruin him before he crushed another one of our sterling clients. I mean, the word, 'extensive'' doesn't begin to cover the level of dirt we tracked down on this man. Just the paper files and photographs we have on the man fills a room. I mean, we laughingly call it the Rheingold room."

The Heiress was near-speechless. "What the heck could one man do to inspire so much fear and concern in your amazing law firm?"

Peter stopped walking and processed how he would articulate what he was about to say. "We track five of the most feared people in Harrisburg to make sure there are no surprises at our firm. Ironically, two of them work for our firm. Two of them are legislators. And the fifth one is Ryan Gold Craven."

"Look, when Pennsylvania was passing their first gaming bill, there were millions of dollars of lobbying fees floating around Harrisburg. The gaming industry and political leader's plan was to give 14 organizations the gaming licenses for free. We had a marketing campaign supported by talking points about job creation, property tax reductions, and tourism dollars. Except for the religious legislators that opposed gaming as a vice, and the free-market legislators that opposed gaming as anti-competitive, the damn legislation was a slam-dunk. No one expected what Rheingold did next."

Peter was speaking almost reverently, "The bloody brilliant jerk holds an unannounced Press Conference in the Capitol Media Center a week after a gaming license was sold at auction for $400 million in Gary, Indiana. Since it was Rheingold, and he said it was about gaming, with 24-hour notice, he packed the Media Center with reporters and TV cameras. He stands up there with a shit-eating grin and announces he was preparing to file his gaming amendment that would hold a Saturday night, Gaming License auction on ESPN LIVE. The auction would permit anyone to bid as much as they wanted to bid on the licenses, as long as they were pre-qualified by a Standard & Poor's financial viability statement. With the cameras rolling, he predicted a gaming license auction would bring in $1.5 billion dollars. His amendment would distribute the $1.5 billion to school districts to fund dollar-for-dollar school property tax reductions."

The Heiress was amazed how Peter could articulate his disgust so eloquently. She stared in admirable silence and listened.

Peter continued, "That Rheingold episode was perfectly timed on a Thursday afternoon, so it would hit the Friday newspapers, and Sunday editorials. That weekend, I never heard more cursing and swearing. Monday morning the bill was amended to a $40 million license fee for 12 licenses and $10 million for two limited use licenses. Literally, through a 20-minute press conference, he raised the license fees over $500 Million dollars against the strongest lobbyists and law firms in the nation." Peter was shaking his head. "In the end, he deep-sixed us by $1.4 Billion dollars. On a whim. On a fucking whim!"

Peter finished his colloquy with a sigh of disgusted veneration. His cell phone buzzed, he excused himself to take a phone call and took a few steps away. His younger partner, Doris Kevin, continued Peter's diatribe.

Rheingold Roulette

Doris started, "Peter isn't the only one impressed by Rheingold. I don't know as much as Peter, but I remember the legislative battle over gaming. While everyone else fighting for and against its passage, Rheingold was studying all the distribution models being developed for school property tax relief from the collected gaming revenues. Even though he was dead set against gaming, if it passed, he was hankering to make sure his school districts finally got their fair share of state funding. That he was friendly with so many of the Capitols top legislative aides was also one of his legendary traits. He treated everyone with respect and decency, and so often those qualities came back to Rheingold in hearts and spades." She blushed, "I didn't mean hearts, like that, like women's hearts."

She continued, "Legislative caucus meetings are private, and only legislators and pertinent staff are permitted inside the caucus room. But everyone learned that evening's gaming debate was heated. For years, portions of the legendary gaming caucus debates were retold many times in bars and offices."

"Apparently, they had a caucus meeting on final passage of the gaming bill. When the bill's details on school district distributions were discussed, several ardent pro-gaming proponents were screaming at Rheingold for his brilliance at being dead set against gaming, but his school districts were ranked #1, #5 and #8 in the gaming distribution formula. One frustrated legislator stood up and yelled something like, "You fucking son of a bitch! You opposed every aspect of this bill. You made us increase the damn license fees from zero to $1.4 billion. You delayed every vote we tried to make. In the end, you voted against gaming, and now, now we learn your damn school districts get the most fucking money in the distribution of the gaming revenue. I'm going to fucking kill you, you motherfucking whore."

"Apparently total bedlam broke out. Rheingold made things worse by laughing his ass-off while this 70-year-old member nearly had a stroke over the whole situation." At first, The Heiress was chuckling under her breath, but she couldn't hold back and started laughing out loud. With Peter walking back towards her, she touched Peter on the shoulder, "I really think I need to read all of his files."

Peter asked, "What do you mean?"

She responded, "I want to read all of your files on him."

A day later, she found herself repeatedly thinking, sometimes giggling, *who the hell is this guy? How the hell does he pull this off?*

A week later ten large file containers were packed and shipped to her hideaway in Montana.

Montana

She whispered into her phone. "Siri, play on repeat, 'The Gulf of Araby', by Natalie Merchant, *Live in Concert, New York City, June 13, 1999.*"

The Heiress didn't do anything half-ass or without purpose. When she needed to escape and refuel her soul, she found solace in the Black Paw Mountains. After her intense training, financials consolidations, and world travels, she started acquiring as much land as she could buy near the final surrender lands of the Nez Pierce and Chief Joseph. For her, at one of the saddest vortexes of civilization, she found her peace. Here, the Indian way of life ended at the hands of the namesake of Howard University, who previously had done so much as the Commissioner of the Freedmen's Bureau.

Drinking coffee at sunrise and wine at sunset she absorbed the energy of the Nez Pierce and their incredible desire to be free. Her soul opened up. She felt whole again by reading and often touching the monument she placed in the center of her colossal ranch with Chief Joseph's immortal speech:

"Tell General Howard I know his heart. What he told me before, I have it in my heart. I am tired of fighting. Our Chiefs are killed; Looking Glass is dead, Toohulhulsote is dead. The old men are all dead. It is the young men who say yes or no. He who led on the young men is dead. It is cold, and we have no blankets; the little children are freezing to death. My people, some of them, have run away to the hills, and have no blankets, no food. No one knows where they are - perhaps freezing to death. I want to have time to look for my children and see how many of them I can find. Maybe I shall find them among the dead. Hear me, my Chiefs! I am tired; my heart is sick and sad. From where the sun now stands, I will fight no more forever."

Chief Joseph - Thunder Traveling to the Loftier Mountain Heights – 1877

At dusk, she was getting settled. She pulled on her favorite flannel sweats, cashmere black socks, and one of her oversized men's sweatshirts that read, "NAVY RUGBY – ELEGANT VIOLENCE."

In Montana and Villanova her extensive wine cellar was always packed with cases of Red Car Pinot Noir.

She brought a bottle of Red Car Heaven and Earth to the table stand next to her reading chair that overlooked the Bear Paw Mountain range. In terms of million-dollar views, this sunset view was priceless.

This red wine from Sonoma County always tasted so good in Montana. As she opened the red wine, the mansion was filled with the haunting voice of Natalie Merchant.

The Heiress picked up the gold file. She didn't know what to expect. But she was looking forward to reading a few of these files.

GOLD FILE #1 Sonoma County, California

File Memorandum

We were asked to rundown the story behind all the Red Car wine in Rheingold's possession. We asked his two favorite restaurants how they always had Red Car in their wine cellar.

We couldn't find anyone that knew the story behind the Red Car.

WAIT.

Immediately, The Heiress grabbed her wine bottle. Indeed, it was Red Car, Heaven and Earth. *Wow. Talk a billion to one. This is so bizarre.* She stared at the bottle. Amazed by the pure coincidence, she continued reading the memo with added interest.

The Memorandum read, *you asked us to research his obsession with Red Car. The best we could find was a short story he allegedly published anonymously in a small journal in Sonoma County, California. From travel receipts we couldn't confirm how many times he was in Sonoma County. We learned that Rheingold often told friends, the best restaurant in the world was in Jenner, California where the Russian River meets the Pacific. No one could confirm if he wrote this article, or who was the Elizabeth he referenced in the story.*

It read:

Sonoma County

"Dutch Bill" Howard wasn't Dutch, and his name wasn't William Howard. Born in 1823, William Howard was really Christopher Thornassen Folkmann, a Danish sailor who jumped ship in San Francisco Bay in 1849 to somehow acquire an unclaimed timber plateau soon called Occidental, California. Today, the railroad station building is a breakfast place called Howard Station Cafe. They use organic foods every chance they get. The coffee is good.

The waitresses have a uniquely fresh attitude. A few moments after you sit down, the place mystically envelopes you. You start gazing around, you soak it all in, and soon you feel there. You get it. We ate breakfast there on day two of our four-day first date in Sonoma.

You don't just jump into online dating. It's a slow-thought process. Basically, you must admit it ain't working. Then, you essentially give-up on normal dating channels, as you start to believe there's a better way through technology.

Anyway, the waitress was actually pretty sassy. My daughter ordered a coffee with cream and sugar, and in all seriousness the waitress quickly asked, “Can I see your ID?” My daughter froze. Then our whole table and the waitress burst out laughing. Busted in Occidental. Still makes me laugh.

Yeah, it was a four-day first date. It’s still hard to believe, but my daughter was there. Over the four days Elizabeth’s three children were there. Oh yeah, Elizabeth’s cool mother were there, too. You can’t make this shit up.

Folkmann, also known as Howard, granted the North Pacific Coast railroad a right-of-way through his property in return for a lifetime railroad pass. Railroads are straightforward. They named the railroad station, Howards.

Before 2016 I had never heard of Occidental, California but those two words are hauntingly sweet music to my ears now. You see, once you walk into Occidental at a fast pace with Elizabeth, that place, that woman, that dream keeps pulling on you, to find a way to get back to her.

When she said we were going to walk to breakfast I assumed it was a mile or so away. In fact, it was more than a couple miles and she and her daughter don't walk slowly, even in the 92-degree heat. Elizabeth has a beautiful flair in her brilliance. Earlier in the morning she asked me to follow her car to town. We dropped my car in what I later learned was the main street of Occidental. We were on a mission to pick-up car keys at her house to drop in her mother's Mercedes at the Sonoma airport.

Now, it's not every first date where your date asks, “So, do you want to see the goats?”

Before that statement, I thought I was pretty experienced in first dates. But I admit I wasn't expecting the goat proposition. For the record it's true, a goat bit me.

Right before that happened two goats were trying to get out of their stall. I grabbed a goat for the first time. Their fur isn't soft like a cat or dog, it's coarse. It’s unpleasant. For a few seconds I was feeling quite accomplished with my goat grabbing skills until the goat turned and bit me. Shocked, Elizabeth looked at me as I heard her say those immortal words, “Oh shit the goats got out.”

Somehow, while we were focused on my goat bite, the darn goats had shimmied their way through the gate and sprinted out. Yes, it's true we spent 20 minutes on our first date walking around the property looking for goats. Despite her PhD and my MBA/law degree, we both laughed when I asked, “What do you yell to get a goat?” That day I learned I have zero skills when it comes to goat calling. Right when she was about to give up, she saw the goats standing on top of a ten-foot tower of hay bundles, eating away. Turns out, those darn goats were hungry. Imagine that. Case closed. Then she coaxed the goats back into their stall by a handful of hay. You learn something every day!

Simply put, she's beautiful. Not the goat, I mean her, Elizabeth. She's radiant in shorts and sneakers, radiant all dressed-up. She's sharp, quick, and doesn't let anything pass her bye. I like that. Union Hotel is also in Occidental. It's explained on their website.

On May 10, 1876, Old Dutch Bill Howard sold Lot #6 to Amelia Jones. The Jones family built a two-story structure and resold it to Howard, who sold it to Giovanni Gobetti and his wife Giovanna in 1891 for $2,000 of gold. In 1925, they sold it to Carlo Panizzera and Carlo renamed the building Union Hotel.

Carlo operated the Union Hotel as a boarding house and restaurant for stopover railroad passengers. One morning Mary Alberigi, his waitress, was carrying a load of linens from the hotel rooms upstairs down the steep, narrow stairway to the floor below. Under the load, Mary tripped and fell. Carlo found her, picked her up and carried her to the doctor. They were inseparable from that day on. The couple married on December 7, 1929, and on September 27, 1930, Mary Panizzera gave birth to their only child, Lucille.

Mary and Carlo's daughter Lucille grew up in the family business, playing in the Union Hotel's restaurant and saloon, as her parents worked. On November 6, 1949, she married Dan "Mahoney" Gonnella.

Dan and Lucille had five children: Michael, Mary Theresa, Mark, Daniel, and Frank. Lucille's father Carlo died on July 31, 1977, and her mother Mary followed two years later. Lucille and Mahoney Gonnella managed the growing business together until March 8, 1992, when her husband Mahoney passed away.

The North Pacific Coast railroad stopped operating in 1929. Mary Pannizzera's great home cooking had become legendary, and the Union Hotel grew. The year 1990 brought the addition of the Bakery/Cafe and the first Union Hotel Pizzeria began serving pizzas and pasta in 1992. Today, Lucille Gonnella is a living link to the history of Occidental. Her children and their families continue the rich tradition of these famous dining establishments, where the past seems to be the present, living on in the authenticity of the food and family.

Elizabeth. She wasn't expecting it. In reality, I didn't know the stairway was made special by Carlo and Mary. But sometimes you just seize the moment and act. We were there, like tourists. Standing in line to pick up take-out Italian food. Elizabeth was standing in front of me. I softly pulled her back into my arms. Her eyes lit up like only hers can do when she realized I wasn't just pulling her back to let a waitress pass. I was pulling her into a long, sensuous kiss. My right hand held her delicate face, fingers caressing her soft skin.

Moments later, a passing waitress jokingly yelled, "Hey, you can't do that here."

And then as the waitress passed by, like magic Elizabeth whispered, "Oh my, don't listen to her, you can do that anywhere."

I still can't get that kiss out of my head.

The Heiress froze. She realized she was breathing deeply. Her heart was pounding.

She never met anyone in politics capable of writing anything like that. In fact, she rarely met anyone in politics that impressed her.

She took a long sip of her wine. She again grabbed the bottle of Red Car and look at it. On repeat play of Natalie Merchant was singing the chorus of, "Gulf of Araby."

In the expanse of her vast ranch, her mind thundered, "*how the hell can we love the same wine?*"

The Heiress pulled out the yellow files and selected a yellow file to read:

YELLOW FILE – Ski Lift Memorandum

Rheingold had several ski areas in his legislative district. A bureaucratic prick that hated skiing was trying to classify ski lifts as elevators. Translation: every time a skier fell off a ski lift, trying to get on it, the lift would have to be shut down until a licensed elevator inspector could personally inspect the lift. The regulation was ridiculous. It would bankrupt ski areas. But no one had the balls to fire the prick. A younger Rheingold would have gone full throttle to get the prick fired. Or, he would have slam-dunked a legislative amendment to final passage to override the regulation. But now, Rheingold knew he was so notorious, a few leaders may block even his well-intentioned legislation.

Instead of leading the charge, Rheingold knew he had to find a champion to help carry the ball to victory.

He explained to the ski industry leaders, "Look if I lead this amendment, a few of my colleagues will rally to block it, just to burn my ass. So, I'm proposing a better path to passage. Major Sandy also has a great ski area. I'm telling you Major Sandy is leadership material. With Representative Sandy leading this effort, a whole set of other champions will begin to emerge on our side. Major Sandy should be the face of our common cause. We'll get this over the goal line faster, cleaner, and better positioned for quick Senate passage as well."

The legislation passed in record time.

The Heiress smiled, *Hmm.* And grabbed a piece of heart-healthy chocolate. She wondered what was in the 9-11 file. It was one of the biggest files.

Memorandum from newspaper articles, blogs, posts, and interviews with legislators.

The 9-11 File

On September 11th I was working from home, up early responding to constituent emails, and working up several bill amendments. I had been in office nine months, after my upset win over a popular 18-year incumbent. My cell rang, and my chief of staff frantically said, "Boss, turn on the TV, a plane flew into the World Trade Center."

Rheingold squawked, "What do you mean a plane flew into the World Trade Center?"

Michael responded, "Boss, I don't think this was a mistake! Something's really wrong."

Rheingold barked at the television and his cell phone, "Shit. Michael, what time is it?"

Soon they learned the planes hitting the World Trade Towers knocked out internet for millions of households in the tristate area, including their office internet and phones. Within 30-minutes, the whole staff was working from Rheingold's house as a command center. Luckily his house was served by the oldest cable company in America, with coaxial cable not connected to the World Trade Center. Food was ordered. Around 2:30 pm, Michael shouted, "Boss, the commuter buses are blocked from leaving the city. The bridges and tunnels are closed. We're getting calls from commuters. They are taking the NJ Transit trains to the last NJ Transit station - 29 miles from Pennsylvania. Right now, there's no way to get them from New Jersey to Pennsylvania!"

Rheingold, already multitasking on a number of emerging issues, stopped. "Wait, how many commuters are you talking about?"

Michael said, "It might be 200 people?"

Rheingold sighed, *Dang.*

"All right people, new project," Rheingold paused, then dictated. "I want Guinevere and Lauren working on buses, how many buses can we get to Mt. Arlington in the next hour. Okay, okay, Michael, call the schools and college, ask how many people they can get in cars heading to Mt. Arlington. We need Jon calling all the schools and sports teams to see how many buses, bus drivers and student drivers we can mobilize. Bob, can you get the Commissioner's office on the phone so I can brief them on what we are doing. I'll ask for their help on the mountain."

The volunteer drivers worked past midnight. Every bus commuter was transported from New Jersey to their commuter parking lots in the Poconos. In the end, it wasn't 200 commuters. It was more than 350 commuters. Rheingold talked to the commissioners at midnight. They were tired and amazed at what their teams had just accomplished. After the debrief, they got choked-up when they started sharing stories of what happened at Ground Zero.

Two days later, the team was still working from Rheingold's house.

At the morning team meeting, Rheingold asked, "Michael, can you get Jerry on the phone, the president of the local Bank?"

Rheingold inquired, "Jerry, this is Ryan Gold Craven. I've got a favor to ask!"

Jerry hesitated and then calmly said, "Representative, thanks again for everything you did the last few days. How can we help?"

"It looks like we have six victims from the County. It's going to be months until everything gets sorted out. Their families need help, right now! We're putting together a fundraising effort. We'd like your bank to serve as host, collecting checks and permitting bank branches to collect funds."

Jerry immediately weighed-in, "Rheingold, of course, that's not going to be a problem."

Rheingold replied, "Great, when can we start?"

Jerry paused, "When do you want to start?"

Rheingold, "If you say yes, we can put together a media announcement as early as 2 pm."

Jerry paused again, appreciating Rheingold was in campaign-model. He was going to tear down walls to help these families. Jerry cringed, knowing full-well the time and resources this effort would take inside the structure of his fast-growing bank. But then without hesitation Jerry added, "No problem at all. In fact, you can host the media announcement right here at our corporate offices."

Rheingold, "Great, thanks so much. I'll see you then!"

Eight days later Rheingold and other county and state officials, somberly presented $26,000 checks to each of the six devastated families. In a week, this small, rural county raised $120,000, and distributed the funds before the families had death certificates.

The Heiress looked out at the Black Paw Mountains. Took a long sip of her velvety red wine. She watched and marveled as the silky wine residue slowly etched its way back down the glass. *Who the hell is this guy?*

The Heiress pulled out another research subfile.

Patton Landers

First Suicide of a Spouse After 9-11

The day after 9-11, before any deaths were confirmed, Rheingold Craven befriended and helped Patton Landers. He sat with her for long hours at her house, waiting, hoping for word on her husband. Joe worked in the World Trade Center. After the 1st plane impacted the WTC, Patton was talking to Joe. The last thing Joe said to Patton was, "I've got to go help, I'll call you back."

As hours turned into days, hope turned into sadness. Rheingold took Patton to the bank, drove her on errands, spoke with her lawyers in Louisiana, and helped her reconnect with family.

The day after her husband's funeral at Trinity Church across from Wall Street, burial place of Alexander and Eliza Hamilton. A gun. A suicide. Interviews with Rheingold saying it was the toughest news he's ever received in his life. A People magazine article. The first suicide of a spouse after 9-11.

Months later, a benefit concert for the victim's families. The guest star was Bill Cosby, in his prime, before the scandals. Cosby called Rheingold onto stage. Cosby was busting on him. The audience, Cosby and Rheingold were in tears laughing – that soon transformed in just plain 9-11 tears. A room bawling. Until Cosby composed himself and miraculously got everyone laughing again.

The last sentence in the sub-file. "You can't make this shit up."

The Heiress put the files down. Thirty minutes had passed. She stood up, stretched her lithe muscles. Despite her extensive training, she was sore from the rugged 14-mile hike she made in the morning. She felt light walking through the now dark ranch to the bathroom. She had every reason and urge to go to bed, but she wanted to read more. She returned and grabbed another set of files. She wondered what the red color scheme would be. She savored another big sip of wine.

THE RED FILES

Inside the first red file was an invoice for $84.93 cents for plumbing services from a Spanish Tapas restaurant near the Capitol. A yellow post-it read, "If you pay this invoice, nothing more needs to be said!"

The file memorandum was in a smaller font.

Over the course of a long dinner, Rheingold and his date had consumed at least four bottles of a Portuguese red wine. It must have been good wine, the way the story flowed through several sources. After dessert they both left their table for the downstairs bathroom. Once they got inside the tiny bathroom, the young lady sat on the toilet. Allegedly, Rheingold offered her his then flaccid manhood. She must have been quite skilled. Despite the multiple glasses of red wine, she woke him right up. The story says he spun her around, placed her hands on the sink. They must have finished strong and broke the sink! Afterwards the restaurant owner found his name, address, and sent him the invoice with a note that said something like, "Please pay the attached invoice for the sink you broke last week, and nothing more needs to be said."

The Heiress wasn't impressed by this file, but she blushed, *Oh my.*

The second red file was also in small print.

You asked to rundown stories about the man. This man or his lady friends must have had a thing for bathrooms, office tables, office chairs, and elevators. Here's another story that was retold and confirmed by several sources:

A blonde connected with one of the state agencies for economic development walked by Rheingold in a crowded bar filled with politicians and lobbyists. Moments later, Rheingold excused himself to go to the bathroom. He was gone for quite some time and his friends were shaking their heads, already busting on him. With all eyes on her, the blonde walks by the men and retorts, "Everything they said about him is true." She kept walking right out of the bar. A minute later Rheingold walks out and sits down at the bar as if nothing happened.

Eventually his one buddy leans over and says loud enough for everyone to hear, "So what? you're not going to say a word."

He turned around and politely said, "I have nothing to say."

They all laughed, and his buddy said, "Dude, you don't have to say a thing, she already did!"

The Heiress wasn't too fascinated or impressed by the male banter. But she again contemplated, *who the hell is this guy?*

A third red file.

Trade School Memorandum

We interviewed another restaurant owner who filled in details of another interesting evening. Apparently, Rheingold was the guest speaker for a trade school graduation. On stage he gets introduced by the female school principal to give the Keynote speech. He met her on stage. Evidently, it was a powerful speech. He was invited by the attractive school principal to an after-graduation reception with her and other teachers at a local sports bar.

The restaurant owner confirmed the sports bar closed at 1:00 am. Around 1:30 am the bar owner walked out. Only two cars were left in the parking lot. One of the cars was definitely steamed-up and rocking. Because of the DUI laws, he had a policy of staying until every car left the parking lot. So, he opened the sandwich he made for his post-work meal. Twice, the owner said he walked over to the car to knock on the window and twice he said the action was so intense. She was screaming so passionately, he felt it would be a great injustice to interrupt them. Finally, he added, after 90 minutes of that intensity, he figured they must have made themselves sober. So, he drove home.

The Heiress paused, then thought, okay just one more. And again, her mind deliberated, *who the hell is this guy?*

She opened a fourth red file:

Memorandum: The Speaker's Office

Again, in small print.

Rheingold was called to the Speaker's Office. He wasn't told why or the topic. He didn't wait long in the outer room but was quickly ushered into the Speaker's Office. Ostensibly, the Speaker was a little embarrassed. He spoke quietly. He said he had a meeting with the bipartisan office leader. She discreetly mentioned that a House member was entertaining a young lady in his office when the cleaning crew was arriving at 0430 am. It wasn't appropriate.

On Session days, the cleaning crew arrived early. Allegedly, the cleaning crew heard unmistakable sounds from one of the offices, with the door shut and locked. The Speaker said he was embarrassed to be talking to the member about such a delicate subject. He wanted to emphasize that members were not allowed to stay in their offices overnight or entertain guests beyond a respectable hour. Equally embarrassed, Rheingold told the Speaker it would never happen again.

This red file had a subfile:

A long-time staff leader, beautiful, auburn hair, athletic, with a well-known temper against any flirting or inquiries by politicians or lobbyists. Happily married. No history with anyone in the Capitol.

Before a staff meeting. A group of female staffers were ranting about various male political leaders with poor reputations with the ladies. Apparently one staffer said something like, "Well I heard Representative Craven is a big, male whore who's slept with half the Capitol."

Then, just as the long-time staff leader walked into the room, she reportedly said, "Shut up Helen, you don't know what the hell you are talking about."

There are conflicting reports, but several staff members insist she winked to a few of her close friends after she raised her voice to the ranting staff member.

Out of curiosity, The Heiress pulled up a blue file, entitled,

Writings By Rheingold Craven Uncovered from Various Sources

Subfile #1

One single piece of paper, that read:

TEACHER

it's quiet.

empty

yet raging so loud in my soul

and ringing

ringing to retell me,

time and time again

I'm once more-

human.

oh,

We hope love immortal.

your hand hold-

suspended

as meaning floats away

just because

just because

just because

it does.

and then

We hope love immortal.

and yet

in giving bliss-filled joy

I'm not once easy.

you read me--

like worn pages

of comfort food

and

We hope love immortal.

Bitten.

wincing

back to rounding-

an old familiar tune

with facts

cold known to me.

Subfile #2

Another single piece of paper

MY ALL

blessed be

my life

my lips touch - -

the tiniest hairs

along the nape

of your soft neck

your

tiny

purr

blessed be

my life

and nobody knows.

if all

I had

was your love - -

know

I know,

I had everything!

I sat-

sat next to you--

hand in hand

an eternity

wrapped

into our-

first kiss

blessed be

my life

I've been so strong.

so strong when I hold you.

my fingers try to grip,

your soul

your

tiny

purr

and I wait.

I wait.

my life

your life

our love

it's not anything-

we've lost-

it's not anything,

until it is!

until we are!

blessed be,

my life

like holding you

holding

a moment

and even time emerges whole,

but I don't.

I wrote a book, a poem, a dream, a life about you.

but

I can't write the ending,

only you...

The Heiress paused. Took a deep sip of her Red Car. In a choked-up voice, she said, "Alexa play, 'God Only Knows', by the Beach Boys."

For reasons she couldn't explain, she rolled-over, and ripped off 50 push-ups as the song started-up. But she kept thinking to herself, *damn, I can't get those three words out of my brain,*

---

your

tiny

purr

Subfile #3

Another piece of paper -

WHAT SHE TOLD ME

We are born.

crying

we grow old

so slow.

lived a fairy tale,

of delusion

trapped in youth.

But

was madly in love,

We were closer than close.

felt her presence.

when she wasn't around

smelled her essence.

across our two-borough town

wrote a thousand,

thousand words

to try and say,

I love you.

And thought I owned the world,

thought we owned the world,

In youth

In life

In love

until the world owned me

after she told me.

in between

lived a thousand, million deaths,

cause once you know,

nothings

whole

Nothing is

whole

when what she told me.

killed me.

She wasn't my first kiss.

didn't pass me a love note in 6th.

didn't hold my hand in the back of the bus.

we didn't hurt that way.

even as the years have passed,

near a summer lake

she emerges from a path

walks up to me, and we kiss.

but I'm a ghost to her.

'cause what she told me.

killed me.

we study a bunch of things,

but we don't know shit.

what's worse than the crime,

is she's gotta live with it.

and knowing they're walking this earth.

and you can't do shit I'm told,

we learned it was hit or be hit,

and I was knocked out cold.

'cause what she told me

killed me.

little girls

precious

little girls

they

should

be

free.

if any man touches them

That man should be shred and dead, no plea!

'cause what she told me.

killed me.

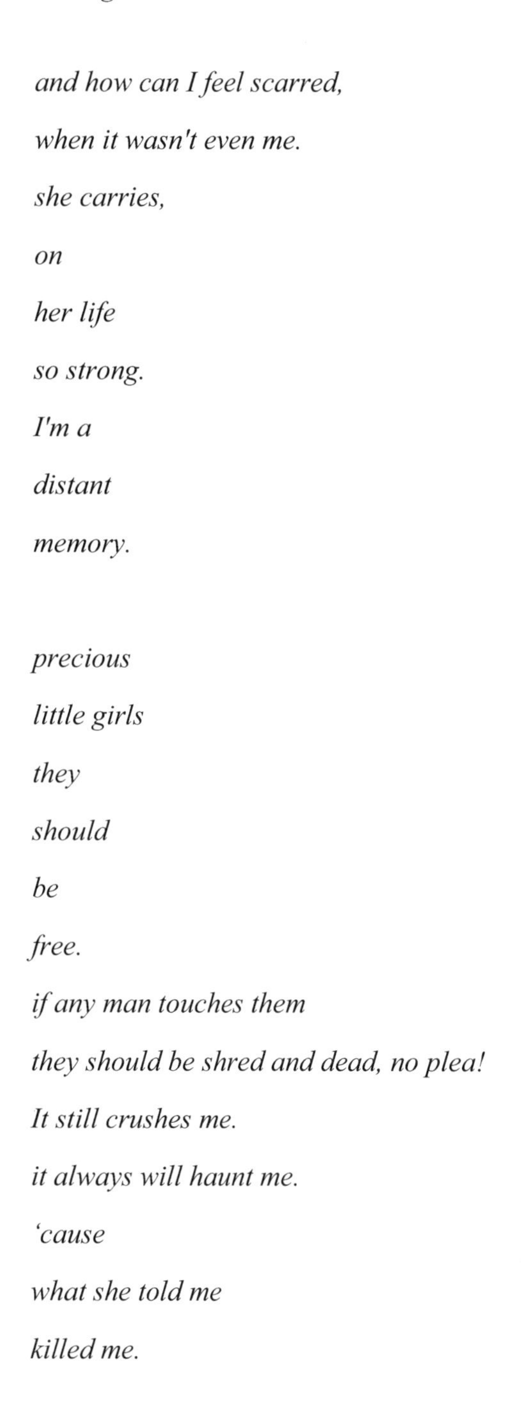

and how can I feel scarred,

when it wasn't even me.

she carries,

on

her life

so strong.

I'm a

distant

memory.

precious

little girls

they

should

be

free.

if any man touches them

they should be shred and dead, no plea!

It still crushes me.

it always will haunt me.

'cause

what she told me

killed me.

Ryan Gold Craven

In response to the August 26, 2020, article

published by The New York Times Magazine,

Convicted of Sex Crimes, but With No Victims

The Heiress took a deep breath.

She was too wired to stop. She re-read the last piece, twice more. It gripped her soul, she felt so torn.

Did all these gut-wrenching things happen to one man, one young man?

She picked up a purple file.

County Delinquent Taxes

County Controller Craven reported today that more than $12 million in delinquent taxes were collected in his unprecedented and unusual effort to publish a quarterly Top 100 list of the county's largest delinquent taxpayers. 30 days earlier he announced his plan to publish the Top 100 list. For perspective the annual county was $18 million so $12 million was significant cash. Apparently, the state's low interest rate for late taxes was being abused by several large property owners using the state's low interest rate as a short-term loan. As he hoped, many of the largest delinquent taxpayers didn't want to see their names on the front page of the newspaper. So, they paid by the deadline.

Concurrently, controller Craven announced his audits of the County Tax Claim office revealed another $65 million sitting in a bank account, not yet distributed to school districts and municipalities. The largest school district reported the funds received by these two efforts meant the school district wouldn't raise taxes for the first time in eight years.

Another subfile in the purple had this article:

County Controller Audit Speeds Funds to Single Moms.

Controller Craven reported his audits of the Domestic Relations office revealed more than $9 million in child support payments were still sitting in bank accounts. These funds that should have been distributed to custodial parents, usually single mothers. Controller Craven reported his office would be mailing hundreds of checks to custodial parents in the next 15 days. He reported 335 mothers would be getting checks of $10,000 or more in delinquent support payments. For years, these funds had been sitting in bank accounts, unaudited or reconciled. *$10,000 for 335 mothers.*

She picked up a White File:

Anti-Forum Shopping

State Representative Craven announced today his anti-forum shopping amendment into the 2003 Tort Reform legislation. He explained, "For too long, medical malpractice and tort litigation cases have been tried in counties delivering the highest verdicts instead of where the actual injury occurred. For too long these outrageous awards have crippled the state's medical malpractice insurance, and the M Care Fund, forcing skyrocketing premiums to physicians. Today, doctors are leaving Pennsylvania because they can't get or afford medical malpractice insurance. Today, one of Pennsylvania's leading exports is doctors that we train in our globally competitive medical schools."

"From today forward, this amendment will force all medical malpractice lawsuits to be litigated in the county where the actual injury occurred. We're confident this amendment restores common sense in our courtrooms and will save billions over the next ten years."

There was a 2019 PowerPoint in the file, turned to page 12.

The Heiress read the slide, “Since 2002, the Craven amendment on anti-forum shopping has saved more than $12 billion dollars and stopped the then massive outflux of physicians.”

She paused again, *who the heck is this guy?*

She picked up an Orange File.

The Legend of Two Glasses of Red Wine

The Heiress thought to herself, *now what the heck is this all about?*

In the dozens of interviews with women that claimed they had romantic relationships with Rheingold Craven an underlying theme emerged concerning two glasses of red wine. Unexplainably this legend intertwined with the crass obsessions of several investigators. In large part these investigators mimicked the antics and frustrations of the crazed Director in the Pink Panther movies who goes nuts over Inspector Cousteau.

After several interviews, these investigators became obsessed with the common observation, “If Rheingold had two glasses of red wine, he was an insatiable stallion all night.” Apparently with Rheingold, something happened with the perfect balance of hormones, resveratrol, and quercetin.

The Heiress noticed there was a thick file devoted to the Scientific basis of Red Wine and Male Performance. She thought, *wow, these guys really were obsessed with him.*

Interview #7, In Pertinent Part.

“So, you’re saying he told you about this so-called legend of two glasses of red wine?”

“Well, yes, I’m not sure he meant it as a boast, curse, or prediction.”

"What do you mean by that? "

"Well, I mean the first night we were together, it was just a blur. We both had long workdays. Over an exquisite dinner we shared a bottle of red wine that he raved about. And yes, I remember, well, anyway that night we really woke up. I mean, I remember thinking I was so tired and 40 minutes later, wow. Up until that point in my life, I had never had sex for more than 30 minutes. He boldly told me he thought 60 minutes was a good first night. He needed 60 minutes. For perspective, I didn't even know what you could do for 60 minutes. So, like, I don't know what he was drinking that night. But, if I could bottle it up, I'd be a billionaire."

Interview #12, in Pertinent Part.

"Do you know anything about his theory of two glasses of red wine?"

"Wait, you know about that? How do you know about it?"

"It's something we are researching. Several of his women friends mentioned it."

"Oh my, wow, I'm not the only one? Wow, that's so awesome and shit. Fuck him. Damn."

"Can we ask again; do you know anything about this theory or boasting about two glasses of red wine?"

"First off, it's not boasting. No, it's not boasting. Look, for months we teased and taunted each other. Ya gotta understand we were knee deep in a legislative fight. He was so brilliant. The weak souls around the legislative situation were so resentful. I mean they were awful, and loathsome against him. But he was gracious to their insults. He just stayed focused on getting the legislation passed. In the end, he won. He got the law passed. Earlier leaders and groups had no idea their dead bill was now law. Yes, I wanted to celebrate with him, because I knew most of the external and internal shits, he had to navigate to get this passed. So, yes, I went to the celebration for the bill passage. Yes, I wanted to talk to him and kiss him because he was so damn brilliant and kind.

"So, I did. Ha, he was trying so hard to talk to me, impress me, and I was like, 'Dude, instead of the small talk can you just take me right now.' Eventually we got there, and it was mind-boggling. Yeah, I'm not sure how much he drank that first night. We both were polluted. But he was so amazing!"

"So that was it, that was the only time you saw him?"

"I didn't say that! No, hell no, I was with him dozens of times. That's how I know about the legend of two glasses of red wine. You could say we proved it. Damn, three summers ago I practically poured two glasses of red wine down his throat so I could ride him for an hour."

Interview #23, in Pertinent Part

"I didn't realize you were so biased against Rheingold. I came here today, imagining you were going to celebrate him, memorialize him, and thank him for his years of incredible service."

"We're sorry you have that impression. We are just trying to develop an understanding about him. Do you remember anything about the two glasses of red wine?"

"Oh, I knew all about him. No surprises that way."

"What do you mean?"

"I knew he was a lady's man. People talked about him in the Capitol. Lots of it didn't make sense. I remember women that loved and hated him, at the same time. So, it didn't make any sense. I started to see him when I was out. He was polite, kind and endearing. It wasn't puppy love, well maybe it was. The first time, we weren't drinking, I just invited him to look at some of my artwork at a local gallery. He was so responsive and attentive to the idea of me painting. He wooed me. Yes, it was magical. With two glasses of red wine, he was amazing. We tried it often, you know, like why risk fate."

Subfile #4a

Another story we captured from an internet link he didn't have completely secure.

Murdering Weeds

An Awfully Long, Short Story by Rheingold Craven

Look. On this planet there are two kinds of people.

People who have picked fucking weeds and people who have never picked a gawd-damn weed in their freaking lives. There is no in-between. There is no sideshow or back door to war. You either picked a damn weed or you haven't. This awfully long, short story is an inspirational and irrationally legendary tale about the people who have picked fucking weeds.

You're Reading a Story about Murdering Weeds!

Let's level-set. You've just started reading a story about murdering weeds. I'm not one to judge, but let's agree you're already as tilted as I am if you're still reading an awfully long, short story called, *Murdering Weeds*. There are a million reasons you started reading this story but most of you fall into one of four categories. Yes, the really cool group is the readers that downloaded this story through a recommendation of a friend, family member, or work colleague. I laugh at the notion that they thought, you must be as tilted as they are, so they aptly recommended a short story called, *Murdering Weeds,* to you. I'm imagining your friend's driving to work, taking a crap, or picking fucking weeds, and they pause to ponder and think to themselves, *damn, in the next ten minutes, I'm going recommend this stupid-ass story about murdering weeds to a bunch of my best, gawd-damn friends.*

That, your friend did, in fact, recommend this story to another fellow human being, makes me laugh and shit my pants.

Right on!

Truly, I wrote this story for all of you fellow tilted shits. Without us, the world sucks. And every time I read this paragraph I'm going to smile, laugh and think, *damn I fucking hate picking fucking weeds.*

Another group saw the story title and thought, *cool yo! A book about weed.* Look I don't want to be a bummer, but this ain't a book about "that" weed. No, this is a damn epic novel about pulling fucking weeds. I mean feel free to visit my Ponderosa, pick the damn weeds, and smoke them. Shit yeah, I'll pay you just to watch. I'm half-curious to watch you smoke thistle, dandelions, poison ivy and whatever shit-weed grows in my flower beds. Damn straight, maybe you can turn this shit into a cash-crop.

Look dude, most of the readers of this story wouldn't want you pulling the weed you're imagining, dude. Relax. Take a deep breath. You don't have to read this short story or even finish reading this paragraph. Everything is going to be just fine. Sit back and fill your little bong with a little "Magic Mojo" and we'll talk about this in the morning.

A third group hates this story. You hated it before it was written. You hate the topic, hate the politics of pulling weeds, hate me, hate life, and generally and succinctly: you're fucking dicks. Many of you were part of the non-stop, nagging prick choir that told me and others like me, that we weren't going to amount to anything in life. You went out of your way to be dicks. Simply put, you were miserable when I knew ya, and ya haven't changed a bit. So, fuck off. That's right dick, I wrote passages in this story specifically to piss you off. Let me rephrase this sentence… parts of this story were written specifically about you, with hopes I could piss the fucking shit out of you. . . basically, I hope you pricks read this book and hate every single word of it. Then I hope you go outside and suck on an exhaust pipe. So, on behalf of several generations of people that you treated like shit, fuck you!

A fourth group is/are friends, family, and work colleagues. Heck, I know this story gets a little personal in a psychic f-bomb kind of way, real fast. I'm sure you can understand and appreciate that it's difficult as shit to write or talk about weeds and not drop a few fucking f-bombs. I'm sure my parents and grandparents are mortified. I am writing a short story with more f-bombs than Uncle Sam's Navy. To family, friends and colleagues, I share my apologies in advance. Let me be succinct and clear: it's all downhill from here.

Dick Disclaimer

I changed a few names because I didn't want the names of dicks in my fucking short story. I changed a few more names, so I could make up a few things and not get called out in front of Oprah. I included some names of people because they're fucking cool and I knew they'd piss their pants seeing their name in a story about murdering weeds. A few people, well, we asked permission to use their names in advance, because, well you know, lawyers and shit.

Finally, I wrote this story for Darby. I met Darby during the virus and our first date was in a Stegman's parking lot. In one of my better moves in life, I brought along a bottle of white wine, two red solo cups and the rest is romantic history. I wish it lasted.

In summary, Darby is smoking hot, beautiful. She's a smart and lovely lawyer-lady, no-nonsense, sassy, and cool. She's got a big handful of the most beautiful black hair and deep brown eyes that glow like fiery amber. Because of the virus, we weren't dressing-up or hitting the town, instead I was wearing crummy jeans and sweatshirts. She was wearing black yoga pants. Dang, I don't know who invented yoga pants, but that human being should be exalted and placed in all kinds of fucking museums and shit. I'm not going to wince words; Darby looks good in yoga pants. Real good.

Yes, dick readers! I did just mention Darby is a lawyer, so yes, I changed her freaking name to protect the innocent, and the universe of cool women on the planet.

Bang!

Then without warning, on Day 33 of our relationship Darby made a declaration, “Today is the day I will kill weeds.” Then, in the briefest amount of time for any relationship, I quickly learned, when Darby sets her mind to killing weeds, there ain’t no mercy. So, we jumped in the car, and off we went to Home Fucking Depot. When we got there, she knew exactly what she wanted to get.

I didn’t know, Darby was a gifted, legal, and scientific goddess in the art of killing weeds. Yes, during this short car ride I quickly learned Darby was well-educated in the zenith of knowledge on killing weeds.

There she was, just a lawyer-lady, standing in front of her boy-toy, asking him to love her, while she revealed her deepest strategies and passions about murdering weeds.

I listened deeply and absorbed the intensity of her research and test-results. I realized I was not alone in my vigil to destroy weeds. After we parked the car, I leaned over and gave her the most romantic and passionate kiss I could muster. I’m talking about a kiss worthy of an Oscar baby. As our lips parted, she whispered, “Wow baby, what was that all about…”

And that’s as much personal shit as you need to know.

Okay Let’s Refresh What We’ve Learned

Joni Mitchell is amazing and *Both Sides Now* is brutally sweet poetry.

We’ve also learned people who have never pulled weeds are different sorts and breeds. They won't ever know or understand what we mean. They can read about it. They can prance outside like weenies, and pretend to pull a few weeds and think, What's the big deal? Therein lies the facts and figures, they don’t know shit.

There used to be two groups of non-weeders. On one hand, you've got the ultra-rich and their aspiring kindred that'll do anything to appear richie-rich. On the other hand, you've got the dirt-poor.

I can guarantee you, ole Bonnie Prince Charlie never pulled a bloody weed in his tortured life, nor did Donald Trump or his kids. Likewise, millions in public housing and subsidized rentals never touched a weed. Oh, good grief, don't bitch and shit yourself just because you never pulled a fucking weed.

The whole point of this awfully long, short story ain't designed to make you feel special. Don't read on to feel lucky or conceited. It's quite the opposite, I suppose. The dark side of this story is, well read the fucking title, it's about murdering weeds. So, listen up. If you're rich or dirt-poor, you don't know shit about pulling weeds. So, unroll your tight wand undies, go back to your world, and, shut the fuck up.

Yes Alexa, the stars of this masterpiece novel know exactly what I'm laying down in ink. Pulling weeds, fucking sucks! You can translate the phrase, "pulling weeds, fucking sucks" into 200 different languages and everyone that has pulled fucking weeds, knows exactly what the fuck I'm talking about.

If you're holding your breath waiting for a footnote supporting the general thesis that "pulling weeds, fucking sucks" from a scholarly, bullshit Harvard study, go shove a rose thorn under your fingernail. Better yet, go sit your ass down on a hornet's nest. In fact, everything laid down in ink here, is my sole fucking opinion. There are no corporate sponsors giving me cash or sucking on my dick.

The average reader of a story about murdering weeds hated math and sucked at calculus. So, let me keep the math and formulas simple as kindergarten shit. Let's just say the richest 10% and the poorest 10% haven't pulled a fucking weed. Shit yes, there's exceptions, move on.

So, my fellow citizens that means 80% of you motherfuckers have been forced to pull fucking weeds. Yes bitch. There are exceptions, move on.

Not Creating False Hope

I'm not articulating in any fashion that pulling weeds builds character, strength, or goodness. And I'm not saying it doesn't. I'm merely pointing out the Captain Obvious facts that pulling weeds sucks.

Home Fucking Depot Part 1

There's something cute about a woman wearing black Ugg's, black yoga pants and a black matching shirt. Maybe that's the woman's dress code for destroying weeds in the new millennium. To me, it's hot, sexy, and commanding. So, like a good boy toy, I followed the little lady past Gertrude the woman at the front of Home Fucking Depot they hired to appease sexist hiring practices. Some corporate dick told her, "Hey just stand at the front door and say hello to everyone that walks in the store. And, if they ask any questions, point them to Rick or Stan."

Oh please. It's cool. I'm all about Gertrude working at Home Fucking Depot. But let's call a spade a spade. It's the corporate dick that said it, not me. I'm just revealing what happened.

Anyway, I digress. I'm walking fast behind the little lady who's clearly on a mission to buy weed killer. We stand in front of the weed killers like we're standing outside of Madison Square Garden for a Springsteen concert. I glanced over and I'm pretty sure I saw her licking her lips. She goes straight for the good shit. You know when it says 365 on the bottle, it's gotta be good. None of this four-month bullshit. I mean if you can buy 120-day shit or 365-day shit, to me, there's no question, I'm buying the 365-shit, and I'm not diluting it.

Most men can't leave Home Fucking Depot unless they clock in two/three hours. I mean this place is fucking heaven. You walk around and there's row after row of all this cool shit. They have 50 kinds of hammers. They have 50 kinds of power drills. Who the hell thinks this shit up!

Unlike every other store in the universe, women in Home Fucking Depot are like, "Look honey, I just want to go in, get what we need, and get the fuck out."

Really? What?

It is what it is. We race to the checkout line, standing 3-feet from the Covid-virus oozing lady in front of us. Then we finally check out. Believe my ass when I say, instead of six feet, we're talking eight inches from the check-out clerks face, because the damn accountants at Home Fucking Depot are too damn cheap to install credit card machines six fucking feet from human civilization. Six feet, my ass.

The Day After the Introductory Bullshit

Now that we got that shit settled, let's get started.

Here We Go – The Primer on Killing Weeds

After weeks of letting it slide, at my own house, I said, *no more.*

It was time to get serious.

For weeks, those wicked weeds had been taunting me.

"Oh, we heard you got a girrrrrlllfriend"

"Oh, look who's here... the lazy-ass..."

I'm like, *Shit, the spineless weeds are making speeches in my front yard.*

I'm pretty sure their weed-speech was something like, "Well done my fellow weed-bitches. At long last, we have brought this lazy-ass property owner to his knees and showed him who's boss."

The bastard weed choir chimes in, "That's right, it's our time. It's time for The Weeds to dominate."

Stop.

I had had just about enough of this bullshit, from a bunch of plants that don't even have a damn back bone! So, I quickly mapped out my own little trip to Home Fucking Depot. Little did I know that Home Fucking Depot had joined the ranks of sissies, too.

There I was, a free resident of The United States of America, being forced to stand in a weeny-ass line outside of the store in the cold fucking rain, while some bastard 26-year-old teenager was limiting the number of humans into the gawd-damn store. I mean the place is a huge fucking warehouse the size of ten football fields.

Anyway, finally the douchebag policy gets fulfilled and I'm walking into the near-abandoned store. Look, I don't need no freaking help, Rick, or Stan, I know exactly what I want.

That's right, wicked weeds. The little lady has told me her extensive legal and scientific research on torturing and killing fucking weeds. Now I am going to use this knowledge to murder weeds. So, standing in front of the weed killers. I go right for the hard shit.

Those corporate shits that really think Americans are going to dilute the freaking concentrate are delusional. You see, I'm getting two different kinds of the hard-shit concentrate. I'm going to torch these bastard wicked weeds. I'll show them what it means to eat shit and die.

I checked out. Yeah, of course I was less than seven inches from the check-out clerk since the pricks in corporate weren't going to pay millions to move their weak-ass credit card machines by six feet, in 10,000 Home Fucking Depots. Dude, I couldn't drive fast enough to the house.

Then it hit me.

Shit. It was 8:35 pm at night. I'm in a business suit, and it's fucking raining. It's fucking dark as shit, there's no sunlight and, to strangle these bitch weeds, the weather conditions demanded the bitch-weeds had to be nice and dry to receive my wrath.

So, I went to sleep.

Look you sick pups, I didn't dream about killing weeds. That's just plain disturbing.

Instead, like every other disturbed American man, I dreamed about my sexy girlfriend whispering in my ear how she wanted me to kill these poor, defenseless weeds that were ruining her world.

Dang, Toto, wake up, wake up.

In the morning, I deliberately had an extra gallon of coffee. I knew I had to move fast and show no mercy...

I grabbed the 365 concentrate! I stabbed the stupid-ass cap thing, and poured that liquid weed death right up to the brim.

I said a silent prayer for all the flowers and bushes that might be casualties in my war on weeds. I prayed for forgiveness for what I was about to do. Soon my nostrils were flaring. I was repeating a football pre-game chant.

It was game on.

As I walked, almost jogged, toward the first flower bed, I fired back, “Good morning. Good morning! It's time to say hello to my little friend.” I was almost giggly, “Looky, Looky, here you go you wicked, wicked weeds. I’ve got a little snack for you to munch on, and it's called, fucking POISON.”

You really think because I've fallen in love that I've gone soft, and turned sissy? Are you fucking kidding me? Well, I've got a nice surprise for you, this here liquid weed death was recommended by none other than my little lady friend, just for you. So, eat this shit and die, you wicked weeds. Oh yeah, that's right, I added the Roundup 365 concentrate with the other Roundup concentrate and you're gonna eat this shit and cry like tiny, little baby weeds.

Rapidly, I moved from flower bed to sidewalk to flower beds. Every now and then I had to reach down and grab a weed by the roots if it really pissed me off. Oh yeah, I was channeling years of aggressive post-traumatic stress syndrome, for stresses I didn't even know I had or recognized.

Or, on the other hand, I just wanted to get this shit done so I could jump in the shower, jump in the car, and drive to see my sweet little lady. I’d let her know, I put our dynamic weed kill strategy into motion. Turns out, telling stories about killing weeds was like porn for us.

I'm kidding, you sick fucks.

Oh my, I was sure she would be thrilled at the eloquent and poignant decision I had made to mix the two concentrates to create the ultimate weed-kill brew. Yes, and she'd marvel at my speed and agility as I glided around the property spewing liquid weed death.

Completed, I walked back to the garage, making sure I squirted a few parting shots to several defiant American thistle weeds. Aye, it broke my Scottish heart to hurt the native Scottish thistle, but this American thistle was ridiculously rude and unrighteous. Yes, this thistle had to go. It had to go down hard. To quench my bloodlust, I grabbed an ice-cold Lord Chesterfield Ale. Quietly I celebrated the groundwork I laid down hard, to crush these fucking weeds for another bloody fucking year.

When Roundup Sucks!

Like most humans, there are a few things in life that ruffle me feathers. Stupidity in government ranks #1. Organizations massively overspending ranks #2. Tax revenue systems that are massively inefficient, wasteful, and corrupt. Popular movies, athletes, and TV shows that suck and yet still create celebrities that believe their popularity has granted them superior wisdom over the rest of civilization. But definitely in the top ten list includes the definitive provision, when Roundup sucks!

That's right, Roundup.

Five days after, I devoted hours of my life to eradicate weeds, weak shit Roundup made me the laughingstock of the fucking universe. In fact, I went out of my way to spend $70 bucks to buy the 365-day shit and wham, it sucked ass.

Five freaking days after I peppered my motherfucking weeds with a shit ton of Roundup, I got back to the house, looked around the yard, and the weeds were giving me the middle finger. I'm like, what the fuck! The weeds were laughing like, "Fuck you motherfucker!"

I was so pissed. I didn't change out of my business suit. I didn't squirt my ass with bug spray. I immediately got into Kill Fucking Weeds mode. Without a moment's pause, I poured the rest of the Roundup 365 into the Roundup Concentrate Plus. Immediately I started drenching my motherfucking, taunting weeds with another round of Roundup. Screw the directions on diluting this liquid bullshit.

First off, who can even read the bullshit directions when they make the font size as small as shit. Most humans need a magnifying glass to read the directions. Me, I'm fucking blind. I need a damn telescope to read that shit. Second, the moment a rational human grabs their reading glasses to decipher what the directions are trying to say. You realize the directions are fucking useless.

Roundup 365 concentrate comes with a plastic cap you're supposed to use to dilute the poison. I'm confident less than 100 customers have used this piece of shit plastic cap. With no scientific way to prove it, I'm convinced 86% of the people buying Roundup 365 have no idea that the attached plastic cap is actually a measuring device. So, they just pull it off, toss-it, and immediately start killing weeds.

Here's the bottom line. I used the Extended Control Roundup and half a bottle of the Roundup 365 concentrate. One might conclude this was a powerful brew. One might conclude if I sprayed this shit on green plants without vertebrate that this plant-venom would rip these fucking weeds to shreds. One might conclude after I sashayed around the property spewing this poisonous mixture that no weeds could ever survive. But here's the final analysis.

Sometimes Roundup Sucks.

Oh sure, read the small print underneath the already small print, and I'm sure there's some weak-ass lawyer language about rain, dew, moisture, sunlight and other naturally occurring events impacting the effectiveness of Roundup's best shit. But here's the thing. In my mind, I already did the math. If I don't dilute the concentrate, and it happens to rain, shouldn't a lethal dose still be received since I delivered non-diluted shit. Wouldn't the rain dilute the brew like the damn tiny directions indicate?

Of course, at 2 am after I hustled around the property to deliver the second application of fucking Roundup, wouldn't you know it was raining, bat-shit-crazy.

The next morning, it's fucking beautiful, not a cloud in the sky. Yup, you could almost conclude the entire universe was fucking with me. So instead of whining like a little baby, I got out there, like a champion, and spewed the remaining gallon of Roundup on the fucking weeds.

Dude, I sprayed so much Roundup, that after it soaked into the earth, it not only killed the fucking weeds in my yard, but it started killing weeds on the other side of the planet in China. Did I mention I hate fucking weeds!

The Heiress scratched her head. *Whoa, what the heck was that all about?*

Subfile #8 immediately restored her undivided attention!

SONOMA

On my horse,

of course.

On our mountain trail's hue.

Of a Pacific view I drew.

To a thinking of him tune.

Sonoma.

Rheingold: Born Fatima

Not right now.

Not right now.

But soon.

Another night of homework.

I'm at full torque.

Morning chores, such a bore,

then Mom asked me to do more

before a Saturday noon.

So no, Ma.

Not right now.

Not right now.

But soon.

Finally, a walk away from chalk

and the talk, talk, talk...

Among the cedars and bay leaves

I breath deep, beyond pet peeves.

Dealing with things, I don't let others a clue.

So many things hurt, I never knew.

Yeah, then like you I'm staring at the moon.

So no, Ma.

Not right now.

Not right now.

But soon.

It's nothing I'm talking about.

Unless you want me to shout.

Just let me be,

I've got my dreams as soon as I'm free.

And I can't get there too soon.

Sonoma.

Not right now.

Not right now.

But soon.

And like to increase my annoy.

You keep asking if it's a boy.

I'm like really, really,

really.

When I keep drifting back to that tune.

Sonoma.

Not right now.

Not right now.

But soon.

I get it, you're doing the mom-thing.

You want a hug and an all-okay ping.

And I know you know I'm older,

some things I'll do on my own shoulder,

and I'm fine until June,

So no, Ma.

Not right now.

Not right now.

But soon.

She Opened a Fifth File.

Oh, this looks like a doozy.

Interview File - Female Companions.

After reading twelve of hundreds of files, The Heiress couldn't believe this large global law firm had conducted such an extensive external investigation to get an edge against a man named Rheingold.

Interview #1

We conducted an interview with an attractive professional lawyer/lobbyist. She willingly agreed to speak with us at The Hilton bar after work. They ordered red wine. Well-dressed, impeccable. Hair-pulled back. Glasses, very stylish.

"How long did you know Rheingold Craven?"

"Ten years!"

"How long before your encounter with him?"

"Six years."

"Do you still have contact with Rheingold?"

"Occasionally on work projects."

"How is the relationship?"

"It's just like it always was, professional and fine."

"Really?"

"Yes."

"So, what are your personal feelings toward him?"

"Well, certainly, I hate him. With every cell in my body and soul!"

"So then, you'll do anything against him then?"

"Well, no. To be honest, I'm also still madly in love with the man."

"Hold on, I don't get it. You hate him and you love him*?"*

"Yeah, that about sums it up. Ya gotta understand. Before I met him, I had men pegged on a scale of one to ten. Ya know, like Brad Pitt was a ten. And then I met him. And it's like this five-year friendship. It's like he's so kind, and nice and genuine. You start thinking about him, missing him, looking forward to seeing him. And, on the one hand, you know, you hear he's like that with everyone. And on the other hand, you just know there's something incredible between the two of you. You start to think it, imagine it. Soon it's playing out, like fate, like it was supposed to be. Yeah, I hate the guy but love the man."

"In case you're not really understanding. Most women hate a man like Rheingold. They figure he's definitely one of those love 'em and leave 'em types. I mean, isn't that what he is, right? But you know they don't know him. They're totally missing the point. See, he still loves me. He knows I still love him. It's understood. You just don't connect with a human being like that, and wake-up the next day and move-on. Like he touches parts of you, he leaves an impression on parts of you, like no one else touches you before or since."

"Oh, so he's good in bed?"

"No. I didn't mean it that way. No! Well- yeah. Well, hell yes, he's good in bed! I mean, but it's so much more than that. Like I was saying before you rudely interrupted me. On a scale of one to ten, it's not that he's a ten. It's that he expands your awareness of what a ten can be and should be. You're left there, knowing that exists, knowing you can't own him, tame him. You can't have him all to yourself. It's an empty feeling that you hate him for taking you there, letting you experience something better than you ever imagined. You love him for sharing that experience with you. Yet, you hate him because now that you know, you know; it might be impossible to ever feel that way again. I mean he connects with you in an intellectual way. Like he really gets to know you inside and out."

"But after reading our statement, we thought you came here today because you wanted to bash him?"

"Hold on, I just bashed him. Weren't you listening to a word I said?"

"Yes, yes. Can we ask a few more questions? How many times were you with him?"

"Well, there was the first time, that was really amazing. After that I didn't see him for quite some time. I mean, we wrote to each other. We spoke every now and then. I know I was in another relationship at the time, with a good man. But, like I said, he totally throws off your whole world. It sounds bad, but I just needed to see him again. But knew I shouldn't."

"So, you didn't see him again?"

"Well no. Well, yes, I saw him again. I yelled at him with everything I could muster. I told him exactly how I felt, truth-filled, why he was wrong, yeah, I told him everything on my mind."

"So, you yelled, stormed-off and never saw him again?"

"Well, no, that night we made love like four times. Whatever I thought about the first night was all wrong. Everything I thought I had felt and experienced, everything. I mean everything was better the second time."

"Hold on, I thought you said you yelled at him?"

"Yes, I really yelled at him."

"But what did he say, how did he react?"

"The sonofabitch agreed with every word I said. He had the nerve to tell me ten other reasons I should be mad and upset at him, all of which I hadn't even thought of yet. He told me all these other reasons I should be mad at him. I realized as he's going down this list, I'm falling in love with him all over again. It was a more intense feeling than ever. I don't know, at some point, I just grabbed his face and started kissing him. Things led to things. Well, you know."

"Look, I'm kind of half-embarrassed to say this, and then I'm not. Before I met the guy, like, I thought I had had an orgasm before him. I mean, like you know, right? And, then I'm with him, and you're like, damn, what the fuck was that?"

"So, what happened next, I mean, did something else happen?"

"Well, yes, I hated him again."

"Wait, I thought you just said he made you feel amazing?"

"Well yes, he did, and he broke the scale again. Like you reach a nirvana, and you think to yourself, *dang it can't get any better than that.* Well, let's just say it was way better than that!"

"So, why hate him?"

"Well, isn't it obvious?"

"One day you're going through life. You believe everything's pretty darn good in your life. Then a man walks into your life and shows you there's a whole second floor to the department store that you didn't even know existed! After he leaves, you're stuck, you're like 'Shit, how the hell do I get back to the second floor?' You realize, *I'm stuck on the damn first floor.*" She paused, reflected, and whispered, "Stuck on the first floor… "so damn straight, I hate him."

"So, after that, then you never saw him again, right?"

"Well, no. The next time I saw him I drug him out of a restaurant, and I really let him know how I felt and how rotten he was to do that to me?"

"So, you were really upset?"

"Hell, yes I was upset! I drug him into my car, and basically ravished him."

"So, if he walked in here right now, what would you do?"

"I'd scream bloody murder. I'd give him a real earful of a riot act. Oh, shit yes, I'd tell him how I really feel!"

"Oh, so you'd yell at him, and then you'd eventually make love to him?"

"No, not in front of you, you damn perv."

The Heiress laughed out loud. She mused, *something about this man makes sense. He must be something special if a Philadelphia law firm went to all this trouble to interview these women, study all these projects. He's just one man!*

She took a moment to pour the rest of her Red Car wine into her glass. After staring at it in the room glow, she savored a long, slow sip. She held the glass in front of her, felt the warm glow of red wine caress her body. *Red Car.*

Interview #5

Yellow post-it notes on the file. The moment this woman walked in the interview room, there was just a powerful presence about her. Her beauty, her mannerisms, her aura, her voice. Two of the men said they couldn't stop looking at her, like it was some kind of trance or magnetic attraction. Yet, the man interviewing her remained unconvinced. In a weird way he was starting to act half-crazed.

"So, you've read our statement, and you've agreed to visit with us today and tell us how you feel about Rheingold Craven?"

"Yes."

"Is there anything you'd like to say before we get started?"

"No, not really."

"So, what is your basic impression of the man?"

"Do you mean how do I really feel?"

"Yes!"

"Well, I hate the motherfucker!"

"Wow, I didn't expect that. So, you want to tell us the ten reasons why you hate Rheingold Craven?"

"No, I'm going to tell you the 100 reasons I hate the motherfucker!"

"Okay, before we get started can we ask just one quick question?"

"Yes."

"If you could, would you sleep with Rheingold Craven if you had the chance to do so?"

"What? Do you mean right here and now? Like, is he here? Is that an option? You didn't tell me he would be here today?"

One panelist remarked in her notes: *You couldn't imagine the total transformation that occurred in another human over the mere mention of a question about making love with another human-being, most especially after that person had just declared they had 100 reasons to hate him. It was spellbinding.*

"No, no he isn't here today. But I'm not understanding? You just told me you had 100 reasons to hate him, but know it seems like you'd like to see him? Do you want to see him again?"

"Hell, no I don't want to see him again! You have no idea. I don't want to see him again. But you specifically asked me if I wanted to sleep with Rheingold Craven again. And I don't know, maybe it was the way you asked it, or that you said his whole name. But no, I don't want to see him again. But would I sleep with Rheingold Craven again if I could? Oh my God, yes."

One panelist wrote on a post-it note: *We all had to chuckle, when the interviewer threw up his hand and stormed out of the room.*

The Heiress twisted in her chair. And thought, *oh my. I've got to admit. Dang. Oh my, my panties. Who is this man?*

Shannon And Rheingold in London

Unannounced on social media, Shannon and Rheingold flew to London on an overnight flight on The Heiress's transatlantic jet. There were three jets like it in the world. None had the modifications she made. Halfway across the Atlantic, the logistics and security, transferred to MI6.

Rheingold later raved about MI6 and British hospitality from the moment they were in their presence. It was another whirlwind, complete with incredible clothes supplied by the British tailors adored by The Heiress. MI6 moved them quickly to a morning meeting with the Prime Minister at 16 Downing Street, culminating with a formal afternoon meeting with the Queen, Prince William, the Duke of Cambridge and his wife, Kate Middleton.

Soon after, Shannon texted The Heiress: *Wake me up, someday, and tell me I just met the Queen and Kate Middleton in Buckingham Palace.*

Little did Shannon appreciate; but when she spoke, The Queen and Kate Middleton listened intently.

Both wrote extensively in their diaries that evening of their lovely meeting with Shannon, describing her eyes, her presence, and her fearlessness against the events of the past few weeks. Queen Elizabeth added in her journal: *While I had been properly trained my whole life to face death, threats of violence, and dear Lord the IRA bombings, this fierce little American appeared as brave our Royal Marines. She was determined to see justice through her life.* The Queen continued: *All my adult life I have known about these atrocities against young women, and we did nothing. I was advised we couldn't do anything. As much as I am ashamed by our historical inaction, now we must use every resource in our Kingdom to end this travesty against women.*

It was a passage the Queen found comfort reading many times over the rest of her life. Appreciating his role, Rheingold stood stoically tall and proud, standing next to Prince William. His brain marveled, *I have absolutely nothing in common with this man, except for the fact that the women in our lives are the most famous women on the planet.*

On the flight to London, Rheingold had lobbied hard for a visit to a British pub. MI6 wouldn't commit and said point-blank they couldn't commit. So, it seemed heroic to Rheingold when they pulled it off. Despite the events over the past weeks, Rheingold still wasn't fully appreciating the scale and enormity of everything in front of him. Certainly, it was happening so fast. It was difficult to grasp. He couldn't know the security surrounding Shannon to keep her alive. It's hard to appreciate. At that moment in time, he and Shannon were the most famous couple in the world.

In an earlier meeting, The Queen asked the Lord Chamberlain, "let us do something special here. Give them a night to remember. Call in a few favors."

The Pub

The Pub was a famous establishment but over the past ten years it was rarely open to the public. It was used by the royal family for entertainment and receiving guests in less ceremonial surroundings. To the rest of the world, the signs out front indicated it was closed for a private party. Shannon was as excited as Rheingold.

Walking into the landmark Pub was surreal. Everything was sparkling. As they walked up to the bar, they greeted the bartender like kids drinking their first beers. Rheingold asked, "can we have two pints of Young's Bitter pumped up from the basement?"

The bartender smiled. The keg had been specially delivered a few hours before on orders of the company's proud CEO. On the plane debriefing with MI6, Rheingold confessed his 20-year desire to return to London specifically to have a Young's Bitter pumped up from the basement. He and Shannon tipped their glasses, laughing that they hadn't ever had a beer together. It was so good.

Then it got weird, like in the coolest sense of the word. Like, Keep-Austin-Weird, kind of cool.

It's hard to describe anyone's impression when Bono walks into a room unannounced. But a man and woman walked into the Pub, and Shannon and Rheingold looked at each other and mouthed, "Holy shit, it's Bono and his wife."

The guests laughed with Shannon and Rheingold. The greetings were so kind. The bartender quickly poured two more pints. Bono and Ali Hewson were so down-to-earth and interested in Shannon's work. They both acknowledged they knew about the FGM. They were embarrassed to admit they didn't know what to do about it. But they earnestly pledged their international support.

Bono enjoyed his moment to talk with Rheingold. After a bit with his Irish brogue, "Dude, they told me about your legendary skills with the ladies." Bono added with his famous smile, "Nice!"

Just as the bartender was starting to pour everyone's second pint, they all turned to watch another couple walk into the Pub. At the same time Shannon, Rheingold, Ali, and Bono all looked at each other and quietly said, "Holy shit, it's Paul McCartney and Nancy."

It was Paul McCartney and Nancy Shevell, who were equally kind and interested in meeting Shannon and Rheingold. They all laughed as the bartender poured Paul and Nancy their first round of Young's Bitter. After polite greetings, Paul and Nancy were excited to pledge their international support. At some point,

Rheingold self-reflected to himself, *Holy shit, I'm drinking beer in London with Bono and Paul McCartney.*

Just as the bartender was starting to pour another round of pints, the six of them turned in unison when another couple walked into the Pub. And before anyone could say anything, Bono called out, "Holy shit, it's James Bond."

Daniel Craig and his wife Rachel Weisz turned and looked at each other and mouthed to themselves, "Holy shit, it's Shannon."

The greetings were equally pleasant. Rachel was ebullient to meet Shannon and learn about her plans and global touchpoints. The four women shared ideas and contacts throughout the major cities where their charitable interests had touchpoints. They were so moved. They told Shannon they would clear their schedules over the next weeks to help Shannon push for 100% eradication.

Throughout the evening, Shannon just glowed. It was all so precious. Deep down, she felt her cause was getting the attention and power she and The Heiress had discussed at their lunch only weeks earlier. Shannon watched attentively and soaked in the beauty of these three gracious ladies. To Shannon they were so comfortable in their skin. Shannon reflected at the pinging déjà vu experience happening before her eyes, remembering The Heiress telling Shannon she was going to meet the most famous and effective women in the world.

As the men gathered on the other side of the ladies, suddenly Sir Paul grabbed Rheingold's chin and whispered a little more loudly than he hoped in Rheingold's ear, "What's your bloody secret mate, the debrief says you're brilliant in the sack." He, Bono, Daniel, and Rheingold started laughing like school mates, and the ladies joined in, as Shannon blushed with her glowing smile.

Rheingold shrugged, "Dude, I have no idea."

Which brought further laughter, and Daniel Craig slapped Rheingold on the back saying, "You just called Paul McCartney, 'Dude.'"

Rheingold winced inside, his shoulder muscles exploding in pain, but no way was Rheingold going to be a sissy in front of James Fucking Bond. It wasn't lost on him that he was laughing with Paul McCartney, Bono, and James Fucking Bond.

A few more pints and an hour later, the hugs were real as four-couples headed home for the night surrounded by security. Ironically, it was the American couple with the most security, as MI6 drove them in armored vehicles to a secret military barracks outside of Heathrow.

Shannon and Rheingold showered and as was becoming common, they dressed into a set of new clothes personally tailored for them at one of the famously exclusive haberdashery shops The Heiress liked in London. They smiled, kissed and Rheingold couldn't let it go, shaking his head, "Baby we just had beers with James Fucking Bond."

She smiled, kissed him, and with the brilliance of love in her eyes she said, "Baby, James Fucking Bond just had beers with Rheingold."

They weren't staying overnight.

Like clockwork, MI6 got Shannon and Rheingold to the airport into an equally special jet chartered by the royal family. To keep everyone off their tracks, upon landing hours earlier, The Heiress jet had immediately refueled and flew back, indirectly, to NYC-JFK, then Philadelphia.

Like clockwork, as their 7.5-hour flight was safely in the clouds, the loyal British press started publishing the media stories proclaiming the secret visit of Shannon and Rheingold with the Queen and royal family. On cue, The Heiress's AI technology picked up the media releases and exponentially distributed the media releases to every media source on earth.

They wanted the terrorists know they weren't going to hide and cower. No, it was going to be full throttle. They were going to build worldwide support to eliminate, once and for all, the scourge of FGM from planet earth.

Sixty minutes later the press published the stories and pictures of Shannon and Rheingold with Ali and Bono, Nancy and Paul, and Rachel and Daniel. Already, exponentially improving, The Heiress's AI distribution got more posts, with greater placement, timing, and eye-recognition capabilities than the first releases only 60 minutes earlier.

Within 24-hours Eagle Brewing Company disclosed they had run out of Young's Bitter after the media releases had included pictures of the four raving couples praising and toasting the brew. Two days later, Eagle Brewing Company was sold-out of every beer they made.

Over the Atlantic

Refreshed by the showers and excitement of flying in another amazingly equipped jet, Shannon and Rheingold were wide-awake, sitting together in the family compartment as the jet started its flight over the Atlantic.

Within the glowing smiles and hand holding during take-off, Rheingold's mind was reeling.

"Shannon," he started in his smooth, deep baritone voice.

He touched her face, "Shannon, we've been running so fast, and I," he paused. "I wanted to take a moment and tell you, my truth."

"Oh baby," she purred.

"Shannon, my love."

He got closer to her. In one motion, he was on one knee, looking up at her, "I want you to be my beloved wife."

"My whole life, my whole being, I've been searching for you."

"The moment I saw you, clear as day. I just knew. It was fate.

"Everything in my life has led to you. You are my oneness."

He stood and pulled her into a long embrace.

"Rheingold, I'm so in love with you," she shakingly whispered. "I was so alone in my life, so alone.

"Rheingold, I read every love story ever written, all the Shakespeare, all the songs, all the movies."

"The bad experiences I had, made me resigned to the fact that I would never find love…

"I'm so in love with you. More than I could I ever say," as she crushed her sobbing head against his firm chest.

Rheingold crooned, "I don't want to wait. This week let's get married. Let's never be apart."

"Oh Rheingold, I can't wait. I can't wait to be your wife and be with you forever!"

Making love is a lot of things. It's passion. It's energy. It's power. It's submission. It's domination. It's parallel. It's procreation. But you haven't made love until you make love with love tears. For so many humans making love is never seen or felt as the great healing gift it can be. Making beloved love.

With sweet love tears, Shannon and Rheingold started kissing each other.

They walked into the jet's bedroom. They were wiping tears from their faces as they undressed. They climbed under the covers, facing each other, holding their trembling bodies close together. His hand and fingers held her face, as they started kissing. Even in the tears and emotions, they naturally slid together. Their bodies retouched the special places as he entered her so softly. His tears fell on her trembling body. She reached up and wiped the tears from his eyes and whispered, "Rheingold, I love you."

They sensuously moved in a loving, tantric unison. It was a moment that touched their souls. And just as slowly, they turned their bodies with Shannon curled up inside his strong arms feeling all of him. And ever so tenderly they fell asleep.

At the Philadelphia airport, Jack was waiting for them with two other armored Lincoln Navigators each packed with four security leaders. They moved in tight unison. No mistakes.

When they returned to the compound they were dropped at the main house where The Heiress, Reed and Kelby were waiting for them. Again, the hugs were real, and like the first morning, an elegant breakfast was laid out before them. After everything that happened, they took time to enjoy the pleasantries and company.

The stark realizations were real. Rheingold was banged-up and his pain was still real. To get around without impacting her sliced stomach muscles, The Heiress was at the breakfast table in a customized wheelchair with technology outdoing anything Stephen Hawking had in his lifetime. A miracle to be alive, her optimized health and lifestyle made her recovery faster than any doctor imagined. Yes, she was hurting. The pain was real. But there she was, defiant and true to her nature, literally at the table, and ready to lead.

Almost to prove she wasn't as hurt as her doctors were describing, The Heiress stood up and walked to get the coffee to freshen up everyone's coffee cups. They didn't see him sit down more tenderly than when she got up.

Without even saying it, they joined hands. They would later describe the magical energy they felt in that moment. The Heiress started clearing her voice to speak when Rheingold bellowed in his deep morning voice, "Dear God. Dear God of infinity and all things. Thank you for bringing us together at this table, for this cause, for this love. Bless us in our days, protect us in our sleep, so we may do the good you have brought us together to do in your name. Amen."

Echoing Rheingold, they squeezed each other's hands when they all said, "Amen."

After breakfast, everyone was speed-briefed on the evolving work against FGM and sex trafficking. Next, Rheingold, gave an update on the global media and marketing campaign. He thought he was in over his head, but now he was leading a global marketing campaign with the most-connected, marketing firms on the planet. Just as The Heiress hoped, his recommendations were making big impacts and the messaging was more focused on results and finding more champions of the cause.

Kelby was holding back and couldn't wait to ask, "So what was it like meeting Bono and Ali?" Instantly, the ladies were chatting about Paul McCartney, Nancy, Rachel Weisz, and Daniel Craig.

Then, just like that they were moving forward into another aggressive week's schedule.

Launching the Daughter's Campaign

Probably the most impressive thing about the Daughter's Campaign was its speed to launch. With the mystery, scale, and excitement surrounding it, even for the world's biggest stars and celebrities were pulled into the suspense.

Everyone was asking, *"What is this?"* and, *"When is this airing?"*

The sheer audacity and simplicity of the campaign was brilliant. With so many millions using TikTok, Instagram, Facebook, Twitter, and LinkedIn, Rheingold pushed the team to use every technology platform. The instructions were clear and basic. Enter the portal, watch the video instructions, record your video, upload it. Everyone on the planet would get the same instructions at 12 noon. The Heiress communications systems were ready to post every video, real-time. Everyone in the communication's center wondered if the world wide web could handle the surge.

The Heiress, Rheingold, Shannon, Reed, Kelby, Roz, Dance, and Kimberly watched from The Heiress's mansion, in the comfort of her sublime Situations Room, accompanied by another rare vintage from The Heiress's wine cellar.

As planned the first 12 posts were launched at 12 noon, alongside the thousands of celebrities who started watching the posts within their recording platforms. Unbeknownst to them, as the stars were watching the video and recording their posts, so was the rest of the world.

The distribution cadence and channels developed by The Heiress's AI technology were unprecedented, They were on a scale never before imagined. The executives from the largest marketing companies just watched in total awe. Equally cool, before 30 minutes ticked off the clock, The Heiress's AI technology had exponentially evolved every aspect of the distribution and the distribution channels, so the results and impacts were more than twice as effective as they were an hour beforehand. Within 60 minutes of the kick-off launch, everything doubled again.

By midnight, 100 million people had recorded and posted their own videos for the Daughter's Campaign. Just as the 12-member marketing team had discussed; this campaign was a raging forest fire.

The spin-offs, no one predicted. Around the globe, people started posting video spin-offs of the Daughter's Campaign. The caring, creativity, and love were extraordinary.

In a friendly competitive spin-off, the CEOs of William Morris Endeavor and Creative Artists Agency used a similar format and famous songs for the Daughter's Campaign to showcase the famous artists and athletes in their portfolios. Combined, just between these two marketing titans, their TikTok and YouTube videos had over 200 million views, in 48 hours.

Shannon Revisits UN

Working in stealth, another of Rheingold's contributions was getting the team to agree to coordinate a global pathway for the co-sponsorship campaign through the United Nations where strong nations without a large presence of FGM, would bring clout, trade, and military power to aid the FGM cause. For the most part, Russia, China, Japan, UK, Australia, and South America didn't have a FGM footprint, so they were good allies at the UN, World Bank, WHO, and other global agencies. While Shannon and Rheingold wanted to revisit New York, it was easily decided for safety precautions that Shannon's remarks would be remote. Everyone knew the gravity of addressing the UN Security Council.

Everyone knew the terrorists would stop at nothing to kill Shannon and block any UN actions. Despite the support of the five permanent members of The UN Security Council, USA, France, UK, Russia, and China, getting 100% support of the whole UN Security Council was no slam dunk. The global team that The Heiress was assembling with Shannon and Rheingold had strong points of contact with every one of the ten temporary members of the Council. Estonia, India, Ireland, Kenya, Mexico, Niger, Norway, Saint Vincent and the Grenadines, Tunisia, and Vietnam.

Several of these nations presented major hurdles. The team enjoyed internal banter on the strategy of avoiding, ignoring, or confronting the UN Security Council. In the end, the team's prevailing strategy was to go full-Monty to discover the ways the FGM advocates were going to react.

And react, they did.

Three of the temporary members immediately tried to delay the meeting. Another temporary member threatened to filibuster any action on FGM matters if this meeting took place so quickly without notice or warning. Surprisingly overnight, both Russia and China were stronger in their support to end FGM than anyone ever imagined. Many dismissed the Russian and Chinese positions as using FGM to advance the decades-long ethnic cleansing so ruthlessly played out in these countries.

Inside Langley, the CIA was delighted, especially female agents, to see the real reasons gleaned from their real-time intelligence gatherings from Russia and China. Just like everywhere else in the world, the Daughter's Campaign was equally effective in Russia and China. Women, wives, and men around the world were uniting behind the Daughter's Campaign. The wives of world leaders were especially moved by the Daughter's campaign. Like America, Chinese and Russian leaders appeared in videos supporting the Daughter's campaign. The intelligence reports may have revealed Rheingold's illustrious past, but dang this guy could really develop, and deploy a branding campaign.

The 11 am UN conference call was quick. In fact, 12 of the 15 nations on the call had national leaders that had already recorded videos for the Daughter's Campaign. As expected, three nations voted no. Niger, Tunisia, and Kenya. After the vote, the long-time Kenyan ambassador respectfully asked if he could add a statement to the official record. The other seasoned ambassadors from China, India, and Ireland, quickly chimed-in, and simultaneously echoed, "Please, please, yes."

Without pause the Kenyan ambassador adjusted his glasses, waivered, and then he spoke ardently about his country's strident efforts to end FGM, but he emphasized and tried to gain sympathy for the political realities facing any leader in Kenya regarding FGM. He stiffened, "Unlike some of you, any Kenyan that speaks openly about ending FGM is immediately at great risk of assassination. Two of my best friends have already been killed for their writings and speeches." He shifted in his seat and started to fumble with his cell phone. An ancient soul revered by his tribe and nation, clearly started sweating, as he again humbly apologized for his inability with technology. Then he held up his phone for all to see. Across the conference call a video started with the ambassador clearly in tears, almost weeping, then with a loud stern voice!

"Please let the world know!

"I'm on my daughter's team.

"I'm on my daughter's team."

The video shifted, and a statuesque woman in traditional garb clearly his wife, joined him in the video. They looked at each other nervously but lovingly, now holding hands.

"I'm on my daughter's team."

"I'm on my daughter's team."

Shannon sat at the monitor crying.

She knew the Ambassador and his wife were taking great risks. Inside her tears she imagined an assassination team was already assigned to kill him and his wife for this global outburst.

The chairman of the meeting, equally affected, hesitantly started to speak. "Thank you, Mr. Ambassador. Thank you. Let us all find strength and courage by your endearing spirit and example." He continued looking at his watch. "Unless I hear any objection… this meeting is adjourned at 11:37 a.m."

The Campaign Updated

By noon, there were more than 250 million posts for the Daughter's Campaign. The world wide web was wobbling with volume spikes. The CIO of Equinix was quoted, "Thank God the post is only five words. If the post had been 12 words, most likely the internet itself would have crashed."

The Workout

Shannon couldn't wait to workout with Rheingold. They had talked about it endlessly, laughing and taunting each other. But nothing prepared Shannon for the Rheingold workout gear. Shannon, of course, was dressed in the most modern, form-fitting gear made for women. Her sneakers were new, shiny, and bright. Quite simply, stunning.

Rheingold, on the other hand, was decidedly old-school. Shannon was sizing him up with a finger on her lips, holding back her laughs. His expression of modernism was worn-out black sweatpants instead of schoolhouse gray. His hooded sweatshirt was ripped, old, faded, torn, and ten years old from Auburn University. That year Cam Newton and Auburn won the national championship. They must have overprinted thousands of thick, high-quality sweatshirts. Rheingold thought it was great to purchase sweatshirts from the $5 dollar discount rack. He also enjoyed the puzzled looks he got wearing an Auburn sweatshirt north of the Mason Dixon line.

His Nike training sneakers looked older than the sweatshirt. Smiling, Shannon gave Rheingold a great big hug, "Oh honey you look so good. I'm so glad you found your best workout gear, because I can't wait to bust your old ass."

Rheingold proudly countered, "Shannon, there's a lot of blood, sweat and tears in this gear."

The deal was Rheingold would try and keep up with Shannon for her three workout songs. And, if Rheingold was still alive after the three songs, Shannon would do Rheingold's workout for his three workout songs! When Reed and Kelby heard about this love-wager, they kidded The Heiress that a medical team should definitely be made available. Everyone laughed. But The Heiress had the most laughs as she watched the workout LIVE from her technology-equipped bedroom.

Of course, the workout room in The Heiress's compound was incredible. The sound system and large video screens were better than any concert venue.

"Are you ready, big boy?" Shannon asked.

With that, Shannon pushed play on her already synched phone. She blasted, "Bloody Valentine" by Machine Gun Kelly. Immediately they both laughed. Knowing they both watched this video when one of The Heiress's Army soldiers mentioned Shannon was as cute as beautiful Megan Fox in the Bloody Valentine video.

They started dancing as the music boomed around the room. They laughed as Shannon got him mimicking Megan Fox's sexy dance in the "Bloody Valentine" video. Shannon started adding cheerleading moves that Rheingold very weakly tried to mimic. They were facing each other, playfully shaking their shoulders, bouncing to the beat, when Shannon went double-time. Rheingold tried to spark his old muscles to keep up. He didn't. She leaped into a backflip, into a somersault, into a leap, landing solidly. Laughing, Rheingold did an awkward log roll, jumped into a raised-arm Texas Longhorn Hook 'em Horn's salute. It was weak.

At this Shannon, really started moving.

Shannon was shining in her moment, dancing with and around Rheingold in double or triple time to Rheingold's occasional moments of weak dance moves. Then, she started showing off with handstands, which Rheingold immediately mimicked with some surprising success (without the leaps she was doing in-between).

Shannon was beaming. Rheingold was sweating like he just walked out of a sauna. She was dancing circles around Rheingold in double-time, and she was loving it.

Rheingold was looking, well, out of his league!

Acting the part, Shannon got serious as the next song started. "Clean", by Hey Violet, had Shannon dramatically reacting to the first notes. She started walking elegantly around Rheingold with yoga like moves, nodding at him to mimic her. Shannon was turning difficult yoga poses into dance. At once she was slowly moving into and holding intense yoga poses for 16 beats. Then leaping high into 16 beats of dance, to 16 beats of a slow groove into her next pose. Her body strength and flexibility were on full display. Rheingold wasn't even close.

Halfway through, Rheingold managed to coax Shannon into some kind of disco dance. They held hands and sashayed back and forth. They were smiling like lovers at the high school dance, mouthing the words that Rheingold didn't know.

Watching, The Heiress smiled. *Dang they even make a break-up song impressively cute.*

Shannon let out a big scream. Her last song started, "Do It Again", by Stroke 9, and she started a sensuous dance in front of Rheingold, that he tried to mimic, very weakly. Shannon turned this song into a hot yoga routine. Rheingold was a hot mess. Putting it nicely, his ability to stretch was limited. Toward the end of the song, Shannon whipped her body into Rheingold and they grinded together with a long kiss.

And then there was silence. They kissed and smiled. Rheingold had survived. Barely.

Then Rheingold parted and said, "Now it's my turn. Are you sure you are ready for the real stuff? You can back out now?"

"Oh my," she said.

He started moving a bunch of benches and weights around into stations.

"Okay, okay, we call these the Ricky Bobby's," Rheingold proclaimed. "These are stations where we're going to do a slow and steady cadence of ten reps of these Ricky Bobby exercises. Okay, first we'll do ten push-ups, then ten squats, then in between the two chairs we'll do ten dips, then its ten mountain climbers, into ten jumping jacks. Then we'll sit, touch feet, and do ten sit-ups. We'll finish with ten alternating curls, where I use the 25lb dumbbells and you'll use the 5lb. Easy peasy!"

Shannon remarked, "Nice, very nice. But how about I use the 10 pounders, big boy."

Rheingold smiled with a shit-eating grin, "We'll see."

"Oh, and we're going to do 'em nice and slow- good. Here I got a little tune to help us get started to get to ten sets of the Ricky Bobby."

He grabbed his phone and laughed to himself, "Let's Get It Up," by AC/DC. It was a tune so familiar to him and something new for Shannon. She gave him a puzzled look when he did a couple of arm pumps.

Rheingold started thrusting his hips…He quickly kissed her and positioned her for push-ups next to him and they started with ten pushups then ten squats…Slowly, they proceeded to complete their first Ricky Bobby set.

____

Rheingold was taking his time, as they started their fifth set. He was going slow, so he could survive. He was taking his time in-between sets, even sneaking in a kiss or two. Rheingold and Shannon were smiling but they were wearing a more determined look after doing 50 pushups, 50 squats, and the rest.

____

Rheingold was pleased with their progress, and smiled when his next fun song came on, "Holding Out for the One," by Tenille Townes.

Shannon yelled, "Oh my God. I love this song." She sang out loud, "Holding, Holding. Holding Out for The One. Holding, Holding. Holding Out for The One." They started grinding back to the ten pushups, and dance moves in between each set.

Wow, Rheingold was impressed. They had completed seven good sets of Ricky Bobby. He felt every muscle in his body and knew he was approaching his limit. Shannon was smiling, showing signs of a workout, but also appearing like she was just getting started. Both were struggling with the dip sets. Getting past the eighth set was going to be challenging. Rheingold was sagging on the sit-ups. To be fair, an eight set Rick Bobby was a pretty darn good workout.

For his last song, Rheingold was going to go old school, thinking he'd decide between two old classics, "Back on My Feet Again", by The Babys, or "Good Girls Don't" by The Knack. But right then, he adjusted, quickly flipped around his phone to pull up another song, "C'est La Vie" by Stereophonics. Rheingold declared, "Baby I'm going to need a lot more juice to get to the finish line, I need some Welsh rock n roll." He pressed play.

Even with the Welsh inspirations, the nineth set was a bear. Rheingold was straining on every set, lamely doing the reps. Shannon, energized by a new song, pounded out the ninth set with a vengeance.

On the tenth set Shannon ripped it out as the song energized her. Rheingold got halfway through the sit-ups and rolled over like a little baby. He watched and marveled at Shannon doing her thing. On the eleventh set she skipped the dips.

She breezed through twelve sets.

Now she was rubbing it in, adding shakes, jumps, leaps, and handstands within her thirteenth set. She had total fun with the thirteenth set, adding a whole bunch of jumps and flips.

After she finished fourteen sets with a tumbling, flipping flourish, she raced over the Rheingold and straddled him as he was lying in a heap. They rolled around. When they finally kissed it was playful joy.

The Rheingold TikTok

After their workout shower, Shannon was still on fire. Rheingold was hurting and moving slowly. Losing the workout bet, Rheingold now had to do his first TikTok. So, Shannon was busy coordinating with the videographers and getting everything set-up. She could barely contain her excitement as they walked back into The Heiress's gym. In minutes, everything was set up.

The presentation was designed to be as simple as possible. Rheingold was going to be dressed as cool as they could make him, with dark sunglasses with black frames. They all agreed something was missing. They made calls and presented Rheingold and Shannon with a cool black felt hat. From the moment he tried on the hat, it was obvious the hat made Rheingold complete. Shannon was dressed in a light flowing dress, with a color matching pair of tight-fitting yoga pants to her upper thighs so she could do the flips and jumps she was planning to do.

They had a blast trying to choose the perfect song for Rheingold's first TikTok. They listened to dozens of their favorite songs. To some, Shannon did dance moves to demonstrate some of her ideas. While so many songs would have been great, they both felt they hadn't found the perfect one. Then Rheingold pulled a great song from the 80's that Shannon knew from college cheerleading. *Your Love,* by The Outfield." Like other songs it wasn't perfect, but it had the perfect line for Rheingold.

With everyone set, the camera and sound system started rolling. With dark shades and the black hat, Rheingold was standing stoic and cool in the center of the frame. Energetic Shannon, was standing behind Rheingold, waiting for the song to start.

Swinging around Rheingold, Shannon mouthed the first three verses of the song while she gracefully moved around Rheingold. She was facing the camera with lip syncing with the music.

Then Rheingold mouthed, "You know I like my girls a little bit older."

Shannon sang the next verse. They both lip-synced the next verse.

When the song kicked-off, Shannon started doing leaps and flips around Rheingold as he just stood stoic with a shit-eating grin. On the right side of the screen, they posted #EndFGM facts and the Action Plan to Adopt #EndFGM pledges across America. They asked for women and men to help. At 57-seconds they hugged like high school sweethearts, laughing and twisting around, in playful love. They let it roll for 65-seconds. Shannon was amazing! Rheingold was Rheingold. The video team kept watching the replay, until the director said to the team, "I don't see any edits, and this is beyond my expectations. Let's release this as soon as possible."

Shannon yelled, "Oh my God, it's amazing."

With that the finishing team took over, and eight minutes later Rheingold's first TikTok was released, and posted. They tagged it into Shannon's Tik-Tok, Instagram, and Facebook account.

Within Rheingold's first 15 minutes of fame, his brand-new account had 12 million views, 10 million likes, and 2 million shares. Within 24 hours, Rheingold had 28 million TikTok followers.

The University of Alabama

10-hours later, in like manner the cheerleaders of the University of Alabama made a TikTok video that went equally viral across Alabama, the South, and the rest of the world. Their gymnasts and acrobats paid tribute to Shannon, her courage, and the fight to #EndFGM.

Their cheer routine started in the endzone of their famous football stadium,

Roll Tide

Roll Tide

We are…Alabama

We call on Roll Tide nation

We call on our brothers and sisters of the SEC.

We call on the USA

Let's #EndFGM in Alabama

Let's #EndFGM in America

Let's #EndFGM in the world

Falling in love with 80's music, the Alabama cheerleading squad quickly shifted gears and used a mocked-up powerful version of The Outfield's song, "All the Love in the World." They started 2:28 minutes into the song. Here, they lovingly spliced in scenes of Shannon's videos and parts of Rheingold's 1st video, while the cheerleaders had a blast lip-synching the lyrics. Somehow, they filled the student section to sing the chorus with them at the 3-minute mark, 4,000 students lip-synching and shouting, "All my love. All the love in the world. All my love. I'll be sending you. All my Love. All the love in the world. All my Love. All My Love. All the love in the world." At the end of the video, the Alabama student section roared. "Shannon, We Love You."

In 6-hours the Alabama cheerleader's video reached two million views, soon after two million likes. Within 30-hours, all the schools of the SEC and Big Ten posted similar #EndFGM TikTok videos. Within 60-hours, similar TikTok videos were posted by cheerleading squads from most of the nation's colleges and universities, high schools, and youth sports leagues.

Across America and Canada, fraternities and sororities started posting #EndFGM videos.

The creativity and video innovations were incredible. The impacts were unbelievable.

No one could remember when college campuses were so united and focused on one issue since the Vietnam War. Within 48 hours TikTok videos crossed the seas by football (soccer) clubs around the world.

Young people were appalled to learn the magnitude and savagery of FGM. Rapidly, all the passions on college campuses were directed at the eradication of FGM. Like the speed of the internet, within days, 60's style sit-ins started to dominate college campuses. The students demanded college and university Presidents and Boards of Trustees immediately sign the #EndFGM Pledge. The reaction was immediate. The students demanded emergency meetings to enact change. Like the pension and investment efforts against apartheid, the #EndFGM Pledge spread rapidly to college/university foundation investment funds, governments, and corporate pension funds.

Penn State University acted first, enacting the #EndFGM pledge a week after Shannon and Rheingold posted the #EndFGM pledge video. Within that first 10-day period, all Ivy League, Big Ten, SEC, and Patriot League schools adopted the pledge.

Taken by surprise at the speed and impacts, FGM nations immediately experienced dramatic drops in their stock and bond markets, and currencies. Already some of the poorer nations of the world, their economies crashed, exports came to a standstill, and their ability to maintain debt payments was immediately questioned.

Within ten days of the Rheingold's 1st video, The World Bank called an emergency meeting with the sole agenda dealing with FGM Nation Debt. With swift reaction, newspapers, especially student newspapers, media and social media posts condemned any nations that supported or harbored FGM nations and called for the strictest economic sanctions ever applied against a nation. The common theme, "If a nation continued to support or harbor FGM, every sanction should be applied to that nation until that nation capitulated or collapsed."

Student organizations started to protest any action or emergency relief action for beleaguered FGM nations. Their common theme was, "Change First, Then Aid." In other words, "No aid until all political and religious leaders signed the #EndFGM Pledge."

The first nations to sign the #EndFGM Pledge were oil nations.

The FGM sanctions were so severe to FGM nations, rich and poor, that the political and religious leaders eventually signed the End FGM Pledge on their National TV stations. The global media celebration of the first oil nations signing the #EndFGM Pledge was so strong, soon other FGM nations signed. But the nations with the largest numbers and percentages of FGM held out.

The excitement at The Heiress's mansion was ebullient. With a group of The Heiress's Army leaders, Shannon and Rheingold watched the news on CNN. Like the rest of the world, they were shaken at the speed and depth of the #EndFGM pledges.

Shannon and Rheingold on the Tonight Show Starring Jimmy Fallon

Again, using all her connections, The Heiress was able to get Shannon and Rheingold on the Tonight Show Starring Jimmy Fallon. There was one condition. NBC had to play the Shannon video featuring the song, **A Moment Like This**, by Kelly Clarkson to introduce Shannon and Rheingold onto the set.

With Shannon's TikTok publicity for the show, Fallon's Nielsen ratings jumped dramatically from roughly one million nightly viewers to over 19 million viewers for the Shannon and Rheingold episode. The internet replays were the most ever.

Fallon started his introduction, "Tonight's guests need no introduction to anyone on TikTok. With an estimated TikTok viewership approaching 77 million, Shannon's audience is one of the biggest in the history of media. Her fiancé Rheingold, with only one TikTok post, has over 25 million followers on TikTok."

As the Shannon video plays, Fallon, the band, and the crowd were all wiping tears, audibly weeping! As the song was ending, Fallon was still wiping his eyes, then he commented, "Wow, I've seen this video, like more than 20 times, and every time, every single time, I get choked up."

Looking at Shannon, "Wow, you are so amazing. It's the biggest honor to meet you, Shannon!"

"It's really a great honor to meet you. Wow, Jimmy Fallon!" replied Shannon.

Still wiping his eyes, "Shannon, we've been blessed to have so many guests on the Tonight Show; celebrities, politicians, and musical legends, but you really are something special. And, brave. My God, you are so brave and fearless. Thank you for everything you are doing for so many women today and in the future."

Holding Rheingold's hand for support, "Thank you, Mr. Fallon. It means so much to me to be on your show with Rheingold. Truly, I believe everyone knows, I wish I wasn't here tonight. I wish FGM, and sex trafficking didn't exist. But unfortunately, they exist, and it's time to end it."

Fallon: "It's difficult to imagine this horror exists and impacts 200 million women on the earth. It's tragic."

Fallon turned slightly to talk to Rheingold. "So, Rheingold. Like everyone else in America, I have a thousand questions. But welcome to the Tonight Show."

"Dude," Rheingold began with his classic greeting, "like Shannon said, it's a great honor to meet you and be on The Tonight Show. Thank you."

"So, Rheingold, I must ask, you never had a TikTok account, and then your first video gets 25 million views, and you have 25 million followers, how does it feel Rheingold?

"Dude, what's TikTok?" Fallon and the crowd laugh in response.

Rheingold chuckled and continued, "Hey man, you have to understand, Shannon is amazing. She's a force of nature, and if anyone on the planet can get this done, it's Shannon!"

"Hey baby, you're pretty amazing in my book!" Adored Shannon, as she and Rheingold snuggled like teenagers as Fallon rolls his eyes.

Fallon: "Okay, okay, so how did you guys meet, like really meet?"

"Well, truth be told, I was able to read about Rheingold, and I couldn't wait to meet him. And, when we finally met, he was exactly everything I dreamed."

"Dude, I didn't know anything. I know nothing!" Rheingold shrugged and Fallon and the crowd laughs.

Rheingold adds, "I mean, the woman is so beautiful. Just look at her! And she's smart, driven, fearless, and cool, what's not to love! I mean, if this is a dream, it's a better dream than I could have ever imagined."

"So, Shannon, what's next?" Fallon asked.

"Well, Rheingold made a great strategy with the UN, and it's working perfectly. Then our last video, his 1st, included the #EndFGM pledge and college students are changing the world. We're starting the Shannon Fund, and with these funds we're going to teach through, Train the Trainer programs around the world. We need to do so much teaching, listening, and learning. This week I am going to Cairo to start efforts in Egypt. As you know, it's ground-zero in Egypt. It's ground-zero where so many really brave women and men are trying to change the world."

Rheingold added, "Plus, we're trying to get Congress to act and use American influence to protect women around the world."

"So, what's the story about the red wine?" Fallon asked with an eyebrow wiggle.

Rheingold spoke plainly, "Oh, you mean the Red Car wine. Yes, it's true, my favorite wine is Red Car from Sonoma County. We learned Red Car was the favorite wine of so many of our friends. So, yes, you could say Red Car brought us all together."

Shannon sassily retorted, "Oh honey, I believe he meant you and the two glasses of red wine. You know, baby, what red wine does to you. Oh yes, yes, yes, you can definitely say Red Car made us come together!"

"So, wow, whoa!" Fallon replied, startled by her response.

Trying to redirect the conversation, Fallon switched subjects, "So, yes, yes what about drinking beers with Paul McCartney, Bono, and Daniel Crag?"

"Oh, you mean drinking beers with Nancy, Ali, and Rachel?" Shannon continued with her witty banter.

"Ouch, touché!"

Rheingold interjected, "Dude, I love that beer! Young's Bitter. It's so awesome. Did you hear they sold out of that beer?"

"Honey," interrupted Shannon, "I believe Mr. Fallon was asking what it was like drinking with James Bond."

"Who's James Bond?" This elicited another round of laughs.

Then Rheingold turned, 'Look I'm here to ask some men to get some ~~balls~~ (beeped out by censors). I won't mince words. This FGM has been going on way too long. We need men to join this fight to #EndFGM."

Shannon interjected, "Honey we need the ladies, too."

"Shannon and Rheingold, I wish I could hang out with you all night. You guys are amazing. Shannon, thank you. My wife Nancy and I look forward to helping you and working together to eradicate FGM and sex trafficking."

"Thanks, Mr. Fallon." They said in unison.

"And, on behalf of the entire team at the network, we wanted to share this video we made for Shannon." Fallon adjusted to face the viewing screen along with the rest of the audience.

The video started with Jimmy Fallon and his wife, Nancy Juvonen:

"I'm on my daughter's team!"

Then the screen split in two with the cast of Saturday Night Live:

"I'm on my daughter's team!"

Then the screen split in three, with the cast from 30 Rock:

"I'm on my daughter's team!"

Then the screen kept splitting adding show after show of the network's programming:

"I'm on my daughter's team!"

No one could remember a 11-minute segment on television that could match the viewership, impacts, or immediate and long-term internet traffic. Like the night the Daughter's Campaign launched, the night the Tonight Show aired with Shannon and Rheingold, the internet almost crashed again.

Back at The Heiress Compound with Reed and Kelby. they discussed Shannon's trip to Egypt.

Rheingold still wasn't pleased. Five days ago, when the opportunity to visit Cairo was presented, Rheingold was instantly opposed. The Heiress was steadfast about the Cairo meeting's goals and adamant against Rheingold joining Shannon on the trip. She reminded Rheingold he needed to be in New York to meet with the twelve marketing executives, on the same day Shannon was speaking in Cairo. Despite her desire to be with Rheingold, Shannon reminded Rheingold they wanted everything to stay on schedule so another global marketing video could launch after the

Cairo speech. Reed emphasized to Rheingold his importance to the global marketing campaign. After further protestations Rheingold eventually relented. Shannon would fly to Cairo that night. In the morning, Rheingold would fly to New York. Jack would drive The Heiress to Washington for a meeting with five senators.

It was their last breakfast together. They would remember it forever. After the ladies ran off to review a few sets of clothes for Shannon to wear in Egypt, Reed, feeling the intensity of fear in Rheingold's voice when he was explaining his concerns for Shannon's safety in Egypt asked, "Dude. How are you holding-up?"

Rheingold paused. It was the first time in a week he was alone with Reed. He was trying to find words in the English language, "Dude. What the fuck!" his voice wavering. "It's all happening so fast."

The words found their path, "I mean, Shannon is so amazing, and it's like wow, how am I here?" He added, "This cause, it's so intense and dude, there's people trying to kill us. It's fucking nuts. I can't even go to a fucking Wawa without getting shot at. It's like I'm in a James Bond movie." Rheingold paused.

"Dude, yesterday I got drunk with James Fucking Bond."

Reed laughed. Like, what else could he do.

He put his hand on Rheingold's uninjured shoulder.

"My man. You know why you're fucking here, right here, right now?" Reed declared.

"Because God knows, you're the only one calm enough, cool enough, smart enough, and caring enough, to pull this shit off.

"Dude.

"You're the only one."

___

They looked at their watches and nodded. It was time for Shannon to leave for the airport for her red-eye flight. As she hugged everyone Shannon cried the happiest tears of her life.

She hugged and kissed Rheingold and whispered, "Baby I am so happy. It's all happening. There's a real possibility Egypt could sign when I'm in Cairo. Wouldn't that be amazing?"

Rheingold held her tight. Then he pulled back to look into her eyes, "I just want you back as soon as possible. I just want you back."

After Shannon left for her flight to Cairo, everyone left for their homes. Rheingold and The Heiress had their first chance to speak alone since they met. Even though they were exhausted, they shared a knowing look that they wanted to talk.

They stood across the exquisite kitchen, and The Heiress said, "Siri play 'Both Sides Now', by Joni Mitchell, on repeat. Sound Level 3!"

"Sorry, I just felt I need her to sing this song right now," The Heiress quipped to Rheingold, as she painfully walked over and refilled his wine glass and then hers.

Like no other song, the song so slowly filled every corner of the room. Watching The Heiress, Rheingold briefly thought the look on her face resembled that knowing look before someone pulls out a cigarette.

Rheingold started, "Everything you predicted about Shannon, was true." He continued, "Just like you said; she's amazing, beautiful, and everything in my dreams."

The Heiress started, "After I learned about both of you, I had a strong feeling you were destined to meet and be together."

Rheingold hesitated, "But the limo ride here, our kisses, they felt just as real..."

The Heiress quickly exclaimed, "Yes, the kisses were real, but more than anything, I needed you to trust me. At the moment, I thought sharing passionate kisses, the music and moments of unbridled emotions were the only way I could pull you in."

The Heiress didn't stop, "This is a war, Rheingold. The evil forces we face are not going to go away without a fight. As I told you before, the only thing that is going to be able to hold us together is love. Everything we know is going to be ripped and torn. The only way we win this war is undying, passionate love." She paused reflecting, "That kind of love is the only reason I'm alive today."

Rheingold sighed, "I hope nothing happens to Shannon."

The Heiress softly touched his shoulder as Joni Mitchell's voice trailed into a blurry saxophone solo. Then she calmly stated, "Shannon is a warrior. She already knows the battles she faces. Shannon is stronger than anyone I know. If I had a daughter…"

And instantly The Heiress paused, looked at Rheingold and burst into tears. And in that same raw moment Rheingold knew exactly why he was here, with her, with Shannon, with this life-mission.

They embraced in knowing tears.

Daughters.

Life.

He hugged The Heiress, ignoring the pain surging from his shoulder. She winced, too, from her own pain, and the years of holding back the most painful thing a mother can know.

The Heiress trying to hold back but failing, sobbing, wailed, "Rheingold, I lost my baby girl, I lost my baby girl."

Her whole body shaking, "my baby's name was Rachel. Her name was Rachel!"

"She was just a little baby."

The pain only a mother knows. The pain that never ever goes away.

Ryan Gold Craven stood as tall and strong as he could, despite his own sorrowful weeping, "I know. I know. It's okay." They stood quietly weeping until that awkward 2nd Saxophone solo burst out in "Both Sides Now" with its twin bursts, almost squeaks, that pierce even the most guarded soul.

With the song bursts of harsh reality, composing herself The Heiress gathered her stronger voice, "You know for all my life, I thought this song was the truth, like it was my anthem. But it's really not true at all." She stood a little straighter wiping the tears from her eyes. "I know love. Love is the only thing that kept me going." She added, "I felt all the emotions and angers. I've had all the money and resources; and the only thing I've learned is time and love are the most valuable assets in the world. Nothing else compares. Nothing else matters."

"All these years, I thought that I really didn't know life or love at all. When it was right in front of me, every day. The love I have for my daughter. The love I have for my family. In the end, I learned I really know life and love so well. "

She continued, "Then I saw Shannon's TikTok video, and soon met her. And her whole life is about love."

The Heiress glowed, "When I met Shannon, I hoped and imagined my daughter would have been like her. I instantly loved her and wanted to protect her and give her the biggest platforms in the world to finish the good fight she started. She restored my faith, gave me hope. At the same time, I was reading all about you and the way you loved, and got things done. I just, I just knew you and Shannon were made to meet and be together. She needed to know great love. I knew bringing the both of you together was her destiny and your fate."

Rheingold joked, "Well you got that right, that's for sure. You've advanced everything further and faster than anyone could imagine."

The Heiress smiled, now back in command of herself, "The best we can do is pray for her safe return, and that is exactly what I'm going to go do right now. Now get some rest Rheingold, we're all going to need it."

With that, The Heiress slowly but proudly walked to her side of The Heiress's mansion and Rheingold walked equally slowly to the room where he first enjoyed Shannon. Tonight, everyone on the team, prayed.

Shannon in Cairo

Flight 1269

(8:03 pm Egypt time)

With great fanfare Shannon and the UN contingency left the last press conference in Cairo and boarded their plane. Flight 1269 was flying from Cairo to Paris, and then hopping over the Atlantic to JFK. Shannon would be back in NYC by noon the following day. She texted Rheingold, "Baby, everything was awesome, and I can't wait to wrap my body all over you, baby. I'm so excited to feel you touch me."

Rheingold smiled. "Shannon, two nights without you is a nightmare. I can't wait for you to be back with me. It's going to be awesome."

She boarded the flight.

1:07 pm, Philadelphia Airport – The Heiress's Hangar

Using the military protocols that The Heiress's commando trainers had mentioned to Rheingold, at noon they used several diversionary tactics so Rheingold, Roz, Dance, and the security team could slip out of Villanova. In six blocks, well past the terrorist's safehouse, the other two Navigators caught up with them.

Rheingold with Roz and Dance jumped on The Heiress's Learjet for a flight to JFK. There they planned to meet with the marketing team for dinner. Instead of returning to Villanova, he wanted to see Shannon as soon as she was back in the States and enjoy a two-night excursion in the Big Apple. He texted her as she was boarding, "Shannon, I can't wait to see you. So, change of plans. It's all approved and has The Heiress's blessings. I'm meeting you at JFK and we're going to hide away for two nights in NYC."

She wrote back, "Oh baby, that's so awesome. I love you and can't wait to see you. I can't wait to be your wife!"

Originally, he pitched The Heiress about the two invisible days and nights at the Algonquin Hotel. After this whirlwind of days, he pleaded that they needed a break, a change of scenery, and heck they deserved it. The Heiress smiled, and imitating Rheingold she purred, "Dude, you're not staying in the Algonquin Hotel but good choice, it's one of the first hotels I bought in New York. No, you're going to stay at my new place at 15 Central Park West. I'm told it's amazing, but I haven't had a chance to visit NYC over the past four weeks."

Rheingold paused, his brain whirling. "Hold on, did you say, THE 15 Central Park West. Wow!" At first The Heiress was surprised and impressed that Rheingold knew about 15 Central Park West. Rheingold asked, "Wait, you really own-"

The Heiress cut him off, "Consider it done. I'll see you when the two of you get back! But let me be clear, I hope you appreciate that you can't walk around Central Park or any part of the city. You just can't!"

Rheingold responded like a first grader, "I know. I know."

Everything was going to plan.

1:07 pm, Washington, DC

Slowly smoking a cigarette, Jack was standing outside the limo. He was awaiting word when The Heiress would be coming out of her meeting in the Russell Senate office building. He wasn't surprised at the level of increased security. He imagined he could only see half of it. He smirked. After all his years of military training he knew you could never remove the soldier from the man. On instinct, you look, observe, look, and find as many potential threats as you can count.

He knew, war, all-out war, is worse than any human can possibly imagine. War becomes the nightmare of your worst nightmare.

What Jack couldn't see, what none of the dozens of highly trained, security guards could see, was the young mother jogging with one of the modern baby carriages designed for jogging with your baby. No matter the years of training, they couldn't know her family was kidnapped, sitting blind folded at gunpoint in a basement in Georgetown. She was given swift instructions. She was told if she didn't follow instructions everything she loved would be killed. They told her to jog with this baby carriage to the green SUV and wait there for them to call her. She never knew the cell phone they gave her was the detonator.

By dumb luck, after Jack saw The Heiress riding toward him in her motorized wheelchair, Jack bent over to pick up a penny with its head-up. Later, he'd thank his dear mother for that one saying instilled in his brain, "Pick up a penny that's heads-up and all day long you'll have good luck." By another blessing, between the green SUV, Jack, and The Heiress was a large concrete flower structure specifically designed to stop truck-bombs and blasts. Unknowingly, the young mother placed the baby carriage where the concrete flower structure could miraculously shield Jack and The Heiress from the main impacts of the blast. Severely injured, with the aid of the best available medical care, she and Jack would survive their wounds.

Philadelphia Airport

At the same time, the pilot bolted through the front cabin. He yelled, “Evacuate, get out of here. Get out of here. Unbuckle and let’s get everyone off this plane, quickly, now, quickly. We need to get you into the bunker. Into the bunker!” He was increasingly hysterical.

Everyone reacted with actions matching the panic in his voice. On instinct, Roz and Dance leaped up and helped get everyone off the plane. The pilot pushed Roz and Dance out the door, and the pilot was the last person off the plane. He slammed the door shut. Racing down the steps, they sprinted to reach the others. As they approached the bunker, they could see the look of fear in the two security teams at the doors. They were screaming, “Hurry up. Hurry up!”

The only non-ultra-athlete Rheingold was sucking wind halfway through the 82-yard sprint.

They reached the bunker, and the security team slammed the iron doors behind them. They were catching their breath, as bottles of water were being handed out.

Dance seemed to get his breath first and spoke in between breaths, “What the hell is happening?”

Ned and Tate, the trusted security guards most often stationed around The Heiress and Shannon stepped forward. Both of them lived in mansions inside the compound with their beautiful wives and kids. They took a special liking to Shannon because of their rabid love of everything Penn State. Tate looked at Ned and took a half-step back. As Ned watched Tate move backwards, Ned lowered his head and, as if intense gravity were weighing him down, he slowly lifted his head and mustered the courage to look at Rheingold.

There was deep pain in Ned’s eyes, “There’s been a terrible attack.”

1:08 pm, Villanova, Pennsylvania

The work crew was just completing the finishing touches on the new kitchen Shannon had designed. With Rheingold spending more time here instead of Harrisburg, she wanted a great kitchen for cooking, and entertaining. She had an exquisite eye and touch.

Gregg Chartmann was an ancient soul with an eye for making cabinets and countertops exceed any owner's imagination. His master work was in some of the finest kitchens, and corporate offices in New York and Philadelphia. Gregg and his team had spent ten solid days trying to get the kitchen completed by the end of her Cairo trip. Finishing today, they were always pleased to be finished and excited to share their work. Keeping with a 30-year tradition, Gregg's partner Mic pulled out a cooler of cold Yuengling's. He passed around a can to everyone as they popped them open for a celebratory beer. The beer always tasted better after a great result. They raised their beer cans and in unison toasted, "Cheers!"

The Heiress assigned a team of twelve of her best commandos to guard Shannon. Even when Shannon was travelling The Heiress insisted on four on-duty, 24/7 at Shannon's house.

Even though there was 24/7 surveillance, and they scanned every box and letter, that morning they didn't scan the three trucks of the cabinet crew. The night before, while Gregg, Mic and their team were parked at their favorite watering hole on the Mainline, The Ruthless One ordered his two remaining assassins to pack the undersides of their trucks with ultra-light C4. It was equal to the detonation impacts of the explosives used in the 1993 World Trade Center bombing.

The explosions at Shannon's house were felt for miles. The house and three other houses around it were decimated. 16 people plus Gregg and Mic, were instantly killed.

Unbeknownst to the terrorists, Rheingold and Shannon weren't there. Instead, Rheingold's best friend from kindergarten was dead, and everything he owned was incinerated. At the time,

Rheingold was sitting on an Heiress jet plane at Philly airport, not at the house.

Cairo Airspace: 8:07 pm in Cairo, Egypt Time

The savagery had happened beforehand. Surface to air missiles (SAMs), were infamous in the 80s. Americans supplied the Mujahideen so they could shoot down Russian helicopters and planes. Except for air-perimeters secured by American drones, SAMs were still lethal to any slow-flying vessel. Jumbo jets filled with jet fuel were especially vulnerable during takeoffs.

1983 from LaGuardia Airport.

The Korean passenger jet shot down near Japan. Through the dark channels they secured the SAM launcher and missiles through Sudanese rebel forces. They snuck them into Cairo. The jet explosion was heard for miles. These motherfuckers didn't care who else they killed as long as they killed her.

The plane, Shannon and everyone on the flight were incinerated and murdered with the initial blast of the jet fuel. No one survived.

After all the butchery that had already occurred in Philadelphia, the world recoiled.

Few could believe sects of Christian, Muslim, and other religions hellbent on mutilating young girls would go to such extreme lengths to try and murder Shannon, Rheingold, and The Heiress.

The students that had devoted so many hours supporting Shannon were devastated, angry, and more driven than ever.

For hours Tik-Tok stood still, no human fully comprehending how to even respond. Then, Rheingold of all people, posted Shannon's first FGM video on Tik-Tok account. Then he posted her second FGM video, featuring Kelly's Clarkson's "A Moment Like This."

Within 15-minutes, a million other Tik-Tok users posted Shannon's two FGM videos.

Part in tears, part in anger, that evening more than a billion users posted the Shannon FGM videos on Tik-Tok, Facebook, Instagram, and other social media platforms.

The internet shook.

The Aftermath

Two days later Rheingold drove slowly to the crater. He sat there weeping.

He played one of their favorite songs, on repeat. "Come Undone" by Duran Duran.

After the song blasted for the ninth time, local police chief Chris Word knocked on the car window. At first startled and shocked, Rheingold rolled down the window. "Mr. Craven, hey, I don't want to bother you, I don't even know what to say, but if you don't mind maybe we could show you something the forensic team found."

Chief Word was one of those cops, people called a policeman. They reverently called him, Chief. Since his first days on the force, he was the one his boss asked to call the next of kin after children, fathers, or mothers were killed in fatal car accidents. Chief Word called the children when elderly parents had passed. He was the cop that drove kids home, instead of DUI convictions. As the years passed, they said he just had a knack for it. A gift. The truth was, he was the only one brave enough to do it. All his close friends knew, it tore him up inside, each and every time.

Together, they walked over to the side of the crater.

"Brother," Chief Word started, "nothing survived that blast except one thing." He choked-up. "Look, I don't know how to say this.

When the jeweler learned, you were going to propose to Shannon, he placed your engagement ring in a special container designed by the Mossad to evade airport security."

He paused, handing Rheingold that black container, "The forensic team found it where the house stood.

"It's the only thing left."

Chief Word's shaking hand reached toward Rheingold. The chief could tell this was the last thing on the planet this man wanted to touch or receive. He put his other hand on Rheingold's shoulder. "Look brother. I've been doing this for 32 years. I've had to tell parents their kids died in car accidents. It's the worst call a man can ever make."

He motioned, "Look, hold this a second," and he placed the engagement ring box in Rheingold's shaking hand. Then the Chief he walked to his nearby police vehicle. He reached in, he grabbed a thermos and two cups. He turned back to Rheingold.

"Brother, I've got these two fraternity brothers. Crazy as shit. I mean, in college we'd piss our pants in our weekly fraternity meetings, hearing about the stories over the past weekend. You couldn't make that shit up. A few days back, a couple of the guys were telling me about you and Reed and your epic stories. I guess you met a few of my guys, the one night the celebrations got a little carried away. And you and Reed walked out and explained to the guys that this celebration was like the 100th tamest party where you were never arrested. Then I guess you started trading legendary stories. Well anyway, I'm sure the stories grew by the time they got to me."

The Chief filled the two cups with coffee mixed with a couple drams of The Whistler Irish Cream. In the warmest possible way, the Chief could tell a funny story, he started, "Damn, there was this one time in college, these two guys decided they were going to ride a cardboard refrigerator box down the front stairway of the fraternity house. They got all liquored up, chugged some beers, bragged about their plan, when one of the seniors yelled, 'Hey how the fuck are you going to turn right when the stairway turns right at the landing?' They both laughed, when one of them yelled back, 'Shit, we're going to lean into it.' Then in time honored fashion they both yelled, 'Here, hold our fucking beers.'"

The Chief smiled, "They were always our famous last words."

The Chief continued, "So, there they go, sitting in this gigantic cardboard box with eight guys watching. And it's classic. At first, they're sitting there in the refrigerator box, and nothing happened. It's like they are stuck. They just sat there. All of us just started laughing our asses off. Finally, a former football player gets low and starts pushing the box and them in it, to the edge of the stairway until he pushes them down the stairs, and shit, this box just flies, straight down and crashes straight into the wall."

Shaking his head, the Chief added, "Damn, they hit that wall like a ton of bricks. At first, we're like, 'Oh shit! Are they dead?' Until finally one of them looks back up the stairs, and yells, 'Holy shit, we forgot to lean into it.'"

Rheingold and the Chief belly laughed until Rheingold barked, "Fucking crazy man."

As the laughs faded back to hurt, the Chief added, "Brother, you've got a lot of good men and women behind you. More than you know. What Shannon was trying to do, it's got a whole world of support."

"And I know it's got to be hard, but man, we need you now. I got you. I got hundreds that got you. We're going to help hold you up. We're going to finish this war! It's the ninth inning and we're going to help you get it done."

Rheingold looked up. "Brother, I really appreciate it." His hand gripping that engagement box as hard as he could. "Just know, I ain't ever stopping. Never. I'm going to get every single one of those bloody fucking bastards."

They pounded fists.

Rheingold brightened up as they were parting, "Chief, when we get this shit done, let's get those fraternity brothers together. I wanna meet those crazy motherfuckers."

Shannon's Funeral

On a scale matching the funeral of any US President or British monarch; Shannon's funeral·was going to be broadcast in 200 countries.

The Heiress, still recovering from the blast's wounds, working again from her hospital bed, she was coordinating and turning her 12-member marketing team into a core group of 36 of the most experienced major-event planners in the world.

In this total, all-out war against FGM and women, The Heiress was determined to make Shannon's FGM and murder by her own kin, the epicenter platform to wipe-out FGM in every corner of civilization. In teams of 12, surrounding the 36, were another 432 fiery ladies determined to make every strategy and tactic come true.

Determined to leave no stone unturned, Rheingold and The Heiress asked several more leaders into the inner circle. In the US, Congressman Elizabeth Coletti, Phoebe Deluca Lane, Sydney Cadwalader Lodestone, Amy Jennings, Ruth Jones, Tanya Van Campen, Kimberly Kelly, Deb Madison Bryan, Teri-Lynn Fearless, Wendy Kress, Nettie Lindsay, Carol Huff Murray, Darla Samartino, Nancy Atholl, and several other women prominent across the United States. Then they went global.

1. Philadelphia, obviously!
2. Rome
3. Cairo
4. Houston, obviously!
5. New York

6. Washington, DC
7. Boston
8. Chicago
9. Los Angeles
10. San Francisco
11. Toronto
12. Mexico City
13. Sao Paulo
14. Buenos Aires
15. London
16. Edinburgh
17. Dublin
18. Paris
19. Berlin
20. Rome
21. Moscow
22. Istanbul
23. Beijing
24. Shanghai
25. Delhi
26. Mumbai
27. Dhaki
28. Karachi
29. Tokyo

30. Jakarta
31. Manila
32. Sydney
33. Algiers
34. Lagos
35. Kinshasa
36. Lahore

With an audience approaching an estimated 1.8 billion people, the funeral ceremony started with a televised prayer from St. Peter's Square in Vatican City, by Pope Francis of the Catholic Church. Next was a televised prayer from Cairo, a mournful prayer for peace by Sheikh Ahmed al-Tayeb, Grand Iman of Al-Azhar.

Both men, leaders of their respective religions, signed The *Document on Human Fraternity for World Peace and Living Together*, also known as the Abu Dhabi declaration [4] or Abu Dhabi agreement, [5] on 4 February 2019 in Abu Dhabi, United Arab Emirates. It was born of a fraternal open discussion between Francis and Ahmed al-Tayeb, and it is meant to be a guide on advancing a "culture of mutual respect." On its base has been established the Higher Committee of Human Fraternity.[6]

In his encyclical Fratelli tutti, Pope Francis stated this document "was no mere diplomatic gesture, but a reflection born of dialogue and common commitment."[7]

Next, another prayer of healing and peace from David Baruch Lau, the Ashkenazi Chief Rabbi of Israel.

After a pause, an unexpected song was played to the nations of the world. It was Shannon's favorite song. Standing on the platform at the Art Museum, Rheingold's body fought every urge to sit and curl-up into a ball.

Madison Square Garden

Lady Gaga

In a packed Madison Square Garden, everyone holding a candle, Lady Gaga emotionally started playing "I'll Never Love Again":

Like so many other women, Lady Gaga was captivated by Shannon, her story and bravery. The Heiress also a fan of Gaga had secretly booked a surprise lunch for Shannon with Gaga that would have occurred the day of the funeral.

Despite her many hundreds of performances, even Lady Gaga was moved by the weeping and wailing in the crowd at Madison Square Garden, stopping midway, to collect herself and continue.

On cue, after Lady Gaga's piano started to fade, dreading every part of this moment, Rheingold slowly stood and walked to the podium atop Philadelphia's Logan Square.

"They say I only knew Shannon for 42 days. They were the 42 happiest days of my life," his voice cracked.

"The Declaration of Independence talks about life, liberty, and the pursuit of happiness. Shannon's biggest dream was happiness, not for herself, but for all people. For young girls. We are all mortal. We only get so many breaths, and so many sunsets. Life is finite."

"I wish Shannon were speaking with you today instead of me. I would have gladly traded places with her so she could be with you longer. Her words, her passion, her love, made her amazing.

Look. There are 4 billion women on this planet. You are all special. You are all blessed."

"And I pray for everyone on every side of FGM. It's awful in so many ways. And, yet, today, there are still women at-risk, and there are 200 million women living with the impacts of this horrible nightmare. I wish we could, but we can't bring Shannon back. But we can let Shannon and her 200 million sisters be the last victims. Let them be the last victims, the last victims."

Rheingold breaks down.

"I loved Shannon. And Shannon blessed me with her great love. Four days ago, I asked Shannon to marry me, and she said yes."

Rheingold paused, weeping. A collective wailing reverberated around Logan Square from the weeping crowd of mourners.

"I hope and pray you love the woman in your life, and the daughters in your lives." Rheingold paused.

"So many times, Shannon said, 'Unless everyone is free, no one is free.' Which I hope is a saying that keeps bouncing around this world until it is true."

Rheingold continued, "It doesn't surprise me that so many loved Shannon. She was instantly radiant, friendly, and kind. She had a way about her that pulled you in. And she was instantly a sister to so many. I know Shannon would say this, 'Let's work together to make everyone free. Let's make everyone free and keep us free for the rest of time.'

"Thank you for your love. Thank you for your energy. Let's make Shannon proud. Let's make Shannon free."

"Let's make Shannon free."

In Madison Square Garden Lady Gaga was joined on stage by Annie Lennox.

"When I learned, "No More I Love You's" was Shannon's favorite song during her teenage years, I was moved to tears."" Annie Lennox expressed to the weeping crowd.

The first time I heard this song sung by one of our warm-up bands, it shook me."

"Forever, this song is dedicated to our Shannon, who gave us love without conditions."

The song echoed across every capital in the world. Annie Lennox, Lady Gaga and their musicians played the most amazing and moving version of this sad anthem, as pictures of Shannon appeared on screens, laptops, and phones for billions to see and weep.

Spielberg

The Heiress cried an hour of intense tears alone in her Oikos hospital bedroom, after Kimberly told her Shannon's place was bombed. When she gathered herself, she called her friend Steven Spielberg, asking him for a special indulgence to create a moving tribute to Shannon, and world's 200 million victims of FGM.

Spielberg immediately arranged a conference call with Kathryn Bigelow, Sofia Coppola, Jane Campion, and Nancy Meyers, asking them to combine their talents to help direct and quickly pull together this vast production.

Under the tightest security a movie production had ever experienced, Spielberg gathered his superstar team knowing they all stood at great risk, if news of this enterprise leaked. He and his team poured their heart, soul, and love into the effort. Simply put, he wanted to make this video the most moving tribute video he ever made.

Spielberg and The Heiress convinced Tori Amos to recreate her brilliant rendition of the song, Philadelphia, she recorded on October 13, 2001, at the Tower Theatre in Philadelphia. The song was from the movie *Philadelphia*, recorded by rock guitarist Neil Young. Nominated for an Academy Award, the song lost the award to another song from the movie, Bruce Springsteen's "Streets of Philadelphia."

Neil Young wrote this song for the Jonathan Demme movie *Philadelphia*, starring Tom Hanks as a lawyer dying of AIDS.

Demme first cut the title sequence of *Philadelphia* to "Southern Man" and asked Young to write a song like it for the movie. Young gave him this song, which Demme used at the end of the film. Still needing a song for the open, he called Bruce Springsteen, who wrote "Streets of Philadelphia." Demme wanted musicians not typically associated with AIDS causes for his movie because he wanted a mainstream audience to take interest in the film.

Demme spoke further about getting Neil Young to compose a song for the film in a Rolling Stone interview: "I thought, what we need is the most up-to-the-minute, guitar-dominated American-rock anthem about injustice to start the movie off. Who can do that? Neil Young can do that. So, we edited a title sequence to Southern Man to help him see how his music could power the images we were working with. He said, 'I'll try.' Six weeks later, 'Hi, it's Neil, I'm sending a tape.' So, in comes this song. We were crying the first time we heard it. I went: 'Oh, my God, Neil Young trusts this movie more than I do.'"

Spielberg took his usual liberties to bring together almost every major female recording artist to secret locations to record portions of the song.

Alone on the piano, Tori Amos poignantly starts the song in front of the billboard picture of Shannon displayed outside the UN, on the day Shannon first testified before the UN on FGM.

As the song grows, Spielberg cuts in scenes of women from every corner of the world. Kelly Clarkson joins Tori Amos to sing the first parts of the next verse. And then as the scenes of women go from one to two to three women in scenes so too, do the number of recognized faces and voices. Mariah Carey, Taylor Swift, Beyonce, Lady Gaga, Adele, Madonna, Rihanna, Joni Mitchell, Stevie Nicks, Dolly Parton, Katy Perry, Nicki Minaj, Britney Spears, Janet Jackson, Cher, Linda Ronstadt, Shania Twain, Ayumi Hamasaki, Christina Aguilera, Shakira, Enya, Miley Cyrus, Gloria Estefan…

Despite serious safety warnings by his team and top national security officials, Spielberg insisted and gained visas to fly in Africa's leading female artists on his and other friend's private jets.

Angelique Kidjo, Onyeka Onwenu, Salawa Abeni, Evi-Edna Ogholi, Yvonne Chaka-Chaka, Brenda Fassie

To the 1.8 billion, Spielberg launched his tribute, *Shannon in Philadelphia.*

He later recounted he never cried more during anything he ever produced.

"Shannon in Philadelphia"

After the song reached a crescendo, Tori Amos sang the last verses to gripping effect. The last notes of the song echoed through the streets of every major city in the world.

Preparing for Amazing Grace

In the same fashion and coordination of the ceremony, video, and broadcasting, Mike Brawn and the Irish Thunder Band of Philadelphia organized the largest bagpipe assemble for the playing of "Amazing Grace" in the history of civilization.

A fraternity brother of Rheingold, Jack picked up Mike Brawn and his wife in the Black Lincoln limo in Collegeville, and they drove into Villanova to visit privately with Rheingold and The Heiress to go over the details and funding. No expense would be spared. It would be a $5-million-dollar budget just for bagpipes. Brawnie would later relate, "Holy shit, Rheingold wasn't kidding when he said The Heiress would be the most impressive person we'd ever met in our lifetimes. She dropped down $5 million for one song and one million bagpipe players. When he told me I'd shit my pants if she looked cross at you, believe me, he wasn't kidding. And yet, except for my wife, she's by far the most attractive woman I've ever seen in-person. Her skin glowed."

Brawnie's wife quipped, "Brawnie, you are ridiculous honey. I luv you, but she's the most beautiful person you've ever seen. She's gorgeous."

It was agreed, every bagpipe band with 25 players would get $5,000, then every band would donate $500 or more to the Shannon Fund, that way The Shannon Fund would have Irish roots from every Irish community in the world. 45 bands in Philadelphia, 52 bands in NYC, 56 bands in Boston, 42 bands in London, 61 bands in Edinburgh, 43 bands in Dublin, 29 bands in Tokyo, 16 bands in Mumbai, and 107 other bands across the globe. All told, if they could find 5-million bagpipe players, they would have played with over 5-million bagpipe players.

Amazing Grace

On cue, after the last notes of Tori Amos echoed around Logan Square, Philadelphia. Brawnie stood and steadily marched alone to the edge of the steps of the Philadelphia Art Museum. The sun was just to the left of his right shoulder.

Brawnie stood solo.

With one deep breath, before all of Logan Square and the world, Brawnie played the first notes and verse of "Amazing Grace." The haunting echoes of Brawnie's bagpipe sounded across Logan Square.

Then, in one uniform motion the rest of his brothers in the Irish Thunder filled-in beside Brawnie, as they majestically marched into place, joining Brawnie in the playing of "Amazing Grace." Then, the 44 other bands standing down Logan Square to City Hall, up and down Broad Street and Market Street, to 30th Street station, and across the City of Brotherly of Love joined them.

By the second verse, every player tried to ensure the entire city of Philadelphia heard the Gaelic soul.

In New York from Ground Zero to Central Park, the bagpipes rang like a funeral pyre. From Trafalgar Square past Buckingham Palace to Piccadilly Square. From Edinburgh Castle Down Royal

Mile to Princes Street, George Street and Queen Street. From Dublin Castle throughout Dublin. Pipers in almost every city in American and Canada, and 190 other countries played Amazing Grace in unison. Every major TV, internet and wireless channel in the world played the funeral, live.

In those moments, the world cried again for Shannon.

Millions of humans called it the most moving moment of their lives.

The Heiress's Army

Some say it takes a village. There were speeches, a female POTUS candidate talking about building a village.

The Heiress said it takes an Army.

200 million defenseless women mutilated.

It was always ironic when the greatest anti-war songs became the rallying cry for total-war.

"Zombies" by The Cranberries. It was always blasting.

Thousands of women training in unison. Ten pushups, ten sit ups, ten squats, ten dips, ten mountain-climbers, ten jumping-jacks, and ten curls. They didn't call them Ricky Bobby's. After the Rheingold and Shannon workout, Shannon had posted a TikTok of her doing an incredible Ricky Bobby set that got 56 million views in the first week.

For evermore, everyone in the world called these sets, Mighty Shannons!

Maybe it was because it was sung by an Irish woman, targeted to women. But "Zombie" reached #1 on the Billboard chart for six weeks. Then, In the seventh week, three cover versions of "Zombie" made the Billboard #1, in three music categories.

After the attacks and murder of Shannon, recruiting wasn't a problem. Retention wasn't an issue. The biggest logistical challenge was training a million women in cities and towns around the world.

The Heiress recruited women athletes from high school, club, college, and Olympic coaches across America, South American, Europe and Asia.

The Heiress asked leagues, conferences, colleges, universities, to stand together with this fight, as she asked for a six-month off-season for every sport and league. Many did.

When the doubters, and old men raised questions on funding or worse, injuries and deaths, The Heiress worked her oratorical gifts to shift to her message and talking points.

All the wars of the past were over what? Money? This was going to be a war of superior strength, womanpower, and technology against savage beasts.

Through a technology system interconnected with 36 training centers in the broadcast cities for Shannon's Funeral, The Heiress commanded her troops, "Ladies, there are millions of women to thank and praise. Every one of you is risking everything to be free," The Heiress started.

"Today, we start the path to the end. And the only end is the complete eradication of FGM and sex trafficking. Today, on this planet, if you stand in our way, we are going to trample you.

Today, if you are not with us, you are against all women. Women of the World! Men of the World that support our cause! Today, we remember Shannon. We remember the 200 million, and the billions of women that have been harmed and mutilated before them.

We asked them to stop. We asked them to listen. We asked them to understand! But they refused, and they killed instead. Every day, we will train. Every day, we will get stronger.

At the same time, they are going to get weaker. We are going to disrupt their food, their funding, supplies, equipment, weapons, their lives, disrupt everything in their world! And know this. marking Shannon's words. We are not going to stop. We are not going to stop until every single woman on this planet is safe, and free. Together we are going to eradicate this scourge forever and ever.

Leaders of the world. We thank every one of you that have stepped forward, lending support, supplies, resources, and your womanpower. Today, we go-forward. We will update you when there are reasons for updates. There will be no questions."

"Thank you."

"Zombie" continued over the sound systems.

Villanova – One Hour Later

The Heiress was anxious, waiting for Rheingold to get back to the mansion. At the mansion, she knew everyone was as safe as they could be. Outside the compound, she couldn't control as many variables.

Her calls to Senate and House leaders from her technologically advanced hospital bed had prompted emergency hearings of the Armed Services committee. Ten short days ago, Washington wasn't acting on her advice and pleadings; now, the whole world wanted swift, immediate action.

Washington, D.C.

For the first time in US history, war would be declared against a cause, not a country or terrorist group. The action was a strong expansion of the War Powers Act. Not one legislator, republican, democrat or independent stood to speak against it. With unanimous consent, Congress sent the President a Declaration of War.

The Declaration of War was short and focused.

"Any person, organization or country supporting the practice of Female Genital Mutilation (FGM), or sex trafficking is an enemy of the United States of America, and Congress directs the President, armed forces and all national, state, and local governments and agencies to immediately exert all efforts to immediately end every instance of this practice in the United States, the rest of the world, and every civilization.

"Further, any person, organization or country that was directly or indirectly involved with any part of the bombings in Philadelphia, at the United Nations Building, Flight 1269, the Russell Senate Office Building, or Villanova, Pennsylvania is an enemy of the United States of America; and Congress directs the President, the armed forces of the United States, all national, state, and local governments, and agencies to use all force, resources, and support to find, arrest, and convict each one of them to the fullest extent of the law."

The House and Senate leaders agreed there would only be one speaker that would stand in support of the legislation in each legislative body.

In the House of Representatives, a packed gallery with every seat filled in the Chamber, US Representative Elizabeth Coletti (R-California) rose to the podium.

The Chair recognizes the gentle lady from California.

"Thank you, Madam Speaker. Colleagues of the United States House of Representatives. Today marks the day in history when the United States finally says no. Today the United States will no longer tolerate terrorism against women. Today, we will end violence against women and their bodies. Today, we end sex trafficking. After the President of the United States signs this legislation, any nation that permits violence against a woman's body, will have six days to remedy, six days to validate compliance, or that nation will see all trade with the United States end immediately on the 15th day.

To all people and nations of the world, let the United States be very clear. This is a declaration of war against any nation, any person, any organization that permits, facilitates, or finances terrorism against women."

"If you are a nation that supports this legislation you will have 30 days to introduce and adopt similar legislation in your country. If you do not, the United States will consider your nation a nation against women, and you will see all trade with the United States immediately end on the 31st day. Madam Speaker, I urge immediate adoption of the Declaration of War against Terrorism on Women."

For a long moment, the House stood in silence as they watched Congresswoman Coletti depart the front podium. The gallery audience and members of the House sat in solemness seldom seen on the House floor before a vote.

The Speaker called for immediate vote of the legislation before the House. Eerily, the chamber stayed quiet as the House voted.

Except for three members on medical leave, the House vote immediately jumped to 472 Yes 0 No.

Minutes passed. It was like watching ice melt. Then as the obligatory House leaders started the traditional verbal cadence to reveal the House vote on the legislation a deep, growing guttural roar started to build within the Chamber. It wasn't shouts or yells, it wasn't cheers. It started to sound more like the growl of a wounded, angry wolf, until it erupted into a battle cry far surpassing the House chamber after 9-11, and Pearl Harbor.

In the Senate, the exact same protocol was adopted. Senator Laurie Deluca Lane presented the exact same speech. Already watching the reactions in the House and post-vote, Senator Lane was clearly trembling with a mixture of nervousness and rage. Her whole career devoted to the extermination of sex trafficking she broke down after the sentence, "We end sex trafficking." She stood trembling unable to speak, until the Senate Minority Leader, her most bitter enemy and political rival, stood, walked to her, and held her up.

He read the rest of the speech with a force and volume he never exhibited in thousands of prior speeches.

In unison, the two of them read the last sentence together. "Madam President, we urge immediate adoption of the Declaration of War against Terrorism on Women."

Like the House, the yes votes were immediate. With all members present, the vote was 100 yays. Bypassing some 200 years of protocol, the Vice President didn't call for no votes. She just banged down the gavel.

Sonya Jennings, The President of the United States was waiting in the Oval Office. Rattled like never before, she was waiting for notification that everyone was seated in the Rose Garden for the bill signing ceremony that would take place immediately following the Senate vote from 1600 Pennsylvania Avenue.

Her walk to the podium was brisk. There were no waves or smiles.

"Ladies and gentlemen, citizens of the United States and citizens of the world. The legislation has been duly read, and unanimously adopted in the United States House of Representatives and the United States Senate. Under my administration, I want the world to know the Shannon Doctrine from here forward. No one is free, until everyone is free."

"No one is free, until everyone is free. Therefore, I am right now, signing this Declaration of War."

The President stepped to the side of the podium to a separate bill signing table. She didn't sit down; her signature was swift.

She returned to the podium. Her face rose slowly into the Presidential pose that would be recorded in millions of photo shares around the globe.

"To the armed forces of the United States of America. This is your President and I order you to immediately commence OPERATION SHANNON RED. To our allies, you are hereby advised the United States of America is at war, and this nation will not rest until every woman on this planet is safe and is free. To the nations and people conducting, facilitating, or financing terrorism against women, and sex trafficking, please be advised, we are at-war with you, and we will win!"

The President turned and started walking back to the White House.

By prior advanced agreement, the nation's television stations immediately switched to a shared screenshot. One-half of the screen was showing the President and her cabinet walking back into the White House. The other half of the screen was showing the largest launch of weaponry in history. Guns were blazing from battleships, submarines, drones, surface-to-air missile pads, satellites, and bombers. Then the half-screen switched to military, reserve and Guard drone-strikes. The main difference between prior wars and these strikes, was the lethality. Unlike prior wars, where there were missed shots and collateral damage. There were 1,600 targets identified, and within seconds 1,600 targets were destroyed.

As one half of the screen showed the President and her cabinet walking into the Situation Room. The other screen converted into three horizontal screens, each showing SWAT teams knocking-down doors. Within seconds the half-screen switched from three to six scenes. In three seconds the six scenes flipped to nine screens, then to 81, then 162, 324, 648, 1,296, then the screen froze on 1,600 scenes, far beyond the view capabilities of the human eye.

1600 Pennsylvania Avenue acted without hesitation.

In 1919, it took ten days to shake the world in Russia. In 2021, it took seconds.

The Ruthless One

Despite their strong technology and communications capabilities, The Ruthless One and their terrorist cells didn't know, the US was already acting with the coordination of nations. While the Iraqi War had 49 coalition nations, this Declaration of War already had 76 participating nations.

The strikes eliminated most of the regimes actively supporting FGM. In the most coordinated strike in history, within the 90 seconds before the strikes, militant leaders were isolated or separated from spouses, children and the uninvolved. Neighborhoods were cleared by Allied Special Forces.

Several allies had urged an international trial against a group of the top leaders, the President overruled. After so much carnage against women, President Jennings determined a trial would be a circus.

Her instructions were clear, "Starting with The Ruthless One, if they took part in any of the murders of the 943 victims and Shannon, I want them dead. There will be no leaders spared, there will be no martyrs."

---

24 hours before the congressional votes, inside the Situation Room, the last recommendation to the President was made by Major General Anne Frank, USMC. After reading the recommendation, President Jennings looked up at General Frank, until the General spoke, "Madame President, I lost 54 good Marines in the last two weeks. The United States Marine Corps wants this, ma'am. Every General here lost good soldiers. We want The Ruthless One to see his cells and operations destroyed. We want him to know, we won, before we destroy him."

The President looked around the room at all her trusted military leaders. Like her, they had steel in their eyes.

All she said was, "Do it!"

Villanova, PA

Sitting in their previously anonymous safe house outside Villanova, The Ruthless One and six other assassins sat watching the POTUS speech. When the POTUS turned and the video screen showed the first strikes, The Ruthless One and six assassins stood in horror and watched strike after strike hit their operations. Then they watched a purposely done, slow-motion hit to their data center and communications center destroy their communications systems and their TV screen went blank. Their safe house went silent. As predicted, they all rushed outside. They heard it first, the vacuum of the sonic boom. Then the last split-second thing they saw was the Tomahawk missile specially delivered just for them.

The Shannon Fund

With the $25 Billion seed-capital pledged from 200 governments; corporations and foundations in the United States contributed another $6.7 Billion. Corporations and foundations from the rest of the world added $3.8 billion. It was determined The Heiress would chair the Board of Directors and Congresswoman Elizabeth Coletti was asked to be the Fund's first President and Chief Executive Officer. Another six directors were invited from the United States, as were seven female directors from the most-impacted nations, and six directors from the rest of the world for the 21-member Board.

In similar fashion and geography, 21 University Presidents were selected for the Shannon Academic Action Council. Sydney Cadwalader Lodestone would lead this Council. 21 Industry leaders were selected for the Shannon Business Action Council and 21 non-profit NGO leaders for the Shannon Family Action Council. In every state or province in the world, The Shannon Fund selected 21 leaders to positively influence and impact that state or province.

76 allied leaders agreed to eliminate terrorism against woman. 76 leaders agreed to proportionately allocate annual funding to The Shannon Fund for Women. $25 Billion dollars a year would be invested around the globe to help the 200 million victims of FGM. Disbursements and staffing of the Fund would be proportionate to a nation's share of FGM victims.

Word quickly spread, like her real-life TikTok videos, that Shannon would have prevented and refused any word, mention, or memorial in her honor. The Shannon Fund and its directors partially agreed. They persuaded by unanimous consent among nations and organizations, that one official memorial in Philadelphia would be raised in Shannon's honor, along with the 943 others that lost their lives during the fight to end FGM with Shannon.

Recognizing the start of Shannon's public crusade, it was unanimously agreed, The Shannon Center would be placed opposite the US Constitution Center in Independence Mall. The Shannon Center would be designed in Philadelphia, constructed using labor from 200 countries with special travel visas enacted to facilitate the same.

Upon completion, the Shannon Fund organization would be housed in the office-section within the Shannon Center.

The Shannon Center Dedication

30 days after #EndFGM Day, surrounded by hundreds of secret-service members, NAVY SEALS, Delta Force, US Marines, and Pennsylvania National Guard members, and a crowd approaching 700,000; POTUS Sonya Jennings stepped to the podium in Independence Mall in old town Philadelphia. Again 200 nations were linked together for watching the proceedings, by one of the largest audiences in history.

Her voice was strong.

"Global friends," she started.

"Today, we rest for a moment, and take time to celebrate the life of Shannon with the groundbreaking for the Shannon Center in Philadelphia. Just 30 days ago, I spoke with you in the Rose Garden.

Just 61 days ago, Shannon spoke here," she paused, not appreciating she would be choked up already.

"Much has happened since that day. To all impacted families, our nation sends our continuing prayers and unrequited resolve. You will never be alone. Across the world, 943 others lost their lives with Shannon during the fight to end FGM. And with Shannon, they will be individually memorialized here for all eternity."

She continued, "Today, The Shannon Center and The Shannon Fund have been designed to make lasting, positive impacts for women, for daughters, and our civilization for the years and decades before us. We remain steadfast and dedicated to the unfinished business before us. We are just getting started, but our goal is the complete adoption of the Shannon Doctrine across the globe. No one is free until everyone is free. No one is free until everyone is free. Shannon, thank you! You inspired the world, and the world and all its daughters will always love you back."

"Philadelphia! I can't hear you!"

"Philadelphia!"

And with that the crowd roared, *"Philadelphia!"* It was one of the loudest roars ever in Philadelphia! *Minutes later the President spoke again.*

"Thank you. Philadelphia for hosting the Shannon Center. To the rest of the world, thank you."

Unlike her speech three weeks ago, her words did not launch the most lethal strike in the history of warfare. Instead, as she had stood to speak, a squadron of Blue Angels had turned North over Wilmington, Delaware. And, as the President said the words, "Thank you," the sonic boom of the Blue Angels was rippling up

Broad Street from the Philadelphia Navy Yard and reverberating throughout center city.

For the next fifty years the Shannon Memorial was the most visited landmark in the world, millions of visitors to Shannon's corner of Independence Mall to celebrate the freedom of all women and marking the end of FGM.

The Celebrations for the Shannon Center

After the Shannon Center's groundbreaking ceremony, the organizers had planned several receptions for the many thousands of visitors that had traveled great distances to attend and celebrate the ground-breaking.

After several events near Independence Mall, Reed, Kelby, and Rheingold jumped in a black Lincoln Limo supplied by The Heiress to attend the function at the University of Pennsylvania, hosted by former Governor Edward Rendell.

They were escorted through a back door to the front table. As they approached the table, Rendell slapped Rheingold on the shoulder, "My man, if anyone could have made all of this possible, it had to be you." He jostled. Talking to Rheingold so all of the nearby guests could hear, "I still remember meeting you for the first time. You were so different from the other legislators and stool pigeons in Harrisburg. After you walked out of the room that first time, I remember saying to my Chief of Staff, 'Who the hell is that kid?'"

They all laughed.

Never one to hold onto a compliment, Rheingold replied, "Governor, it's great to see you. Dang, you look like you are working out with the Eagles again," as he grabbed the Governor's triceps. Rheingold bellowed. "The best was seeing you in Boston to watch UPenn in the NCAA tournament, when we skipped town, and Harrisburg was having a hemorrhage over you watching a basketball game in March."

Reed and Kelby shook hands with the Governor, and they exchanged stories. As planned, Sydney Cadwalader Lodestone and several of the other board members of the Shannon Fund made a few remarks greeting the guests and honorees.

After Sydney's remarks, Reed handed Rheingold an envelope.

"Dude, you're not going to believe this, but this envelope is for you, and contains a ticket."

"I'm telling you; you don't have a choice. You don't need a thing. The instructions are in the envelope and Jack is waiting outside to take you. Right now!"

The ailing Governor reached up and shook Rheingold's hand. "Take care my friend. Thank you for loving Philadelphia as much as I do."

Kelby jumped up into a warm embrace, "Rheingold, you know I freaking love you. I can't wait to see you again."

Reed stood directly in front of Rheingold gleaming, "I'm so sorry about everything that has happened, but I've never been prouder to know ya man."

Reed smiled his patented, shit-eating grin, "Dude, I remember telling the epic stories of you, and people doubting they could ever be true. And now. Now, you made those stories seem so small and trivial. Come here, man. Love you, dude." As Reed grabbed Rheingold by the shoulders that turned it into a big bear hug. They both held back tears.

Pulling away, Rheingold smiled and laughed, "Look, dude, I ain't making any speeches." And they all started laughing.

He looked down at the envelope, shaking his head.

"Well, let me see where this takes me," and he turned and started walking out.

As he passed Sydney Cadwalader Lodestone, their eyes met. They smiled that smile. As they passed, they high fived. Then they hugged for a long moment like the long-lost friends they would forever be.

Leaving Philadelphia!

Outside, Jack was a welcome sight.

"Mr. Rheingold, a pleasure to see you again." Jack confidently smiled. "I'm looking forward to taking you to the airport." Instead of the usual nod, Rheingold kept walking toward Jack and gently hugged the man that had been with Rheingold since the very beginning of this adventure and was so injured in the Washington blast.

Riding down the bottom of the Schuylkill, a path Rheingold had travelled so many times, they talked about cars and the Eagles as they drove past the stadiums and oil refineries then Interstate 95 and the lights of Philly airport.

Rheingold smiled and softly said to himself, *Fucking Philly. I love this fucking place.*

The Flight

As Jack opened the limo door, Rheingold immediately noticed this wasn't the same aircraft he had flown beforehand. If it were possible, this jet looked even faster. He walked up the stairs to greetings from the captain and two beautiful flight attendants. They showed him to his seat on the eight-seater plane, with an office or maybe a bedroom in the rear.

As expected, the envelope had just enough information to know he was going somewhere, but little else. The flight attendant added a little bit more information.

"Mr. Craven, I've been instructed to open a treasured bottle of Champagne and play some of your favorite music. With the speed of this jet, our flight won't be long," she turned and started pouring the already opened bottle.

And like that, the sound system started playing, "Sensa Un Perche" by Nada.

After his first sip, he thought *damn, how is it possible that this Champagne could be better than the flight from Harrisburg?* Again, he couldn't know that he was drinking one of the rarest and most acclaimed French Champagnes produced in the last 25 years. As he watched the flight attendant started to close the jet door, he looked around and was a little disappointed he didn't see The Heiress.

He sat back, taking a deep long breath, marveling at the bubbly, and took another good long sip.

Soon after, "Video Games" by Lana Del Ray started to play as the stewardess poured his second glass with a big smile.

"Grew Up at Midnight" by Maccabees…

His second glass of Champagne was so perfect. He took a few sips but didn't remember falling asleep, or the flight attendant rescuing his tilting glass.

As she had mentioned, the flight was short. She was softly touching his shoulder as he abruptly woke, and asked, "Where the heck, are we?" She assured him everything was okay.

The touchdown was so smooth it was like they weren't landing but were floating over the runway.

The captain shook his hand, "It was an honor." Embarrassed, Rheingold said thanks and turned his back to the pilot and flight attendant while holding on for balance as he sleepily walked down the flight stairs.

At the bottom of the stairs, he saw a black Rolls Royce was awaiting his arrival.

He looked out, and his first sight of the ocean was the bluest water he had ever seen.

"Sir, my brother, my name is Jerry Harris and I want to welcome you to Bermuda. We are very confident you will enjoy your stay and vacation. Everyone in the world knows you have earned it. My family and I share our thoughts and prayers with you. It will be 18 to 20 minutes to our destination. Please enjoy the ride."

Soaking in what Jerry said, Rheingold responded by whispering, "Thanks, Jerry."

He did enjoy the ride. Uniquely, the vehicle was a convertible as well. Rheingold soaked in the salt air and the sights he had always envisioned about Bermuda. As they drove, Jerry pointed out a few of the landmarks and history. Rheingold always liked to learn about a place's history.

They slowed. As they approached the gate at the end of the peninsula, the gate swung open automatically. The long driveway went slightly uphill to another simply incredible mansion.

Rheingold thought, *Where the hell am I?*

He smiled and laughed to himself, *we're definitely not in Kansas anymore.*

Quickly, Jerry jumped out to open Rheingold's door. "Sir, please follow me," as he led Rheingold to the front door.

As the door opened, it was pretty obvious this ultra-white mansion was going to have the most amazing ocean view he'd ever seen. As he walked to the front step, he could see the entire ocean-side of the house was spectacular glass windows. *Dang,* he thought. *Wow.*

"Sir, my name is Sam, I will make sure everything you want is at your fingertips." Sam was finely dressed and articulate, with Sam's accent and Rheingold's quick glance he thought he was former MI6 or British special forces. Sam continued, "We've been instructed to show you to your room where you will find the steam shower most invigorating."

Well, that's an interesting detail.

"Then we have prepared an exquisite dinner for you. But, after your relaxing shower, we would like you to consider having a drink on the veranda. We're told it's the most amazing view anywhere in the Atlantic."

The steam shower was incredible.

He imagined, *damn, is there cocaine in this water?* He stretched his arms in the air. *Wow. I feel like a million bucks and I'm pretty sure I only had four hours sleep the past week, or was it, months...*

On what had to be the best stereo system ever installed, he heard the start of The Hooters "And We Danced."

Then he smiled again, that a whole new set of clothes had been placed out on the bed. This time the clothes were white linen, draping softly over his sore body. The cloth was the softest he had ever worn. Everything he wore was white, even the soft sandals. Everything, the room, furnishings, and furniture were all ultra-white.

Of course. Of course!

The Veranda

After he dressed, he left the bedroom, and Sam took him down to the veranda. As he walked down the ocean-facing stairway, his mind raced, *who the heck designed and engineered this place? It's simply amazing.*

Outside a waiting area that reminded him of the Scottish mansion he visited years ago, Rheingold walked out onto the veranda. He was glad the music system from his room seemed interconnected with these rooms.

Like the corporate boardroom and the rest of the house, the veranda was ultra-pure white that lit up with the sunshine. The furniture and furnishings were ultra-pure white. The only color on the veranda was the red wine.

He sadly smiled when the next song, "A-ha - Take on Me (Live from MTV Unplugged)" started its haunting melody.

He pondered as he smiled, *who the hell stole my playlist*?

Rheingold's mind started to flow, *What a view. The bluest, clearest water God ever made. I really wish Shannon were here to see this, she would love this so mu*ch. The thoughts lingered, then seared. *Oh, my Shannon!*

His mind argued back, *Shit. Shape it up, dude.*

He smiled again when he recognized the open bottle of red wine that his nostrils also recognized from 12 feet away, Red Car! *Really. Are you kidding me? Great song, and my favorite wine.* He tipped a strong pour of his favorite wine.

Sam walked out and showed him a selection of fine cigars, from Holts of Philadelphia. He selected an Ashton ESG, 23-year Salute. Very cool.

Sam wasn't kidding when he said I'd appreciate the wine and cigars. I love everything about this place!

For sure Rheingold was hurting physically and still feeling the shock of Shannon's murder but sitting here with this bottle of Red Car wine and his favorite Ashton cigar, he thought, *I'm just going to sit here and do absolutely nothing but enjoy this.*

I'm just going to relax and enjoy.

Red Car

He sniffed the glass of Red Car red wine, and his sip turned into a gulp.

He stood before the Atlantic Ocean as a breathtaking sunset was preparing to take center stage and burst on the horizon.

He shook his head. *Man, this is the first time I've had a moment by myself since...since I got on that plane from Harrisburg to Philly.*

His mind drifted, *The Heiress. Man, she is incredible. Truly the most amazing women on the planet. She organized everything. She planted every seed on this incredible journey. She almost died, twice. And she just keeps coming back stronger.*

He soaked in the Bermuda sunset, as the *a-ha* song ended.

There's always that silence in-between songs, when your brain stops processing the end of the last song, and starts to anticipate the next song, where literally millions of neurons anticipate the first notes of a song so the brain can process, remember, and guess the next song.

The first chords hit, and while Rheingold hadn't heard this song in years, he knew it instantly.

"Love Grows (Where My Rosemary Grows)" by the Edison Lighthouse

He shook his head, remembering the high school and college days, watching the video with the Dancing Girl.

The chords started their enchanting flow.

As The Heiress walked out onto the veranda, Rheingold's surprised eyes immediately caught her eyes. He also noticed the limp she was trying to mask.

"I thought you'd like a rare French Bordeaux, but they say this Red Car has goopy, mystical powers," she smiled, as she elegantly filled her glass with the Red Car.

Rheingold added, "I'm pretty convinced all the mystical powers begin, and end with you."

And as he spoke, he felt that magical thing starting to happen to him once again, like every time he was around her. Time - just started to slow down. The sensation was obvious, you felt something happening, but like gravity there was nothing you could do. He breathed her in, the way any man would do in front of a woman he unabashedly admired and loved. He felt that feeling a man feels deep inside his soul, when he could be asked afterwards what she was wearing, what color of shoes was she wearing, and he wouldn't have a clue. When they say, love is blindness.

Her smile widened as the song she selected hit the chorus parts she wanted to reverberate in his beautiful mind.

Like Rheingold, The Heiress was wearing the same all white linen. On her, the outfit was breathtaking, straight off the cover of *Vogue*.

Slowly, elegantly, she walked toward Rheingold. Instead of stopping in front of him, The Heiress reached Rheingold, and gave him a long, urgent, loving hug. Her warm body touched his body. As their bodies parted, they glanced deeply into each other's eyes. Pain, hurt, love, and comfort overflowed.

Both emotionally torn, their embrace turned into a standing pillar of sobbing and heaving tears. For so long, they had held so much inside, until the lightning flash love of Shannon reignited their destiny, fate, and faith.

Rheingold had no idea she hadn't been held, kissed, or made love since her life and love were stolen from her on a rainy night. Then, she was running late and drove separately to dinner, when a drunk driver killed her parents, husband, and little baby girl. He didn't know she did nothing for 6-months, when she suddenly energized to consolidate all her financial holdings into one of the strongest financial enterprises in the world. He hadn't been briefed on her Special Forces training center yet or Project Poppy. There still was so much he didn't know. She thought she'd have more time, or she thought she had no time at all.

She didn't care that her tears started to flow. Rheingold pulled her closer to him. He could feel her shaking. His fingers were running over her hair. He was sobbing too.

Like their bodies, the music seemed to ebb and flow.

Rheingold spoke first, “several times Shannon insisted if anything happened to her, I should embrace you, hold you, comfort you, and never let you go. She loved us both.” Surprised, The Heiress remarked, “Rheingold that’s exactly the same thing Shannon said to me. She was so worried about you if something happened to her.”

Slowly, they swayed together as the “Love Grows” song was coursing through their veins and souls…

As the song was fading, instead of another song they could hear the magical sounds of the ocean reaching the beach, wave after wave. Until she said to Rheingold, “she wanted you to know my name is Rosemary!”

Important References:

[1] PCAR, 2018; The Institute to Address Commercial Sexual Exploitation [CSE Institute], (2016) https://pcar.org/human-trafficking

[2] https://constitutioncenter.org/

[3] Read More: Cracking down on female genital mutilation in New Jersey | https://nj1015.com/cracking-down-on-female-genital-mutilation-in-new-jersey/?utm_source=tsmclip&utm_medium=referral

[4] https://www.catholicnewsagency.com/news/42104/pope-francis-lends-support-to-committee-on-abu-dhabi-declaration

[5] https://religionnews.com/2020/10/04/five-things-to-look-for-in-new-papal-encyclical-fratelli-tutti/

[6] https://www.forhumanfraternity.org/

[7] https://catholicherald.co.uk/pope-francis-releases-encyclical-letter-fratelli-tutti/

About the Author

After reading a book about Dietrich Bonhoeffer, Kelly Lewis started writing a series of books designed to address civilization's worst crimes against humanity. This book is his first release. For more information visit, www.RheingoldSeries.com.

Made in the USA
Monee, IL
07 February 2022

34dbff92-1d9a-461b-ad9d-1d7c495bfdbdR01